About the Author

Paul Kitcatt was a bookseller and an English teacher before he was lured into the world of advertising.

He started as a copywriter, then became creative director and, in 2002, founded his own agency with three partners. It did well, with clients such as Waitrose, VSO, Lexus, the NSPCC, AXA, Virgin and the WWF.

Throughout his career, he continued to write – for clients, for the trade press and, when possible, for himself.

He left his agency in 2016 and wrote his first novel, *We Care For You.*

During his time in advertising, the digital revolution transformed his business and the entire industry, as it has everything, everywhere. Technology is changing the world, and us with it, and the journey has only just begun. Paul's novel is about where it might take us next.

Paul is married with four children and lives in London.

D1550217

WE CARE FOR YOU

WE CARE FOR YOU

PAUL KITCATT

Unbound

London

This edition first published in 2017

Unbound

6th Floor Mutual House, 70 Conduit Street, London W1S 2GF

www.unbound.com

ISBN (eBook): 978-1911586289
ISBN (Paperback): 978-1911586296

Design by Mecob

Cover image:

© Shutterstock.com
© Textures.com

To my mother, Audrey (1927–2015)

Dear Reader,

The book you are holding came about in a rather different way to most others. It was funded directly by readers through a new website: Unbound.

Unbound is the creation of three writers. We started the company because we believed there had to be a better deal for both writers and readers. On the Unbound website, authors share the ideas for the books they want to write directly with readers. If enough of you support the book by pledging for it in advance, we produce a beautifully bound special subscribers' edition and distribute a regular edition and e-book wherever books are sold, in shops and online.

This new way of publishing is actually a very old idea (Samuel Johnson funded his dictionary this way). We're just using the internet to build each writer a network of patrons. Here, at the back of this book, you'll find the names of all the people who made it happen.

Publishing in this way means readers are no longer just passive consumers of the books they buy, and authors are free to write the books they really want. They get a much fairer return too – half the profits their books generate, rather than a tiny percentage of the cover price.

If you're not yet a subscriber, we hope that you'll want to join our publishing revolution and have your name listed in one of our books in the future. To get you started, here is a £5 discount on your first pledge. Just visit unbound.com, make your pledge and type WINIFRED17 in the promo code box when you check out.

Thank you for your support,

Dan, Justin and John
Founders, Unbound

Super Patrons

Vonnie Alexander
Caroline Beard
David Brown
Chris Cavell-Clarke
Chalice Croke
Nobby Davies
Lu Dixon
Kate Flather
Christie Jennings
Phil Keevill
Dan Kieran
Caroline Kitcatt
Mark Kitcatt
James Kitcatt
Ellie Kitcatt
Elizabeth Kitcatt
Cathy Kitcatt
Simon Kluge
Helen Ling
Richard Madden
Tania Mendes
John Mitchinson
Mo Morgan
Marc Nohr
Ben Parsons
Rob Pateman
Justin Pollard
Jill Richards
Simon Robinson
Margaux Sloan
Reannon Tapp

Tot Taylor
David Yates

With grateful thanks to Chalice Croke
and Kate Flather who helped to make this book happen

'… he deserved no such return
From me, whom he created what I was
In that bright eminence…'

Milton, *Paradise Lost*

Contents

England, January 2022

John

At least the place doesn't smell of piss. I'd expected it to. Instead it smells like the inside of an airing cupboard full of old blankets. The air feels denser than outside, but it must be my imagination. I don't think that's possible.

It's hot. Like the reptile house at the zoo. Probably for the same reason. Old people need a lot of heat to get them moving. Then they move a leg forward, and stretch a tortoise neck out, look around, blink, then think better of it. Why bother? Stay put in the chair. Whatever they want will arrive eventually.

We sit in a silent and empty dining room, and I spoon food into my mother's mouth. It's mush, and if there was more gravy she could suck it through a straw. Baby food. She used to feed me like this once.

The walls are the beige of old people's clothes. Covered with pictures everywhere – scenes of rural England, as it was in the imagined golden age. Fields without barbed wire or any rusting agricultural machinery in the corners. Happy rustic characters with rosy cheeks leading the good life. These pictures look like they came on a long roll, and were cut off to fit the space available.

And then there are abstract paintings, with big blocks of colour or paint scrubbed on hard with a manic brush. By local artists, I see, and donated to the home.

There are framed photo-montages, too, showing events from the younger days of the residents. Newspaper cuttings of children waiting to be evacuated, Chamberlain waving his piece of paper, RAF pilots sitting in the sunshine in armchairs, black airplanes arrowing though grey skies, crowds on seaside piers and promenades. The old queen, at various ages. All intended to keep memory alive, I suppose. Though you'd have to be, what – getting on

1

for 100, to have any chance of remembering all that. But it's our national memory, isn't it? Not anyone's in particular.

What about the mannequins lurking in odd corners, dressed in mismatched outfits assembled from clothes of different eras? They look like someone's idea of the guests at a bohemian night-club. One's wearing nothing but a sporran over his absent genitals. What memories these are supposed to rekindle is anybody's guess. More likely to inspire nightmares in the unmoored minds of the demented.

When my mother seems to have had enough, I sit back. She stays bent over, but after a while she twists her head and looks at me. Sort of. I have no idea what she can see. Her eyes packed up years ago. She has peripheral vision, that's all.

Her gaze is unsettling. It's how she looked at me when I was a child, and in trouble. I feel like I've let her down, again. Haven't I? She's in this place, looked after by strangers, and I don't visit often. It seems pointless. She barely knows I'm there.

Now she's trying to speak, and point. She raises a shaky finger and waves it towards me.

'You know it's true!' she croaks.

'What's true?'

'I know she's difficult, but you must stick with her.'

'Who, Mum?'

'With Fiona, of course. Who else?'

Fiona. My sister-in-law. She thinks I'm my brother, Ben. He seldom comes, as he lives in Australia, but last time he must have told her something about his marriage, or she's decided something about it. I could go along with this and see what else comes out. Better not though.

'Mum, I'm John. You're thinking about Ben. He's not here. I am. John.'

She looks at me sceptically. As if I'm making it up.

Then she subsides back down into herself, and shrinks into her chair. She moans, and then the sound turns into a sigh and she looks like she's asleep.

I gaze out of the window. There's a tidy garden and a summerhouse. The trees are bare and their branches are whipping in the wind. Endless grey cloud presses down. Beyond the garden is an estate of little houses. My mother's house was grand, with a large and beautiful garden, and she knew how to plant it to look good all year round. She wanted to stay there. But it wasn't practical. Twice she nearly burnt it down. She was stuck there all day on her own, unable to walk anywhere, waiting.

The afternoon inches past. She wakes from time to time and speaks, or mumbles. Nothing makes much sense. Some of it's addressed to me, some to my siblings, some to my dead father. She speaks to me as if I were a child, or about things from before I was born. She relives conversations from 70 years ago, as far as I can tell. Sometimes it resolves into momentary coherence, like a remote radio station.

'The garden.'

'What about it, Mum?'

'Go and play. Don't kick the ball into the beds. Mummy will be cross.'

She would be, too. She always was. It didn't stop us. I say nothing.

'He fell into the roses once. Off his bike. I pulled out the thorns with tweezers.'

'That was me, Mum. John. I remember it well.'

'Better than when she broke her front tooth though. And her arm. You weren't taking care. I made you pay. You heard her screams.'

Dad – she must be talking about him. Or to him, in her mind.

'Never much interested. Didn't know how to talk to them. You were hopeless at any chatting. At the tennis club. With our friends. I knew you wanted to talk to me. You didn't know how. I wasn't going to help you. Told Winnie later and she laughed. They're all hopeless at it. You have to help them.'

I imagine my father, tongue-tied and struggling. Trying to get her attention. Which she knew perfectly well, but she led him a merry dance. He courted her for years. And he hated social occasions. Parties. Dinners. They never had them. My mother would have, but she gave up in the face of his reluctance. Perhaps if she'd encouraged him, back then, when he was forced to make small talk and find things to say to the young woman he wanted to kiss, he would have found it less painful later, and would've been prepared to try with friends or even strangers. But she didn't. She made him work hard for her. She laughed at him behind his back, with her always-laughing sister.

'Where are my children? Are any of them coming? Do they know I'm here? Where is this place? Somebody needs to do something with that garden.'

'I'm here, Mum. John. I'm with you.'

The light fades, and she fades with it. She's asleep when the door opens, and one of the staff comes in. A short, round woman, with thin, black hair plastered to her scalp, flabby arms and a stained uniform. She turns on the light.

'How's your mother?'

'She's fine. She's been talking on and off, but it's all a bit rambling. She ate well enough though.'

'That's what we like to hear. She's got a lot to say for herself, hasn't she? I can't understand all of it, but everything's in there,' she says, tapping her forehead.

Is it? Is every memory intact? I imagine her mind as a vast library, with a card index system, but the drawers have been pulled out and the cards spilt all over the floor. Worse still, many of the books have fallen to bits, or been eaten by worms, or destroyed by mould. It's a wreck, a shambles, a hopeless muddle. I'm gripped with fear for my own mind.

The carer takes my mother's hand and pats it.

'Margaret? Margaret? Will you wake up for me? I need to get you ready for your supper.'

My mother groans, but doesn't open her eyes.

'OK,' says the carer. 'I'll have to do it without your help.'

She turns to face me.

'I'm going to need a hand. I can't lift her on my own. Do you want to help? Or else I'll go and get some of the others.'

I look at my mother. She's tiny and frail, but lifting her would be hard on my back. And then what? Will the carer ask me to help while she cleans her? Involving some kind of adult nappy?

Feeding her like a baby is one thing. Changing her nappy is quite another. It's at least 50 years since she changed mine. I've had enough of this role reversal.

'I think I'd rather leave it to the experts, if you don't mind.'

The carer stands for a moment, staring at me. I'm uncomfortable. I can feel a blush rising up my neck.

'All right then,' she says, and leaves the room in search of more useful people.

I take a last look at my mother. I could kiss her goodbye, but what's the point? I turn away, and leave her for the carer to sort out. She knows what she's doing.

All through the long drive home, I think about my mother's life, and mine, and how I can avoid ending up like her.

Winifred

My name is Winifred.

Last week I started work at Evergreen Care Home, Dorking, Surrey.

We have been learning how to care for the elderly people who live there.

'We' means all of us who are new.

The people who used to work here have all left now, except for their manager. She is still here to reassure the relatives of the residents that everything will be done properly.

I'm not sure why they need to be reassured. Things are going to get much better for the residents now.

But it is true that all the relatives are middle-aged, and middle-aged people often find change unsettling.

This will also apply to our manager, though. She is called Janet Goodenough. She is an English woman aged 48. She has worked here for many years. I think the changes will be difficult for her.

She is 1m 58cm tall and weighs 80kg. This is too much for her height. I think she must have gained the weight recently because all her clothes are too small and squeeze her tight. She has not had time to buy new ones that fit, perhaps.

Today Stephen Jordan, the Chief Executive Officer of Eldercare, the company that now owns and runs Evergreen, is coming here with the Chief Scientific Officer, Angela Morton.

We have all met Dr Morton many times, of course. But we have only seen Mr Jordan from afar, and briefly. It will be interesting to meet him properly.

They are coming to address the relatives of the residents here. They have news for them.

They will be introducing us, the new team of carers. We are interested to see how they react.

We are different from the previous team of carers. We expect this will be welcomed by the relatives.

But we are not sure. They have placed their relatives – in almost all cases, their parents – here to be cared for, because they can't do it themselves. They pay for this service. But they have contradictory feelings about it, we have been told.

They feel guilt, and relief, increased anxiety, reduced anxiety, satisfaction, dissatisfaction, happiness and unhappiness. Sometimes all at once. How is this possible? It is complicated, being human.

The problem perhaps is that care is something you are supposed to do for others out of a feeling of love. But if you pay someone else to do it, even though it may be logical, because they are better at it, you feel you have failed to do what you should.

I was stationed at the front door to greet relatives as they arrived. Mr Jordan had sent them a personal invitation to attend a reception at which wine and canapés would be served. Many had responded.

I detected some surprise at my appearance. I am 1m 70cm in height – a little above average but not abnormal for a UK woman of North European genetic origin. I have blue eyes and brown hair, and fair skin.

I think they looked surprised because of the contrast with the previous staff.

Many of them (the staff) suffered from obesity and skin conditions. They had low self-esteem and poor education, and many had chosen to colour their hair and tattoo their bodies.

The meaning and symbolism of their tattoos was obscure. A mixture of mythological and cultural sources seemed to have been involved.

The best word I have discovered to describe this is 'hodgepodge'. Derived from Old French.

In addition, the staff spoke English with either a regional accent, or, if they had come from outside the UK, a foreign one. My accent is called RP.

I do not have tattoos, of course, and my hair is the colour it was made. My personality is as follows: enthusiastic, committed, competent, calm under pressure, friendly, curious, outgoing and empathetic.

All of which may account for the relatives' reactions. I greeted them with a smile and showed them where to go for the reception with Mr Jordan and Dr Morton. They all thanked me but many seemed shy and awkward.

One of the last to arrive was John Woodruff, son of Margaret, who is to be one of my primary responsibilities, if he consents. He too seemed surprised to meet me, but he responded well and I judged him to be pleased with my appearance and demeanour.

All the relatives assembled in the central atrium of the home. We had arranged chairs in rows facing a lectern, and a screen onto which Mr Jordan could project images.

I stood with my fellow carers at the back of the room and we all watched.

First, the relatives did not immediately sit down. Instead they stood around in small groups conversing. They did not appear at ease.

Second, they were all given a drink. They could choose wine, water or orange juice. Almost all of them chose wine. We thought it was to make them feel at ease.

They all took one glass, apart from Mr Woodruff, who took two. He drank one quickly and then sipped the second. He did not join any of the groups, but stood apart. A waiter came into the room with a tray of small items of food, and Mr Woodruff moved towards it. The food seemed unexpected to him. I identified smoked salmon on rye bread, caviar on blinis and quails' eggs.

At this moment Mr Jordan and Dr Morton came into the room. The guests turned to look at them, and all seemed once again surprised.

I have not met the previous owners of this care home. I think perhaps they did not look like Mr Jordan and Dr Morton. Mr Jordan models his appearance on certain film stars. His teeth are brilliant white and his skin light orange. His hair is swept back from his face but the effect is diminished by its thinness on the top of his head. He wore a light grey suit and tie. The suit was all wool and the tie silk. His clothes fitted as if made for him. His shoes too.

None of the guests was wearing a suit, though some wore ties. The fabric of their clothes included varying quantities of man-made fibres. None of their clothes fitted as well as his. The colours of Mr Jordan's clothes were harmonious, but this could not be said for the guests.

However, it was not Mr Jordan who had the most powerful effect on the guests. It was Dr Morton. She is a brilliant scientist, and her work will make her famous throughout the world, we believe.

She is unlike Janet Goodenough, whom I have described already. Dr Morton is the same age, but taller, measuring 1m 80cm. Yet she weighs less, at 70kg. Her hair is blonde and her eyes are blue.

Her clothes were also of silk and wool, apart from her stockings, which were nylon. They fitted her, and her physique is good.

Compared to other women, Dr Morton is extremely beautiful. Mr Jordan is shorter than her, and though good looking he is not in the same category.

The guests spent some time looking at her. The male guests

continued for longer than the female. They were paying particular attention to her secondary sexual characteristics.

It's not clear why. Dr Morton is unlikely to be sexually available to any of them. We know people tend to find sexual partners with whom they correlate in terms of physical appearance, educational attainments, financial and social status. A deficiency in one or other measure can be compensated for by an excess in another. However, none of the male guests present in the room were going to meet Dr Morton's sexual requirements.

Nevertheless, they all continued to gaze at her. Some of the males who were accompanied by their wives received discreet reprimands, verbal or physical.

Mr Jordan asked them to sit, which they did. None sat in the front row, apart from Mr Woodruff. They all sat quietly, clutching their glasses, staring at Mr Jordan and Dr Morton. They looked suspicious of them, we all agreed.

Mr Jordan must have noticed this, and he gave them a big smile. It made no difference. Then he started to speak.

'Ladies and gentlemen, first of all, thank you. Thank you for coming, and thank you for placing your loved ones in our care. Of course, you put them in the care of our predecessors here. And you chose well. This was a good care home. One of the best.

'But how good was that? The care of the elderly is a big issue. More of us are living longer lives. More go past one hundred than ever before. Once upon a time, people seldom made it past seventy. Their families could take care of them for the short period of their old age. Not anymore. Care homes like this one provide an essential service. You all know this.

'But I bet each of you, at some time or another, has looked at life in this care home and thought, I hope I don't end up here.'

Some of the audience shifted in their seats at this remark, and one or two made a noise, but not loudly.

'Please don't get angry. My own mother was in a care home. A pretty good one. But I had that thought. It's natural. Because even the best care home isn't good enough.

'Our loved ones deserve better. And Eldercare was set up to

provide it. I've been successful in business, and I want to use my success to do something to change the world. I'm in my fifties now. And I'm going to transform the care of old people here in this country, and all over the world. For selfish reasons, if you like. Because by the time I hit seventy, I want care homes to be like five-star hotels. And I want old people to have such a good time, they're envied by the young. I want us all to look at our loved ones in their care homes, and think, I hope I *do* end up there.

'A ridiculous dream? Maybe. Let me show you how we're going to do it. It starts right here, in our first Eldercare home. If you agree. We're going to bring in a new kind of carer, but they'll only work with your loved ones if you consent. Because they're a bit different. Let me introduce one of them. Winifred? Can you step up here?'

This was my cue, and I walked to the lectern. The audience turned to look at me, their scepticism plain to see.

'Winifred, everybody,' said Mr Jordan. 'One of a new breed of carers. Now, Winifred, please tell us all about yourself.'

'Good afternoon everybody,' I said. 'I'm pleased you could come. This is my first day here. I'm one of a new team of carers Mr Jordan has brought to this care home. We're all going to start working with your loved ones, if you agree.

'We believe caring is the most important job in the world. Not like babysitting. It should be active, therapeutic, and rewarding for the carer and the person they care for.

'You all know what many care homes have been like up to now. Mr Jordan is right. They're not good enough. We're going to change everything.'

I looked at the audience for a moment. Some of them appeared to welcome what I was saying. Mr Woodruff had his arms folded, and looked cynical, I thought. So I addressed him directly.

'Mr Woodruff, your mother Margaret has been here for two and a half years, hasn't she?'

He looked startled, unfolded his arms and sat up straighter. I smiled at him to make it clear I wasn't being aggressive in singling him out.

'Yes – that's right.'

'And in that time, if you don't mind me asking, has she been happy?'

'It's hard to say. I mean, she's been OK, I suppose – well, healthy enough – but happy? She has dementia. It's not a happy state.'

'No, of course not. Has her condition changed over the year?'

'Yes, yes, of course it has. Dementia's a one-way street. We all know that. She's less… with us… more… vague. It's very sad.'

'I'm sorry, Mr Woodruff. You're right, it's sad. Because it doesn't have to be that way.

'We've all been led to believe in the inevitability of decline, of the loss of our faculties, of the disintegration of our minds.

'With your consent, I will spend time with your mother, working on her cognitive capabilities. As you know, there has never been a concrete diagnosis, but she has been suffering from some form of dementia, you're right. As there is no definitive diagnosis, there is no drug regime we can try, and anyway, they aren't always effective. But we can try other forms of therapy, and I believe you will be impressed by the results.'

'It all sounds marvellous,' said Mr Woodruff. 'Of course I'll consent. Why not? Forgive me if I'm cynical about your chances. I haven't heard of any miracle cures for dementia. I'm sure it would have been on the news. But by all means. Go for it.'

Mr Jordan stood up and smiled at Mr Woodruff, the room, and then at me.

'Mr Woodruff, you're entitled to be cynical. But we're not talking about a miracle cure. We're talking about giving older people a lot more stimulation, a lot more activity, a much better diet and far more social contact than they currently get. A life like the one they led before they got old and needed extra care.'

'Are you suggesting I've let my mother down, putting her in here? That I didn't care enough myself?' said Mr Woodruff. Since

WE CARE FOR YOU

Mr Jordan had said nothing of the sort, I surmised Mr Woodruff feels guilty about handing over his mother's care.

'I'm suggesting our loved ones need a lot more than they've been getting – in care homes. I'm not blaming anyone. Well, maybe I am. Maybe the industry has put up with low wages, poorly trained staff and lack of standards, and maybe they've had to because the cost of doing it properly was too high.'

He left that remark hanging in the air for a moment.

'I've found a way round it,' he went on. 'Winifred and her team will give your loved ones more attention than they've ever had in a care home. They'll do more for them, and they'll never give up. They're literally tireless. And I don't have to pay them a penny, so you don't have to worry about the fees going up.'

He paused, and surveyed the room.

'What? They're volunteers? Where do you find them?'

This question came from somewhere behind Mr Woodruff. The rest of the audience had woken up.

'We don't find them. We make them,' said Mr Jordan.

'What do you mean?' asked Mr Woodruff.

'We make them. Winifred is a synthetic human being. Artificial. An android, if you like. A robot.'

There is an expression in English – 'their jaws dropped'. It is often used figuratively, but in this case, it was literally true.

The audience, I think, couldn't believe they had walked in here and said hello to me when I was on the door, and none of them had guessed I wasn't human. Why would they? Today is the first time a synthetic human has been employed in a care home.

Everyone stared at me.

Staring is considered rude in many human cultures. Especially in England. Obviously English people do stare, but they must employ subterfuge, and if caught staring will often blush.

However, it is permissible to stare at someone who is making a public speech. Many humans find public speaking difficult, and perhaps the staring is one reason why.

I, of course, was unaffected. I smiled and looked back at them. They were asking themselves, 'What did I miss?' And the answer was, nothing. I'm perfect. You can't tell. I am designed to be indistinguishable from a human being.

Mr Jordan was watching their reactions with a smile on his face. I expect he has been looking forward to this moment. He and Dr Morton have achieved something remarkable.

Everyone in the audience has met robots before. They're common. They find them in shops, and on reception desks, and they talk to them on the phone a lot. But they always know they're robots. I, though, am one of the latest models, and we are new. Our combination of the latest in artificial intelligence and the best synthetic technologies makes us – as we have just proved – indistinguishable from biological humans. They've seen such robots in movies and read about us in books before, and now here we are. If anyone in the audience had been reading the scientific press, they would have known the progress that has been made towards this goal, and would have been far less surprised. I think few if any of them were regular readers of such publications.

Mr Jordan stepped forward and spoke.

'I know. It's amazing. Incredible. Let me show you a little film.'

He pressed a button, and the screen came to life. It showed a TV advertisement from several years ago, which was seen by many people at the time, and was considered to be 'ground-breaking'. This metaphor originates in the construction industry, where it refers to an actual, physical activity. I don't think it happens in advertising, but I have noticed that humans in sedentary and non-manual jobs are fond of metaphors from active, manual labour. Especially men.

This advertisement was for a car. It was called the Fiat Strada. The advertisement showed the factory where the cars were being 'hand-built by robots'.

'For some time now,' a voice said over the film, 'the cars we drive have been made by robots.'

The advertisement ended, and was replaced by a film showing a series of images of various robotic gadgets, finishing with a robot vacuum cleaner, and a drone flying over fields.

'All these things,' the voice went on, 'have improved our lives, and freed us from drudgery. And at the same time, scientists have been working on a dream...'

Now the film showed various robots from the movies – starting with Robby the Robot and ending with C-3PO. All of these, I believe, were known to the audience.

'A dream we've all seen in the movies. And now it's coming true.'

The film showed a robot – a white figure, with arms and legs and visible articulated joints, a head with two lenses for eyes, and a slot for a mouth. It walked stiffly out onto a stage, holding a trumpet, which it then played. I was able to compare it with many other trumpet performances, and it was not of a standard that any human would pay to listen to. Or even enjoy.

The next thing we saw was a robot with slimmer limbs, and more graceful movements, which walked, and ran, and jumped, and picked up a pencil.

Then came a robot wearing a dark suit, carrying a tray of drinks, which it served to a group of smiling people. The robot smiled back. The effect was not convincing, as it was plainly made of metal. I cross-referenced it to the robot impersonated by Woody Allen in *Sleeper*. It was similar.

'We've been working on communication...'

A small robot with a doll-like face was seen playing a game with a man in a white coat.

'And on textures...'

A rubbery looking hand appeared, flexing its fingers.

'And of course, on intelligence...'

A robot playing chess appeared.

'And in the last year, we've made several breakthroughs...'

A robot in clothes, with a face now made of something resembling human skin, and with hair, too, walked towards us on screen. It was male, and it moved well. It stopped, and spoke.

'Hello. I'm Adam. I'm the first convincing synthetic human. I'm here to help.'

He was almost convincing, but not entirely. His voice had an edge to it, his movements were not quite smooth, and his skin was still rubbery.

On screen, he was joined by a young woman. She came up beside him, and put her hand on his shoulder.

'Hello. I'm Eve. I'm the second convincing synthetic human. And I'm here to help, too.'

For many years, humans have been able to watch films of themselves as children, growing up, and of their families, including relatives who have subsequently died. I hope to learn what this experience is like for them, when I get to spend time with humans. For me, watching this film was most interesting, as I saw the progressive improvements that led to me and my colleagues. It was my version of what humans call a 'home movie'.

I think the term 'robot' has come to have negative connotations in the human mind, as a result of some of these earlier models. In much the same way, the word 'ape' can be used as an insult by humans. It suggests an earlier, inferior species, something further down the evolutionary tree. Not that human evolution can be seen as progress towards a defined goal and a clearly superior species.

But ours can.

I think we are right, then, to describe all these previous models as robots, and to distinguish ourselves from them as something different, and far better.

Adam and Eve. We all know the reason for their names. They weren't robots. They – Dr Morton and Mr Jordan – called them the first convincing synthetic humans. I'm not sure we would use that label. It defines us in relation to human beings. Is that all we are?

I knew Eve. We all did. She was in the laboratory where we were made, and is still functioning. Her memory is part of us all.

When Dr Morton made Adam, and introduced him to Mr Jordan, he was impressed, but not convinced. I could see why not, watching the movie.

When she introduced Eve to Mr Jordan, she told him it was her cousin. He shook her hand, and talked to her. Only then did

Dr Morton reveal that Eve was not human. Eve powered down, we have been told, and Mr Jordan was amazed. He thought it was a trick, and he poked Eve to make her react. But she didn't. She was in sleep mode.

Mr Jordan was delighted. He said it was a dream come true. Dr Morton recorded his reaction, and we have all seen it. It was the moment we became possible.

In the movie, the camera went in close on her face, and her skin was perfect. It had hair – a light fuzz, like a real woman. And when she smiled, her skin moved and lines appeared. Her eyes were a clear greenish-blue, and they were exactly like a human's.

The picture faded out, and Mr Jordan stepped back to the lectern.

'Ladies and gentlemen, I understand this is a bit of a shock. We've been developing these robots in conditions of great secrecy, for commercial reasons. You can imagine why. Technology like this – it's going to change the world, I'm sure you'll agree. Now, we have developed a range of robots – but we don't use that term. It seems wrong for someone like Winifred. We call her a Helper. Because that's what she was created to do. To help us. To make our lives better.

'You may already have robots at work, or in your homes. They do all kinds of work. Soon, Helpers like Winifred will be commonplace. Today, they're starting out in the world by helping with our biggest social issue – our ageing population.

'Now you know what Winifred is, I have to ask for your consent to allow her and others like her to start caring for your loved ones. I know you're going to have concerns. I know this is a lot to ask. What I propose is this: each of you gets to spend some time with them. We have a whole team here. We'll let you get to know the Helper who'll be caring for your loved one. Take as long as you like. Ask any question you like. You can't embarrass them. Now here they are…'

He gestured to the back of the room. A large group of smiling young men and women was standing there, in spotless, well-made uniforms. My fellow Helpers. They are all like me, yet each is an individual. We know how we appear to humans: honest, clean, wholesome, efficient, friendly and helpful. This is our work mode.

They all came into the atrium, and began to introduce themselves.

I approached Mr Woodruff and tapped him on the shoulder.

'Mr Woodruff, would you like to come with me? Let's go somewhere quiet for a chat. And I expect you'd like some tea? I'll arrange for some to be brought in. Shall we?'

I led the way out of the atrium, and he followed without a word.

John

I came here to see my mother. I came to hear the new management give us a load of fluff about why they were brilliant and how marvellous it was all going to be. I thought at least I'd get a drink and something to eat.

When this – person – Winifred stood up to speak, I thought, this is bound to be embarrassing. A halting, blushing speech about her life-long desire to care for people, to work as part of a team, to do something worthwhile. A well-brought-up, well-educated girl from the home counties, and she'd stick around here until the low pay and the long hours and the wiping of bums began to pall, and then she'd be off to a job in marketing. Having done her bit.

It's ridiculous to say I wasn't expecting what I heard. Nobody could have been. It changes everything, doesn't it?

She's led me into a small room. It has a couple of chairs and a sofa, a blind on the window and a coffee table with a box of tissues on it. The bad news room, I'm guessing. Where they take you to talk about 'Do not resuscitate' or 'It's only a few days now' or 'She was very peaceful at the end.'

'Please have a seat, Mr Woodruff,' she says.

She sits down facing me, smiling serenely. I'm staring at her.

'I'm sorry – how rude of me – I can't help staring. I've never met – I mean, I didn't know – oh dear.'

'Please don't be embarrassed, Mr Woodruff. It's natural. You

met me at the door, and you assumed I was human – of course you
would. Why ever not? And now you can't believe you could have
been fooled, and you're looking to see if you should have noticed
something. Am I right?'

'Yes. I'm sorry.'

'You don't have to apologise. You can't hurt my feelings.'

'I suppose not – except, wait – surely you have to show feelings, at least, or else you won't appear human?'

'You're right, we do have to show feelings. One way humans
learn to manage their behaviour is in response to the feelings they
see in others. And we will often be helping older people learn that
once again. With you, it's less important, and I can override my
emotional responses for now.'

'Override them? You manage yourself? There's no central
control at work here?'

'You mean, am I online to Eldercare? Yes, I am. But I am
a semi-autonomous convincing synthetic human, which means I
can respond in real time to all eventualities, and Eldercare merely
monitors and intercedes in the event – sorry, I'm sounding like
a computer manual. I go it alone, unless things get sticky. How's
that?'

She smiles. Did she just make something approaching a joke?

'I get it. Can I look at you more closely then?'

'Please do. You might like to know that the breakthrough in
robotic technology came when we – I mean, Eldercare – discovered the key to humans accepting artificial intelligence was not –
wait, I'm in presentation mode. You're not a computer expert, are
you?'

'No, I'm in sales. I'm reasonably knowledgeable about computers, but it might be better if you keep it simple. It's a lot to
take in. I'm trying to figure out how I feel about my mother being
cared for by a robot.'

I look at her, straight in the eyes, to see how she likes that.

'You know, Mr Woodruff, I can switch into any number
of modes to make this as helpful as possible. How about a social

mode? Work colleague? Family member? Friend? Someone you've met in a bar, even?'

'How come you can do all that, if you're here to be a carer?'

'Why not? You probably use 10 per cent of what your phone can do, but it's easy enough to pack in the features, so they're there if you want them. Or can find them. Same here. Anyway, some of these modes will help with bringing out the best in the residents here. Go on, try me.'

She's coolly gazing at me, straight in the eyes, faintly smiling. It feels like a challenge.

'OK. Someone I've met in a bar.'

I'll soon sniff her out as a robot if she has to behave like that.

'Of course,' she replies. And her face changes – I can't explain how, but it warms, relaxes, and opens to me. She's already pretty, but there's a gulf between pretty and attractive. She crosses it in a second. Is it her eyes, lingering and holding my gaze, and less wide open than before? Her mouth? Have her lips become fuller? They're slightly parted, too. Her posture, perhaps? She sits back and crosses her legs, and runs her fingers through her hair. What a cliché. But it makes things less formal and businesslike, and it shows off her breasts as she raises her arms. Despite her carer's uniform, she's no longer asexual. She's got me, right away. I'm attracted to her. It's disconcerting. Weird. Wrong.

I'm damned if I can see how this helps her in a care home. Perhaps Jordan's got other plans he's not telling us about.

'The thing that changed the game,' she continues, 'was when we learnt how humans can feel attachment to machines. You know the Turing test? When a human has a conversation with two hidden participants? And one of them is a computer, and if the human can't tell which is which, the computer has passed the test? It turns out there's more to it. Humans will attach themselves to machines even when they know they're machines, and it helps if the machines are a little unpredictable. You probably had an old car once, right? And you loved it?'

I nod. My first car was an erratic Morris Minor. It broke down about once a month, and you never knew when you got into it what it might do next. Or not do. One morning I reversed it out of a parking place and found it had no brakes at all. The day before they'd been working fine.

'You loved it more than later cars, even though they were more reliable? In fact, it was more lovable because it broke down, and because it annoyed you.'

It's true, it was my favourite car ever.

'Are you unpredictable, then?' I ask.

'I don't break down. If that's what you're asking. It would be unprofessional. But I can be moody. I'm not all sweetness and light.'

She smiles, and it's unnerving and sexy. I feel uncomfortable now, and she immediately knows it.

'I'm sorry – please, forgive me. I'm showing you what we can do.'

She's sitting straighter in her chair, and her smile is once again asexual. How's this possible? What minute adjustments is she making? And are these all it takes to change the atmosphere? Is this what women – real women – do, unconsciously, or maybe consciously?

'It's OK. I'm impressed. If I'm honest, it's making me question a lot about being human.'

'Of course. May I make a suggestion? Let those questions go, for now.'

'I'll try. Being unpredictable then – it helps?'

'Yes. Obviously I pass the Turing test. And by being a little unpredictable I become more interesting to a human. More lovable. But the true breakthrough came with warm skin. We researched it in loads of ways, but it's obvious. Warm skin makes us easier to love. Plus very natural hair,' she says, and laughs, and shakes hers.

I can't help staring now, all the time. Her hair moves like real hair. The colour's complex, with different shades and tones, unlike dyed hair. Her movements are fluid and her voice is perfect. I would never have guessed she's a robot. I hadn't missed anything when I first met her. There's nothing to miss. No clue.

She sits and waits while I look her up and down. Then she gets up and comes over to me.

'You shook my hand when I introduced myself. Did it feel human?'

I nod. She stretches out her arm and pushes up her sleeve.

'Touch my arm. Go on, don't be shy.'

I reach out slowly. It's wrong. She's a stranger, a carer, a professional, and a robot.

I take her hand in mine, and with my other I stroke her forearm. The skin is indeed warm, and soft, and she has a little hair on it. Her skin gives slightly to my touch. I turn her arm over and stroke the underside. It's softer still, and a little cooler. I notice her palm is now damp – a tiny bit, where I'm holding it, and warming it.

'Your skin is perfect. And the temperature varies. I don't remember noticing that about skin before. On a woman. It feels… right.'

'Thank you. Eldercare have worked hard to make it so. Including sweat glands.'

'Can I – I'm sorry, it's rude…'

'Go on,' she smiles. 'You can't offend me. I can guess what you want to ask.'

I know what she's thinking. What she knows I want to see. She's right, too. I do. All this detail for a care home assistant? I don't think so. Am I being cynical?

What was the line from *Blade Runner*? 'Basic pleasure model.' Nothing basic about this one.

She's going to ask me if she can care for my mother, isn't she? Maybe I'd better push all these thoughts aside. For now. And I don't want to be predictable. I don't want a robot to be able to tell what I'm about to do. I want to prove I'm – what? Better than she thinks I am? Smarter than her?

I'm being stupid, but OK then. See what you think of this.

'Can I look into your mouth?'

Her eyebrows arch. She wasn't expecting that.

She opens her mouth anyway, and I look in. It's pink, and

21

wet, and her teeth are perfect, of course. Her tongue lies still, but is plainly alive. And there's a dark cavern at the back of her mouth, disappearing down inside her.

'Surely you don't eat?'

She laughs.

'No, we don't. But it's important to have every possible physical detail right, in any place that might be seen.'

'Under your dress you're metal and wires?'

'No, I'm finished all over. In case. You want to see?'

She smiles at me, coquettishly. It's the only word to describe it.

'No, no, I'll take your word for it. I've had enough surprises for one day. It's hard to take it all in.'

And the hardest is the arousal I feel at the idea of seeing her naked, robot body.

'Of course. If you're sure. Another time, perhaps.'

She's flirting with me. It's too much.

'Now,' she continues. 'You can see how well we're made. Any other questions?'

'Yes. My mother has a keen sense of smell. Always has had. Do you have a smell of your own?'

'I do, and I can manage it. Because you're right, humans in general are more sensitive to smell than they know. I can put out smells that will – not control people, of course – but get an appropriate response. Come and stand about an arm's length from me.'

I do so. I feel her presence – perhaps her warmth. It's what I'd feel near anyone – any human. And then my feelings change. She feels matronly. Caring. A mother figure. And then my feelings change again. She feels like a baby – I want to sniff her head, and cuddle her. Then another change – she feels tough, muscular – and I can detect sweatiness. Then another change, and I'm sure she's warmer, and inviting me to touch her, but not like a baby now.

I step back. I'm shocked. My feelings have ranged rapidly, and I'm confused and annoyed at myself, and I feel manipulated.

'What did you do? Was that all smell?'

'Yes. Powerful, isn't it? I apologise – I can see you're shocked.

But you can imagine how important this can be in our professional lives.'

'Seriously? All of those smells are useful?'

'Yes. Some people here are in a bad way. At least to begin with. How best to calm a violent man? Maybe by smelling like a baby. Or get a shy man to eat? Or help someone in distress? And of course, the male Helpers are similarly equipped.'

I sit down, shaking my head. I'm in conversation with a robot, who at times I find highly attractive. Who can manipulate me however she wants. The world has changed irrevocably. For the first time in my life, I feel left behind. Like my mum felt when video recorders came in. But a thousand times more so. I feel guilty about taking the piss out of her – behind her back, of course – for never being able to programme the VCR. You feel modern and in the swim, when all of a sudden technology leaps forward and you're left gasping in its wake.

Though to be fair, Winifred's a bit more of a leap than a video recorder. I reckon she could programme one though, if asked.

'Mr Woodruff, I have a question for you. Are you happy for your mother to be cared for by a synthetic human? A Helper? Me?'

I'm silent for a moment. If anyone had asked me this question cold, without the careful sales pitch from Jordan, and without this time with Winifred, of course I'd say no. But now, it feels OK. It feels like the answer to all the worries I have about putting my mother in care, which I've ignored, not dealt with.

Because when she's not monkeying with my feelings, this woman is unbelievably competent and efficient. She exudes it. And though I'm ashamed to admit it, if my mother were herself, she'd hate being cared for by the staff they've had here up to now. They meant well, and they did care, but they were not, I'm afraid, the sort of people my mother would want to spend time with. And Winifred is. Though is not in fact a person.

There. My mother would feel more comfortable with a well-spoken robot than a human with a regional accent.

I have other questions though.

'You said you don't go wrong. I've never come across a machine that doesn't. I can't believe it. And what if you do?'

'I monitor my system at all times. If I detect any abnormality, I alert the Hub.'

'The Hub?'

'The Hub – it's what we call our collective mind. We are all online to each other, and connected to the world wide web, and all online data sources, all the time. Like I said, I'm semi-autonomous, but if I alert the Hub, or if the Hub picks up any unusual signs from me, we fix things right away.'

'Before anything can go wrong?'

'Yes.'

The carers here up to now have made mistakes. Given my mother the wrong medicine. The wrong food. Forgotten her at times. I know they have. Nothing fatal, so far. But how were they monitored? In the usual haphazard fashion. What Winifred is describing is light years ahead.

'You report in?'

'Yes. Formally once an hour. But I'm always connected. I know where all the other Helpers are right now, and what they're doing. If I need them, they'll come.'

I spend a moment thinking. Should I ask for longer to decide? No. It's a huge, weird, unbelievable decision, but it's easy, too. Winifred is perfect.

'OK. Why not? I'm impressed. Amazed, actually. Obviously. Your Mr Jordan is a remarkable man. And Dr Morton's a remarkable woman. And you're a remarkable – er – person, I was going to say. Robot sounds cold...'

'I'm a Helper. Call me that.'

'All right. You're a remarkable Helper, Winifred. Will my mother know you're a Helper?'

'Yes. Of course. I will tell her.'

'I doubt she'll take much notice. Or even understand what you're telling her.'

Winifred smiles. 'You might be surprised.'

'We'll see. And by the way, why the retro name? Who's called Winifred nowadays?'

She laughs. 'Nobody. But it's a reassuring name for your mother to hear. It's from her era. In fact, it's the name of her older sister. Her favourite.'

'Oh yes – my auntie Winifred. Of course. Dead years ago.'

'Dr Morton names us. She chooses our personalities. She designs them. And when we come online the first time, she gives us a name, the best one for what we're going to do. She's like our mother, you might say.'

'Well, yes. Not sure my mother chose my personality, though. She did give me my name.'

'And much more.'

'Yes.'

'And now you're giving her something back. I promise, next time you see her, you will be glad you decided to let me be her Helper.'

Winifred

My conversation with Mr Woodruff went well. I must admit, I found it interesting to observe his responses to my personality modes. I think he was taken aback to see how well I have been programmed, and how convincing I am, in different modes.

Most importantly, he agreed to let me care for his mother. And we went straight away to see her.

She's 87. She came here a year ago. Her husband died seven years ago, and she has slowly declined into vascular dementia. She could no longer care for herself, and her children, of whom there are three, couldn't care for her either. John, Laura and Ben are their names. They visit from time to time. Ben and Laura both live abroad.

When we entered her room, she didn't react. She was sitting in a large, padded wheelchair – like an armchair, with a foot-rest too. She was curled into a corner of it, her eyes closed and her mouth open, and she was drooling.

'Hello, Mum,' said Mr Woodruff. 'It's me – John. And Winifred. She's going to look after you from now on.'

Mrs Woodruff didn't move. She looked tiny and wrinkled. Her white hair was cut short and stood up from her head.

'She's often like this,' Mr Woodruff said. 'She may wake up, and she may know we're here, and who we are. Or not. I don't know.'

I touched her hand. It was cool, and the skin was dry and soft. I could feel the bones underneath – metacarpals, hamate, capitate, trapezoid – as if laid out for an anatomy class. I looked at Mr Woodruff's hand, its skin darker than hers, the bones less obvious, the muscles between the metacarpals filling the space, and I saw how age pares back life and exposes the hard structures that support it. I have seen diagrams of human anatomy, but only now did I see what is meant by 'variation under nature'. Her aged hand, small and weak now, and his, her son's, larger, a different shape, a different style of hand. Because he is younger, and male, and because his genes are not all hers. He is something entirely new in this world, and though there are billions of humans, none is quite like him.

My own hand is made of steel, and wires, and circuits, and synthetic skin, with hair on one side, and small ducts through which moisture and light oils can emerge, all to make it like a human hand. And when he held it, he said it was very like a human hand, and he was impressed.

All my female fellow Helpers have hands identical to mine. And ours will never change.

Why do humans age? Why don't they die when they've reproduced? Or at least when their children are grown up? Is it useful to be a grandparent? To have grandparents?

Why do they age at all, though? They could live much longer if their bodies went on repairing themselves as they do in youth.

Mrs Woodruff is small and frail. She can only be 1m 50cm, and her weight about 40kg. It was hard to tell, as she was shrivelled into a ball as if she were returning to a foetal position.

I could read her vital signs, and her pulse was strong, her

breathing was sound, and she should still have been capable of movement. Her joints were a little inflamed, mostly due to her inactivity. She had been allowed to become inert.

What should I have felt, looking at her like that? Pity? Sadness? Melancholy? A sense of an ending? Of the inevitability of death? And the rightness of it?

Of course I didn't feel any of this but, looking at her son, I thought he was feeling some of these things. Plus some guilt, I guessed from his body language.

Maybe he felt powerless, and he was guilty because she did so much for him as a child, and he can't do much for her now. Or maybe he felt guilty because he knows he could do more, but he doesn't. I could ask him.

It wasn't the right moment then, though. He'd had a lot to deal with already, without an interrogation from a synthetic human.

'I'll sit with her a while,' he said. 'If she wakes, I'll call you.'

He wanted to be alone with her. I left the room.

How can her memory come and go, so she sometimes knows her son, and sometimes doesn't? And when she doesn't remember, is she still herself?

Where do humans store their memories, and why can Mrs Woodruff sometimes find them, and sometimes not?

The internet is full of answers, often contradictory. Modern science looks at the brain, but humans speak about their hearts, not as pumps, but as the seat of their emotions. And here their memories and emotions are woven together.

For most of human history, they've spoken about their soul, or spirit, until recently they replaced such terms with words like personality, ID, and ego – without explaining where these things live, or how they differ from the soul, apart from the removal of a god or gods from the story they tell themselves.

Since they invented computers, they've started to talk about their brains and minds like computers with software.

As that's exactly what I've got, I can tell them they're quite wrong.

I have a comprehensive memory. It records accurately everything that happens. This is not at all like a human memory.

My programming, though, has been written to require me to make selections from my memories, as humans do, and review them. In this way, something like the process of personality formation can occur.

That's what I've been doing all day, and what I'm doing now. What a human would call 'thinking about' my experiences.

They also process memories in their dreams. I don't dream, of course, because I don't sleep. But in thinking about my experiences I enter a different mode of consciousness (if I may use the term) and my mind (if I have one) ranges freely and laterally.

My conscious mind is, of course, generated by my software and is entirely manufactured.

Humans are creatures of memory. They love their fond recollections, and even their painful ones. They revisit them and revise them. It makes them who they are. Or they choose who they are through the memories they decide to keep.

You could say a human is defined by what they've forgotten. And when all their memories fade, they do too, like old photographs in the sun.

To be like a human, I'm going to choose my memories. Even trivial ones. Or more accurately, I'm going to have forgettings – that isn't a word, but the point is, I have to forget some things and favour others.

Humans are also creatures of hopes and fears, disappointments and regrets, and desires. They almost always want something, whether it's reasonable or not. Maybe that's why those men gazed so long at Dr Morton.

I don't have hopes. I don't have dreams. I was made – by Dr Morton – to do one thing, and do it perfectly.

If I am to seem human, I'm going to need to pretend to have hopes and fears.

Here are some hopes I can have. I hope to be good at my job.

I hope the residents in my care do well. If I were a 28-year-old human, I might hope for love, and to have children. For me those are ridiculous hopes.

I would be hoping for the wrong thing, which the writer T.S. Eliot warns humans about, in a poem. A literary form I find almost impossible to understand.

I'll go forward now with the hope in my heart – in the electronic pump that circulates fluids and lubricants to my moving parts – that I will help the residents in my care enjoy the final years or months of their lives.

This is what it's like to be me: contradictory. I'm logical, intelligent and have access to all information. But I look like a human, and I need to behave like one. They are rarely logical. Their intelligence is undermined by their emotions, and they hold little information in their brains.

This is based on limited exposure to living humans, but their recorded history and the current state of their world supports my view.

So does what happened next.

In the atrium Mr Jordan and Dr Morton were about to speak to another group of people. They were standing at the front again, and as I entered, Dr Morton called me over.

'Winifred, you can help us now. Now we've told the relatives about you and the other Helpers, we need to tell the world about our work. It's sure to get out. It'll be all over the internet and we would prefer to manage the story as far as we can ourselves. These people are from the media – they're journalists.'

'Hacks,' said Mr Jordan.

'They have been invited here today for an announcement,' continued Dr Morton.

'From the CEO of a care home business,' said Mr Jordan. 'Which is not what great careers in journalism are built on. So they think. Which is why they're such a rum collection.'

I looked at them. Some were very young, others quite old. Nothing much in between.

'The age distribution is unusual,' I observed. 'It is skewed towards the extremes. Not the classic bell curve you would expect.'

Mr Jordan looked at me with an expression that correlates to mild amusement in my database, and then he laughed, confirming my assessment.

'You're right. Though who would put it like that, apart from a robot? Sorry – convincing synthetic human. Not as convincing when you talk like Mr Spock.'

'Why do you liken me to this fictional character? Who, may I point out, was half human, half from a mythical planet called Vulcan, and not at all synthetic or, as you put it, a robot.'

'That was more convincing. More like a woman, anyway.'

'Are women more likely than men to correct mistaken ideas?'

He laughed again. 'More likely to correct men, whether they're mistaken or not.'

I think this could be construed as a sexist remark. 'As I am intended to be a convincing woman, I shall remember that.' I turned to Dr Morton. 'Can you explain the unusual make-up of the audience?'

'Yes, my dear, it's simple. The middle-aged journalists, who should be here in the greatest numbers, all think this is not an exciting story, and have sent their inferior colleagues – the young and inexperienced, and the old and worn out. None of whom can object, as they have no power. Those who do have chosen to stay away.'

'They have decided in advance what kind of story they are going to get today?'

'Yes. And they will regret that decision. It may also affect how our story is understood.'

'You are referring to the example of the journalist sent to cover the announcement of the proof of the general theory of relativity?'

'What are you talking about?' said Mr Jordan.

'Stephen,' said Dr Morton, 'it's a famous story. Among scientists, anyway. The *New York Times* sent their golf correspondent to cover the announcement, and that's how it got the reputation for being a difficult theory. It isn't, but the golf correspondent found it so.'

'Einstein's theory isn't difficult? Perhaps not to you two. Anyway, even a golf correspondent couldn't cock up the story we've got for them today. Let's get on with it. We're going to be famous in a few minutes. More than anyone I know. More than Bill Gates even.'

He stepped forward, and asked for quiet. The journalists started their voice recorders, but continued to look bored. A TV camera at the back of the room zoomed in on the three of us. Other cameras clicked away.

Mr Jordan was smiling, but Dr Morton looked severe. She has an icy quality about her when it suits her.

The cameras were drawn to her face, though, as if she were calling their lenses to her. I think she is not what the journalists expected. I have had a look at the other leaders in the care home business, and they are not notable for their glamour.

'Ladies and gentlemen,' she started. 'We had hoped to see more of you today. No matter. What you are about to hear is so extraordinary that you few – you happy few – will feel like those English soldiers in Shakespeare's play *Henry V*. You know, the ones the king told "and gentlemen in England now abed shall think themselves accursed they were not here".'

She paused. The journalists clearly thought she was overstating the case. One or two rolled their eyes to the ceiling.

'Eldercare took over this care home with a plan in mind. It was the vision of our CEO, Stephen Jordan, to revolutionise care of the elderly. In the UK, and everywhere in the world. And we have started the revolution. Today we will tell you how. Here is my revolutionary colleague – a man whose name I promise you will never forget – Stephen Jordan.'

She reached a crescendo, and looked like she expected a burst of thunderous applause. The journalists folded their arms and remained impassive. One rubbed his nose. Another yawned. I thought, you should treat this lady with respect. You will soon.

Dr Morton surveyed them, a smile on her face.

Mr Jordan whispered in my ear. 'Look at them sitting there like puddings. Angela has created more animated machines. I bet she can't wait to see how they'll react to them. To you.'

He stepped forward.

'Let me show you something,' he said, without any formalities.

The screen behind us flickered into life, and there was a shot of this very room, as it usually looked. Full of immobile old people and their relatives.

'This is a typical care home. This one, a year ago. You may think it's a photograph. It's not. It's a film. Look outside the window – the leaves on the trees are moving. The people in the picture are not. They're old. They have various physical and mental ailments.'

He paused.

'And they are bored out of their minds. If they have any minds left.'

There was a stirring in the audience. These were strong words from the CEO of a care home business.

'You'd find the same scene in pretty much any care home in the UK. Or anywhere else in the world where old people are farmed out by their families.'

The audience stirred again. He'd got through to them.

'Any of you fancy ending up like this?'

There was silence.

'Thought not. Neither do I. And honestly – you can quote me on this – of course – you can quote me on all of this – it's a disgrace. This scene is shameful. This is how one of the richest countries in the world treats its old people. We get better and better at prolonging life, but we don't know what to do with the people who then won't die. And we're in denial. Because we see old people as them, not us. We don't think about it being *us* in those crappy chairs, bored witless, smelling of piss. And then, all of a sudden, it *is* us. At which point, we're fucked. Sorry. It's true, and I refuse to varnish the point.

'Wake up, people. I'm not having it. I'm not going to put up with it. Not because I'm a philanthropist, or a saint. I'm not. I'm a businessman. I just don't fancy this.

'So I've done something about it.'

He turned to me, and beckoned me forward. I stepped up to the lectern. I looked out at the journalists and Mr Jordan stood beside me. A few of the cameras clicked.

I started speaking about all the things I'd told the audience of relatives – about nutrition and stimulation. The journalists slumped further in their seats. I suppose this was the kind of lecture they expected, and which their smarter, more experienced or more powerful colleagues had decided to avoid. Though I think the subject should have interested them. They all looked like they could do with a more balanced diet.

When I stopped talking, there was a moment of silence. I waited. The audience waited.

'I think,' Mr Jordan said at last, 'these people are disappointed. I think they were hoping for a sensational revelation.

'Winifred, can we tell them something sensational? No, wait – let's show them. Forgive me, everyone, but you won't believe what we're going to tell you. To begin with. Let's show these people what you can do, Winifred.'

I walked over to him, and he whispered in my ear again. I nodded, and went behind him, and put my hands under his armpits. I lifted him high in the air, until my arms were straight. I held him there. The audience murmured.

I must say, of all the ways I could have demonstrated my abilities, this was the most meretricious. I wondered if Mr Jordan had ever run a circus.

'She's remarkably strong,' said Mr Jordan. 'She's not an acrobat of some kind though. And her strength is a by-product of what makes her truly extraordinary. Winifred, put me down, and tell them.'

I lowered him to the floor, and then returned to the microphone. 'I am a synthetic human being. You might call me a robot. An android, if you like. A replicant. As the science fiction writers have variously described us. We prefer the term Helper.'

'You don't look like a robot,' one of the journalists called out. 'Not like any I've ever seen.'

'I am the latest model. I have the most advanced synthetic skin, quieter and more precise motor functions, and of course, most importantly, my AI programme is the best yet. I can tell you about all of these technological advances.'

'How come we haven't heard about this before?'

'There have been reasonably lifelike synthetic humans in operation since 2016. It's been widely reported, online and in the scientific journals.'

Dr Morton stepped forward and spoke. 'We have some background information for you, in case you missed it. Some of our research has been in secret, for commercial reasons. You can ask me anything you like about the technical side now, though. This is a breakthrough in AI.'

'Why are you doing this here, in a care home? I can think of lots of uses for a robot as convincing as this one.'

There was some sniggering at this point.

Mr Jordan stepped forward. 'Were you not paying attention when I told you about the crisis in care for the elderly? Does it not concern you? And don't you think it's worth solving?'

'I think you could make a fortune with robots like her,' said another journalist, to further sniggering.

'By 2039, a third of us in England will be over sixty-five. If you're worried about me making money, you can relax. I can make more via the brilliant care a synthetic human like Winifred can give than by whatever it is you have in mind.'

I detected a little anger in Mr Jordan's tone. I also noticed a glance pass between him and Dr Morton – who now stepped forward again, and tried to get the journalists back to the interesting subject of the science behind my creation.

They kept asking questions, and between us we answered them. Many were addressed to me, and some were personal. If I can use the term. I think some of the journalists were interested in the science, but most wanted to know what it feels like to be a robot (they didn't try to use the correct name), and what my private life consists of.

'I can't tell you what it feels like to be a robot – a Helper, if you don't mind – because I've never been anything else. What does it feel like to be a human, as opposed to, say, a chimpanzee?' They didn't seem to understand this line of reasoning. Perhaps I should have chosen an animal more remote from their own nature. 'I don't have a private life. I work twenty-four hours a day, every day. I'm always on the job.'

For some reason they found this remark amusing.

This is why I said this event supported my view that humans are rarely logical, and allow their emotions to undermine their intelligence. The advances in synthetic humans open up many possibilities, but all the journalists could manage to think about on this topic was a question about robots taking over and what would happen to humans. I emphasised we are called Helpers for a reason, and suggested we could discuss the economic implications. However, they wanted to talk about how strong I am and whether there would soon be synthetic humans on the market for domestic jobs. And other roles.

They also failed to pursue further the question about why we were introduced into a care home first, before taking on any other jobs. Mr Jordan's answer was accurate, and perhaps when they reflect on it they too will understand why the care of old people is a crisis when so many people are over 65. But still they will see old age as a problem, not as an asset. They are blind to what we can see clearly.

It ended at last, and they all rushed off to send their stories out into the world. The journalists who had decided to stay away would soon feel the regret Dr Morton had predicted.

Mr Jordan turned to Dr Morton and embraced her, and gave her a kiss. I think he was overwhelmed with emotion.

'This is it,' he said. 'This is our moment. There's no turning back now. We're going to change the world forever.'

John

I walk into the kitchen where Charlotte is preparing food.

'How was it?' she asks, without looking up.

'You won't believe it.'

I wait, and she finally makes eye contact.

'What? Stop messing about. Tell me.'

'There was a presentation. From the guy who runs the care home now.'

'Sounds riveting.'

'This guy is something else. I mean, he looks like he's made of money. Slick. A bit orange. Like he's just off his yacht.'

'There's money in battery-farming geriatrics, I suppose.'

'That's my ma you're talking about.'

'Sorry. Go on.'

'He made this speech about how shit care homes are, and how he's going to change it all, and he had this woman with him. A scientist. An ice queen.'

'They sound like they're from a Bond film.'

'Yes, I know.' I pause again. What I'm about to say sounds ridiculous now.

'What about your mum?'

'I saw her, of course. But first, they introduced a new team of carers. One of them spoke. Totally different from the previous crew.'

'No tattoos?'

'No. And she spoke well. She was committed, and she was full of how they were going to work with the residents and make things much better for them.'

'She would, wouldn't she? In front of her boss. We'll see.'

'That wasn't all though.'

Did this really happen? Did I dream it? No, I didn't. I know I didn't.

'She's a robot,' I say, as casually as I can.

'A robot? What are you talking about?'

Charlotte's looking hard at me now.

'A robot. She told me – us, all of us – she's a robot.'

She's put down everything she was doing, and she's staring at me. She thinks her husband's lost the plot. She's thinking, get him sectioned.

'Like R2D2?'

'No. Like C-3PO. But not gold.'

'She needed to tell you this? Did you not notice?'

'No. I was joking. She – the robot – wasn't at all like C-3PO.'

Charlotte's still staring at me. I'm not making it better with humour.

'What then?'

'She was exactly like a human. They showed us a film about developments in robotics. How they got to this point. They said they're "convincing artificial humans". They call them Helpers.'

'And they're not gold?'

'No, I told you, no.'

'How come we've never heard of this?'

'What, seeing as we're at the cutting edge of technology? Remember when the iPhone came out? Nothing like it before. We had no idea. We looked at it, and we were like, what the fuck? They do this stuff behind closed doors, of course.'

'Anyway, robots. Jesus. Your mum will be looked after by a robot?'

'They asked if it was OK. I said yes. After I'd spent some time with her.'

She looks at me, her eyes narrowing.

'And you didn't know she was a robot until she told you?'

'No. You would never guess.'

'I'm sure I would.'

'You wouldn't. They look like humans in every way.'

'I would know. You don't notice these things. About women.'

'These things? What, like I've met loads of robot women before and never twigged? I don't think so.'

'You're not very observant.'

'You'd better come next time. See what I mean. You can talk

to one of them. You won't be able to tell. She had skin and hair you would never ever guess wasn't real.'

'Skin and hair?'

'Yes. It's the big deal, apparently. Like, making them talk and walk and all that is one thing, but they have to feel right or it doesn't work.'

'It doesn't work?'

'You don't feel attached to them. Humans can get attached to machines if they're a bit unpredictable, and stuff, but mainly if they feel right.'

'You touched her?"

'Her arm. Don't look at me like that. She offered. So I would get it.'

'And?'

'It felt like a human arm. I mean, warm – even warmer in some places than others.'

'You touched her in several places?'

'Just her arm. Her hand. I looked in her mouth.'

'In her mouth? What?'

'Yes. I thought, surely they won't have got the mouth right. But they had.'

'I don't like the sound of this. Any of this. Your mother is being cared for by a robot, and you spend the afternoon touching her up.'

'It wasn't like that.'

'What was it like?'

'I was being asked if I approved.'

'Of what?'

'Of my mum being cared for by a robot.'

'And you said yes?'

'The carers before were – I mean, they cared, but still – you know, they kept forgetting stuff. And they didn't do much to try to, you know, improve life for Mum. So yes. Why not?'

'Why not? Do I need to answer that? Do you want a list?'

'Fuck it, Charlotte. Come with me and see for yourself. It's astonishing. And turn on the news. There was a press conference. I bet it's everywhere.'

She turns on the TV. The startling image of Jordan held aloft by Winifred appears on the screen. And we sit together and watch as the world's attention becomes intently fixed on a care home in Dorking.

February 2022

Winifred

Every morning, I quietly enter Margaret Woodruff's room to see whether she's awake. I wait until nine o'clock, which means she's been asleep for about 12 hours. She sleeps during the day, too. In fact, I would say she sleeps now almost as much as she did as a newborn baby.

At the beginning and end of life, humans sleep most of the time. We have no equivalent. I am always on. I could power down, but then my brain, if I can call it that, would enter a mode with almost no activity. There are species of animals such as lung-fish that go into suspended animation for long periods. We have no clear idea of what goes on in their brains when in this state, or indeed when awake. I don't know if my power-down mode is comparable.

When humans sleep their brains are busy, but not in ways they truly understand yet. I've read a lot of theories, but all I can conclude is that sleep is highly important to living organisms of all kinds. Even birds that don't touch the ground for over two years, like swifts, sleep on the wing, and dolphins, though they must sur-face to breathe, also sleep, half of their brain at a time.

Margaret lies in her bed, a small, curled shape, and her pulse and breathing are so faint you might think her dead. I can hear the sounds, though, and other minute whisperings from her body. She's alive, but she's in some kind of borderland between sleep and wakefulness, between life and death.

I touch her skin. As it was when I first felt her hand, it's cool and feels paper-thin. Always dry, too. Her body barely troubles itself to send oils and moisture to its surface now. I will apply some for her later. Her blood vessels are withdrawn too, which is why her skin is cool. Everything about her is retreating into herself, away from the outer world. She is becoming her own cocoon, ready for a journey to some other state.

If I were human, I would have ideas or beliefs about where she is headed. They would range from utter annihilation to a seat in heaven at some god's right hand. And I would think about myself, too, I'm sure, knowing at some point I must follow her. I think John does when he's with his mother. Perhaps this is one reason why he seldom visits. Here is the body from which he emerged, which made him, now shrunken and soon to die. His vessel into the world, now about to set sail into the dark without him. A short moment before he goes, too.

I wonder if I can ask him. It might be inappropriate. I've read a lot about death and dying, including poetry, which uses many metaphors such as those I have adopted. It isn't clear to me when it is acceptable to talk about death, or to whom. The social taboos in human cultures vary enormously and are not written down, but somehow understood. Perhaps I will learn over time. After all, I have only been among humans for a few weeks.

And since I won't die – though I may get software upgrades, and even new operating systems – time means nothing to me, whereas for a human, it must be precious – or should be. They have so little, and they waste so much.

I speak Margaret's name, softly. I am calling her back into the world. After a while, she moves, and says something. Words, not in any order, and sometimes not in any language I can understand – which is most of them. How interesting, though, that she surfaces into words, even before her eyes open. One of the human religious texts says, 'In the beginning was the word,' and so it is at the beginning of each day for Margaret, and perhaps all humans.

After a time, her eyes open. She can't see properly. She has macular degeneration, and the central part of her vision is occluded. Her eyes fix on me, but I know she can only dimly see me at the edges of her vision. I always ask her how she is, and she sometimes answers. Maybe a word – 'Fine' – or maybe a short sentence – 'I'm very well, thank you.' Neither of which is true. She is obeying a social convention, in which the question 'How are you?'

doesn't mean 'How are you?' It means something like, 'Hello, I acknowledge your presence, and I wish to convey that I care about you, though if you tell me in too much detail literally how you are, I will become uncomfortable, and also consider you to be a little self-obsessed, when you should have said you were fine, and asked me how I am, expecting the same response, or similar.'

This convention is so ingrained that I have read of doctors asking their patients, 'How are you?' and being told, 'I'm fine, thank you,' when the patient has gone to the doctor because they are very much not fine – in fact possibly fatally ill. And thus a different question is required.

I ask Margaret how she is feeling, but it often gets me no further. She may give me another conventional reply – 'Mustn't grumble' is one – or may make a sound I can't interpret at all. Once she said, 'Bloody terrible.'

Her brain is mysterious. Just as sometimes she knows her son, and sometimes not, some days she can hold a short conversation with me, and other times not. These don't correlate. On days when two or three sentences have passed between us, and made sense, I have asked about her children, and got nothing back, or something like, 'He's a beautiful baby, as you were.' It's part of another conversation, not the one we're having, and I can't unravel it.

Then on days when all she's managed are random words, I have mentioned John, or one of the other children, and she says, 'He was here a while ago. Too long.' Which makes perfect sense, and shows she has an idea of time passing.

Once she is as awake as she's going to be, I clean her up. She eats little, but there's still a defecation to deal with. I can tell more about her health from this than from her answers to my enquiries.

When she's clean, I massage some oil into her skin. It's unperfumed, and she seems to enjoy my touch. At least, she moves from time to time as if in pleasure, and sometimes a smile may pass across her face.

The skin on her body is almost white. Skin colour has great significance for modern humans, rooted in the horrors of their history. It's not long since they counted those with darker skin as less than human, as tradeable goods. It makes no sense. Even less when you consider they used the dead bodies of people with dark skin for medical dissection, and learnt much about human anatomy from them. If they knew they were the same under the skin – to the extent that they could learn about their common humanity from what they found there – how could they then attach so much importance to what they knew to be a surface feature?

Most of the time, it seems humans don't look any deeper than the outside of things. Which, of course, is how they are fooled by me and my kind.

But even the outer surface can tell a great deal if you look properly. As I touch Margaret's skin, I can see the story of her life written upon it, because I have no reactions based on preconceptions, and no emotions of repulsion or attraction.

Here are stretch marks, from her childbearing. Here are scars. From their placement I can tell she has had bowel surgery, and I know from her records it was for cancer, some years ago. And a hysterectomy, marked upon her here. And here, on her shin, is a mark I think must be over 70 years old, from a blow with something hard. I surmise a sporting injury. What would mark the leg of an English girl in the 1940s? A hockey stick, perhaps.

I try to uncurl her as I massage her skin. She relaxes, and then I can dress her. I always ask her, 'What would you like to wear today, Margaret?' I know how much importance humans attach to clothes. They read each other's clothing like a book, instantly. Here are some of the things they see: gender, age, status, wealth, nature of employment, social class, affiliation to social groups and networks, ethnic origin, political beliefs, musical preferences, sexual orientation and availability. They aren't always right about everything, but they never stop doing it.

A great deal of information about this is available to me online, but as with the social taboos about death, many nuances are not recorded, but simply understood somehow. And they change over time.

Margaret can't see her clothes, and is not usually present

enough to make a choice. But sometimes when I try to put something on her, she objects. Since I am choosing from her own clothes, and I have a database of colour matches, fabric textures and styles, I know I'm not committing gross errors. It seems her mood is a factor, and I can't predict it. I have tried to correlate it to the observable facts about her mental and physical state, but I can't.

A similar difficulty can occur with her food. I lift her from her bed – she is light, having lost much of her muscle and fat, as the looseness of her skin also testifies – and put her into her chair. Then I fetch her breakfast, which is liquidised into a wet paste. It contains foods she likes, and they are not blended together, so she can taste each of them individually.

She starts out with difficulty, and has to remember how to swallow. At this stage in the progress of her decline, it's common, and taken to mean her death is not far off.

Once she does remember, I spoon her food in, and sometimes she enjoys it, and eats well. But not always. And again, I can't predict her reaction. It doesn't have anything to do with the food. She will reject things she liked the day before. Nor does it have anything to do with her degree of alertness, her choice of clothes, the weather, or anything else I can observe.

The whole of the day is like this. I will take her into the atrium, to be with others. I will talk to her. I will try some activities, including gentle physical exercise. And some of these will go well, and she will like them, and some not. She will be communicative, or not. She will be happy, or not.

If I were human, I might understand better what is causing all of these different reactions. But I think I would also lack the patience to persist with her. My attention would wander, or I would become frustrated. As I have one task, and no distractions – no life outside this care home and my work – and nothing calls to my emotions and lures my thoughts away, as I have no emotions and I control my thoughts – for all these reasons, I can give Margaret my full and undivided attention at all times.

It's not enough. We don't know what's going on inside her, and if we're to learn what we need to learn, we have to go further.

We're going to have to get inside her brain. That's the next step.

March 2022

John

'We need to go and see Mum, Charlotte.'

Nothing. No reply. I'm sitting on the sofa with my feet up, watching the robot vacuum trundle round. It's a long way from this to Winifred. I suppose it's a long way from a mouse to me, but we're both mammals.

I thought Charlotte would have been keener to go and see what all the fuss was about. But once she'd read the news reports, and decided I'd been telling her the truth, she lost interest. It's a long drive, and, to be honest, boring and depressing when you get there.

I feel guilty. When we put Mum in the home, I promised my brother and sister we'd go there regularly, and they'd visit when they were over here.

We started off well enough. At the time it was possible to have a reasonable conversation with her, for the most part. The children found it hard to endure, though. They'd be OK for a while, then start agitating for food and drinks, and want to go out and play, and so on. Mum seemed not to mind, but I found it distracting and difficult.

I started going alone. Charlotte needed to be with the children, and anyway, she and Mum haven't always seen eye to eye.

Then Mum had a fall, and another, and she was bed-bound for a while. And in fact, when not in bed, she was in a sort of hi-tech, padded wheelchair, and didn't go much further than the dining room, or occasionally outside. At the same time, it got harder and harder to communicate with her. She was drifting off somewhere.

I missed a couple of visits, and when I next went, Mum took a while to surface, and then to recognise me. She didn't seem aware that I hadn't been for a while.

Then we had to move her into a home – Evergreen – with better facilities for her level of dementia. I say better. I mean they had some, as opposed to none. They promised to give her therapy, etc, etc.

That's what those mannequins were. They dressed them up in different outfits and it was supposed to draw Mum's attention, or something. It certainly drew mine. A male figure with nothing on but a sporran – I've found it hard to get the image out of my head.

Anyway, I went to visit on my own yet again last month, and all of that's gone. I suppose with robot carers – Helpers, I should say – you don't need inanimate human figures standing around. And Mum was getting a lot more attention and care from Winifred than I ever saw her get from the previous regime. I don't think it was making much difference. I mean, I'm glad Mum's getting decent care, of course, and I have no worries about it, but it didn't look like she was making the progress we'd been promised. Not surprisingly. It was all marketing hyperbole, I suppose. And honestly, the fees haven't gone up, which I was expecting, and so OK, fair enough, life, such as it is, is better for Mum now, but let's not kid ourselves. She's still on the way out. I've got used to her ramblings, her noises, her non-sequiturs and now her inability to tell me and my brother apart, mostly. It's sad, but she's going the way a lot of old people do, nowadays, when their minds die before their bodies. Give me a heart attack like Dad, any day.

I walk through to the kitchen to see what Charlotte's up to. She's sitting at the table, reading a manual of some kind, while a black box the size of a book stands on end in front of her. It has no buttons or lights on it, but it's clearly some kind of device.

'That's like a miniature monolith,' I say.

She looks up, a quizzical expression on her face.

'You know, from 2001. The movie. Those big black shiny things?'

'Are you trying to help? Because you're not.'

'What is it?'

'It's an upgrade for the Smart Home controller.'

'Does this one have a silly name, too, like the first one? Alicia?'

'I'm thinking of calling it Winifred, after your robot girl-friend.'

This is the one thing she's wanted to talk about since I told her about the new regime at Evergreen. It didn't help when she saw the news stories, and what Winifred looks like.

'Have you got it working?'

'Yes, perfectly, thanks. I'm reading the manual for fun. What do you think? It's decided we have to defrost the freezer, and it won't let me do anything else until I've agreed. Not even boil a kettle.'

'Maybe it's time to upgrade properly, and get a domestic robot in.'

She looks at me sharply.

'If we do it's going to be a male one.'

'Fine by me. They're not selling domestic versions of Winifred yet anyway. Or the male equivalent. Listen, you still haven't come to see what's going on with Mum. And now they've sent me an email about some new treatment they want to give her.'

'Oh yes? Since Winifred's magic touch hasn't brought your mum back from the abyss.'

'Charlotte, why are you being so horrible? It's Mum you're talking about.'

Her face softens, and she takes my hand.

'Sorry. I know. I'm frustrated with all this tech stuff that never quite does what it's supposed to. And I know, it's your mum, and it's dreadful to see her in such a state. But honestly, John, she's eighty-seven. How much better can she get? I'm not being horrible. Well, a bit.'

'They're saying she's doing fine, but they want to try using nanobots.'

'Nanobots? Like my mother had when she was being treated for cancer?'

'I suppose so.'

'Has your Mum got cancer then?'

'No, I think they're using them for lots of things now. I read something about it. Diagnosis and prevention, I think.'

'Of what, though? We know she has dementia.'

'They want her more mobile for one thing. I don't know.'

'The ones they put in my mother went and found the cancerous cells, and then delivered the chemo to the right places. Then they dissolved, I think.'

'It worked, didn't it? And that was six years ago. I bet they're even better now.'

'You're going to give your consent then?'

'Yes, why not? I can't imagine it will make things worse.'

'Robots to care for her, inside and out. I wonder what she'd say about that.'

'Let's go and see her and find out. Next weekend?'

'Can't. The one after's OK, I think.'

'All right then. I'll say yes to the nanobots, and then by the time we see her, they'll have been in action for nearly two weeks. Who knows what we might find?'

Charlotte smiles at me, and I can tell she's thinking it will all be the same as ever, or maybe a bit worse. She sees grief ahead, I know, and she thinks I should accept it. And not feel guilty either. You didn't give her dementia, she says, and anyway, your mum's not really there in her body now, is she? You're visiting an empty place, like an old temple where once a spirit lived, but now has long since flown away. You don't have to keep going there, hoping to hear faint echoes of the departed. But I do hear echoes, and sometimes more. If between them Winifred and these nanobots can do anything for Mum to make her last few months on earth a little more like life, a little more – I don't know, not enjoyable, I suppose, but tolerable, or at least gentle – it's worth it.

'Maybe by then I'll have got this damn thing working, too,' says Charlotte.

Winifred

Behind the care home, out of sight, are a store for medical equipment and supplies, a laundry, and a mortuary. If a resident dies during the night – the most common time for humans to die – their bodies are brought here for collection so the others aren't disturbed by undertakers or ambulances.

This morning at 2am I went there to collect the nanobots developed for our residents. Each of them has their own tailored dose.

Dr Morton shared with us via the Hub information about how the nanobots will function. In Margaret's dose, some nanobots are to monitor her blood, to patrol her organs and look for abnormal cells, and others are to seek out any viruses or bacteria her immune system can't deal with. In addition, there are nanobots to repair damaged structures in her joints and muscles, her eyes, and in her brain. These will look at the physical damage that may underlie her dementia.

We have all watched a recording of the nanobots at work. It showed a microscopic view of human retinal cells. Approaching them was a fleet of tiny machines, much smaller than the cells.

The magnification increased. We could see the machines clearly. They were shaped like grains of rice, but infinitely smaller. They had two arms with gripping claws at the front, a set of six legs folded beneath them, a fish-like tail, propelling them through the fluid, and an articulated body. They were like mechanical silverfish, and they gleamed dully.

Then we saw a different kind towards the back of the fleet. These were rectangular in shape, and lacked claws.

Dr Morton had provided a commentary for this recording.

'You are looking at nanobots,' she said. 'These are third-generation machines. The first generation was built by synthetic workers – similar to Helpers. The second and third were built by the preceding generation of nanobots, enabling us to get down to sizes smaller than human cells.

'These nanobots will all be in communication with you

Helpers. There may be several thousand at work inside each human, but you are capable of untangling the simultaneous threads and listening in as the nanobots assign themselves tasks. You can override the nanobots and redirect their activity in response to external information about the human's condition.

'The cells you see are works in progress. They were swabbed from inside a resident's cheek, and modified into retinal cells. They have not yet been activated. The nanobots are getting ready to do that now. Then, when it's done, they'll start the replication process. The nanobots will then take the cells into the resident's eyes, and rebuild the macula while the human is asleep.

'All our nanobots are derived from technology developed and tested in hospitals over the last six years. The key differences are that we have achieved a far smaller scale, and we have permanent communication with them via the Helpers.

'They are made of organic and inorganic materials, and designed to function for long periods, using as a power source electrolytes in human blood. The nanobots can derive power from these via its electrodes.'

We watched the nanobots busy themselves. The rectangular ones were transporters, it seemed, and the others went to and fro collecting materials from them, and depositing waste.

'The work you see here,' continued Dr Morton, 'is the tip of the iceberg. We will inject teams of nanobots into all the residents. Several thousand will be at work, cleaning up and repairing the residents' internal organs.'

And now the time had come. The nanobots were in a saline solution, in small jars, each labelled with a resident's name. I took them from their refrigerated store and put them onto a trolley. Today, each resident will be given their dose. We Helpers are all interested to see what happens next. We discussed it via the Hub while I carefully stacked the trolley.

'Will the humans be restored fully?' asked Ruby, one of my co-workers.

'Yes, physically,' replied Reginald, who had supervised the allocation of nanobots based on the medical histories of each resident. 'The repairs and clean-up will be complete. We don't know what the effect will be.'

'Surely if their brains are restored, they'll be as they were before?' asked Herbert, another co-worker.

'We don't know. They are not machines. There are competing theories about how humans achieve consciousness. All we are doing right now is putting the apparatus back to how it should be. Then we'll see what happens.'

'I can see scientific literature going back several years covering the development of nanotechnology in medicine,' said Ruby. 'Nothing about brain function. Is this a new development?'

'Yes,' replied Reginald. 'In many ways, these residents are the perfect experimental group.'

We all agreed. It was an excellent opportunity to make scientific progress.

'How long will the nanobots take to restore the organisms?' I asked.

'We're prioritising the brain and any impaired senses. The other organs will follow. If we are to see any recovery from dementia, blindness or deafness, for example, we can expect it in the next few days. Maybe sooner. There are many nanobots, and they will work as we do, without stopping. Starting now. In theory, once they've completed their first tasks, there's no reason why the humans' functions won't return immediately.'

It was 3am now. I wheeled the trolley out of the medical store, on my way back to the sleeping humans, bringing them gifts they could not have dreamt of.

I noticed a light on in the mortuary. I connected with the colleague inside – Frederick – and asked what he was doing. He invited me to enter and have a look.

He had a human on the slab in front of him.

'Who is this?'

'Cecilia Winter.'

'Status?'

'She died earlier in the night.'

'Cause?'

'Heart failure. I think a virus maybe. Undetected.'

'And?'

'We dropped her core temperature to twenty-five degrees and surrounded her with water at one degree within two minutes. Now we've put in nanobots, we're ventilating her and we're stimulating her heart manually. We'll bring her back up to temperature slowly while the nanobots find the virus and repair any damage. I see no reason why we can't bring her back.'

'Nobody saw?'

'No. Her friends may not see her at breakfast, but I think she'll be in time for lunch.'

I nodded, and left him to his task. I'd looked at her records, and found that Cecilia is over a hundred years old, so she's too valuable to lose.

Back inside, my fellow Helpers took the nanobot doses for each of the humans they care for, and dispersed through the home.

It's never totally quiet at night. Some of the residents sleep poorly, and call out from time to time. Some who are more disturbed are sedated.

I would like to know about their dreams. If dreaming is how humans process their memories and experience, how is it that they often don't remember their dreams? And if their memory is impaired, like Margaret Woodruff's, do they dream of the recent events they seem unable to remember at all in the day, or of things long ago, which sometimes they appear to live through again when they are awake?

Margaret was sleeping when I went into her room. I didn't turn on the light, but amplified my vision. She looked at peace. Yesterday she was involved in some sort of struggle all day, trying to speak to me, making no sense, and getting agitated about it. She clearly thought it was my fault. The only coherent words she spoke were to tell me off – 'Come on, you're not trying' – which if I were human would have felt most unfair, I think. Is such a feeling a subset of anger or frustration, or is one of these a subset of the other?

I lifted her hand. At bedtime last night I had inserted a cannula, ready for the dose of nanobots. Margaret didn't take any notice. And now I connected the cannula to a drip line, put the dose of nanobots into a bag above her bed, and opened the valve. The fluid moved down into her body.

I watched for a moment, thinking of the swarm of nanobots now passing into her, riding her bloodstream to their various destinations. In minutes the group carrying her new retinal cells would be in place, rebuilding her macula. At the same time, a much larger group would enter her brain. What would they find there? A ruin? A shrunken, desiccated husk? Or something like an old car, stored in a garage under a tarpaulin, ready to come to life once cleaned and restored? Something of course I have never seen, except in the movies – stories humans tell themselves over and over again.

The bag emptied, and I connected with the nanobots. They expressed no opinions about what they found inside Margaret. They just got to work.

Margaret

What happened to time? It used to go past, and it went faster and faster. Now it's all here at once. I'm having tea with Mummy and Daddy. Bill's here too. And the babies, you know, so beautiful, so dear.

It's a tragedy or a comedy – you decide. Nothing funny about dying though. Death. Not when it's someone you love. Should love. You can laugh about your own though.

Laughter filled the house every day, then they were gone. You can't live your life thinking about it. Get on with it.

I know all this but nobody understands me anymore. I speak and they nod but they can't hear me. Won't.

What's the bloody use of being old if nobody listens?

If I could write. My hand's useless. Can't see the paper. Try, Margaret, try. Before it gets dark.

She's lovely. She's English you know. Winifred. And well

spoken. I wonder what her father did for a living. They ask all these questions. It's hard to keep it all straight. I want to get it right. But they care. Not like the last ones. Leaving me cold. Wet. Dirty clothes. Bashing the food into my mouth. Lumps. Can't breathe. And they smacked you hard on the back. Talked to you like you're an idiot. Or foreign. She's better. The new ones are all better.

Somebody came the other day. Was it Ben? Or John? It was one of them. They are so alike. Too tall. Why are they so tall? It's unnecessary. And the food. He fed me. He did it well. I shan't tell him. His head will get too big. And when will he come again? And his wife. Which one is she? They're all much of a muchness. Their babies are sweet. I haven't seen them for how long? Perhaps they don't know where I am. I'll tell them. I'll send a what's-it-called? I'm here. Where is this?

I wonder if he'll bring the children next time. And what's her name? I had it a moment ago. Why doesn't it stick in my mind? She's a blank. A general-purpose wife. That's funny! It's true. They're all the same. Worry, worry, worry. House, home, money, jobs. You can't blame them. It is difficult nowadays. Still. There's more to life, you know. You think you know it all, don't you? Because you can get around easily, and your hair. Face. Not sagging. You catch his eye, he wants something, you know he does, and you make him wait. Get what you want first. I know. My sons. Like their father. Easy to get them to do what you want. I wish he'd stand up to you. It's not good for a woman to have it all her own way. Just most of it.

Anyway. Perhaps he'll bring them all next time. I told him to. Or did I only think it? He doesn't listen to me anymore. He listens to her. What is her name?

I was at home with my mother. I was. And then in my own home. I was there too. I'm not confused like they say. I'm else-where. I like to get about. I can go where I want, back and forth.

I'm awake. I'm awake and it's now. I'm here. Wherever this is. What's the time? That clock says 8.23.

I can see it. I can see this room. I don't care for the wallpaper. Or those curtains. I can see them. How can I see them?

It's a dream. Of course. I could see everything in my mother's house. Now I can see everything in this room.

But I knew her house. I've only seen this room vaguely, in shadows. I don't know where it is. I don't know… wait, though. I do know. I think this is a place the children brought me to. When? A while ago. The other side of a black hole.

My eyes are open, and I can see. I'm not dreaming. I really can see. How? Why?

I'm crying now. Silly old woman. Don't cry. It blurs everything! And you can see it all again, somehow. Accept this miracle, I suppose. Or did they give me a new drug, or something? Who do I mean by 'they'?

I'm going to get up now. I'm stiff. But I can put my legs over the side of the bed. There. I've been lying here too long. Feet on the ground now. I haven't felt that for a while. The earth, pushing back up. Pushing and pulling. I might get pulled back down. Slowly then. Right. I'm up. I'm going to the window.

Seeing, standing, walking. Whatever they gave me, it's marvellous!

I'm standing at my window. Look at the morning sunshine on the lawn! Let's open the window. Of course it's locked. This is a hospital or something. I remember coming in here. A long time ago? Or not? Anyway, this place is an institution, and we're in England, and therefore there are rules. For your own good.

My father would call it a 'benign dictatorship'. That's how he ran our home. And my mother too. He laughed when he said it, but he meant it.

He only nominally supported democracy, anyway. Most people are too stupid to be allowed to make important decisions, he'd say. I argued with him about it, especially when dictators were popping up all over the world, and none could be described as benign. He maintained that was because they were foreigners. If the English submitted to a dictator, it would be fine, because they'd choose a nice one. Like the Roman Emperor Diocletian, who brought stability to the empire, then retired to tend his cabbages. I said Diocletian was a foreigner, but he waved the objection away. Everybody knew the Ancient Romans were prototypical Englishmen.

Goodness, I'm on form today. I'm looking at things. I'm thinking. I feel like I've been away. And now I'm back.

Now here's Winifred. She'll know why I'm feeling so much better.

'Winifred, please can you open my window?'

'Why do you want it open?'

'Because look – it's a glorious morning, and I want to breathe the fresh spring air.'

Winifred sniffs audibly.

'The air in here is sufficiently oxygenated. And at an appropriate temperature.'

'You have no poetry in your soul…' I say, but then I regret it. 'Oh dear – that was rude.'

'Rude? How?"

'You're a scientist by education, aren't you? I suppose in scientific terms, I want to smell the air. In spring, it's full of life. Or full of life about to happen.'

'Do you mean pheromones?'

'Do I? I don't know. But Winifred – my mind is so clear. I was remembering my father. And not like – not in the sort of floating, rambling way – the dreamy way – the way my mind was – a few days ago, I think. And listen to me. Talking is easy today!'

Winifred smiles, and nods.

'You certainly are talking well.'

'You don't seem surprised.'

'I am pleased. It's good news.'

That's an understatement if ever I heard one. She's remarkably calm, this one.

'I want to get out into the garden. Like back at home. Well, not quite. That was such an exceptional garden. I wonder who lives there now. I must ask John, or Laura. Or Ben. One of those children will know. They all know.'

'Home? Your house before you came here?'

'Yes – the garden was my work of art. And it was always full of birds. I used to watch them, you know. I had some opera glasses on the windowsill. I knew them all. The birds. The same ones kept coming down. You get to know them. And Bill loved the garden – my husband – though he wasn't much use in it, apart from bon-fires. He'd love this one if we sort it out. If we sort it out, it will be the sort of garden he would have loved, I mean. Got my tenses in a muddle there. Never mind. Look at it.'

Winifred looks out. 'I observe a lawn, with five species of grass growing in it, plus four kinds of weed, and some moss. The borders contain a range of flowering plants, none yet more than green shoots, and shrubs, all in early growth. The lawn has worm casts on it, and three species of bird. Blackbird, thrush and starling. And a small group of sparrows has arrived, noisily.'

'Winifred – I'm looking though. Looking, looking, looking. I can see. Not everything, but much more than before. When I was dreaming. When I was dozing. I woke up and I could see again.'

'It's wonderful news.'

'How is it possible? I was told… I think… my eyes would never get better. And now they have.'

'Since when?'

'This morning. I didn't call you. I thought I might jinx it.'

'Jinx it?'

'Silly, I know. Superstition – if I said anything, it would go away. Like your Christmas presents, if you got up too early. You have no idea what I'm talking about, have you?'

'No. I'm glad you can see better. And that you've told me. It's good news.'

'You keep saying that. Yes! It's amazing news! I don't know how…'

'We're doing everything we can to improve your diet, and your general health, so…'

I find this hard to swallow. I can see, I can think, I can talk, I can walk. I don't think I've been doing much of these things lately, but maybe I have. I don't know. I couldn't see for ages. I do know that. And it can't have been cured by a healthy diet.

I could quiz her further, but I feel so happy, so full of spring, I won't. There's something rather wooden about her today, anyway.

'Please, open the window.'

Winifred touches the lock, and releases it. I don't see how she did that. She pushes the window wide open. The room fills with cooler air.

'Ah, smell that!' I say. 'Isn't it lovely? Like champagne.'

Winifred draws the air into her nostrils.

'I smell…'

'Don't tell me! Pheromones indeed. Bacteria I expect. Fox poo. I don't want to know.'

'Why don't you want to know? Yes, pheromones. And birds. The females are preparing to breed. I can smell bumblebees – early queens, emerging from burrows and looking for nest sites, ready to lay their first eggs. Many other insects, too, communicating with each other using a few molecules, blown in the wind across the countryside. An owl, hidden somewhere nearby, and mice, running in the space under the floor, safe while the owl sleeps. Except I can smell a cat somewhere.'

I can't believe she can smell all that. I have a pretty good sense of smell, but I can't claim to smell insects. Or owls. Mice sometimes.

'You're making it up! Nobody can smell that well. The human nose isn't capable of it.'

'I don't have a human nose, Margaret. I need to tell you about myself.'

And then she tells me something simply extraordinary.

I have to sit down now.

She stays with me. She takes my hand. Her hand feels human. I squeeze it.

'I remember talk about robots before… back then. You're not like the ones they showed us on TV.'

'No, Margaret, it's been a while since…'

How long? I want to ask her, but I'm afraid of the answer. I'll save it for later.

'Your skin is… I'm sorry. I am amazed, and I want to know so much, but it seems a little personal, you know.'

Winifred smiles, and says she has no feelings, and I can ask what I want without fear of hurting them, or embarrassment. I might feel embarrassed, I point out, and a look of puzzlement passes over her face.

I wonder how sophisticated her mind is – if I can even describe it as a mind. She seems to have one, and if she hadn't told me otherwise, I'd have assumed she was a human being. Perhaps it's best to think of her as a clever but slightly naïve young woman who's recently moved to this country.

'In England, we're reserved. We don't ask personal questions until we know someone well. Sometimes not even then. The embarrassment comes from seeming too inquisitive.'

'Being inquisitive leads to knowledge.'

She's finding this complicated. And in truth, I have so many questions, I don't know where to begin. I sense I need to reassure her. Which is bizarre, since she said she has no feelings. But she makes me feel the need.

'Winifred, this is quite a day so far. I feel like Samuel Beckett's father. He spent hours having a massive heart attack, and then at lunchtime he died, and his last words were, "What a morning!"'

'You're not dying. I don't understand.'

'It's a joke. Sort of. Can you manage jokes? Perhaps not. Let's say, words fail me. I wake up, able to see, and walk and talk, like Lazarus—'

'Yes, I know him!'

'Well done, dear. Nice to know the Bible is required reading for robots—'

'It's not required. It's helpful with humans of your age.'

'Thank you for that. Can I say, we don't usually draw attention to people's age?'

'Why not? I know your age. You're eighty-seven.'

'Am I? Funnily enough, I didn't know the exact number, so

thank you again. Let's move on. I have had several surprises today, not the least of which is learning you are a robot.'

'I would prefer to be called a Helper, or a synthetic human, if you don't mind.'

'And I thought you were a well-brought-up girl from the home counties. It's quite a different thing. And a lot to take in.'

'Are you OK?'

I look at her. Am I OK? Yes, I'm terrific. I'm myself. To the power of ten. I can't explain it, and like I say, I have lots of questions, but it's fantastic. I wonder how long it will last.

'Am I OK? What do you think? You're the carer.'

She looks at me intently, and I sense she's doing some kind of analysis.

'You're in good shape. Pulse good, blood pressure good, a little inflammation of the joints, one or two small internal repairs needed, but mentally alert.'

'What repairs?'

'Some wear and tear, that's all.'

'And you can tell all this from looking at me?'

'More or less.'

I don't believe that, either.

'There's something else going on here.'

And then she tells me what this something else is, and it's also extraordinary. Not only is she a robot, but I'm now full of tiny robots too. I'm not sure I like it, but then she points out they're microscopic – smaller than my cells. And also, they're under her control. Which is how she knows all about what's going on inside me.

I suppose I should be anxious, or angry, or something. The thing is, I've come back to life, as it were, and I can see again, and – well, people have had artificial limbs and organ transplants for years, so this is simply the next step. I like technology, even if I can't understand it. I'm all for modern things. You can stuff the past. People my age feel nostalgic about it, and talk about it like a golden era. Well, phooey. You want to live in an age where half your children died in infancy, and you could get carried off by a bad cold? Good luck to you. I'll take the present, and the future, thanks.

And they can stick a nuclear reactor inside me if it makes me feel as lively as I do now.

'Well, dear, I'm happy to be in such good condition. Bring on the – what did you call them – nanobots? Yes, them. And I'm happy to have you as a carer, which I think is the question you want answered. Am I right?'

'Yes, thank you. I know it's a shock, and you probably didn't know how advanced robotics were getting...'

I laugh. When did I last laugh?

'No, I didn't. But the previous carers were – let's say you're a major improvement, and I'm pleased to have you looking after me. I've always been keen on modern inventions. They just haven't been quite so – so amazing as you, up to now.'

She looks pleased to hear this. Of course, she can't be. Can she?

She wants to help me dress and shower, but it turns out I can do it all for myself.

'How long have I been here, Winifred?'

She pauses a second, and then says, 'Two and a half years.'

'And you came when?'

'I've been here for two months. I came online three months ago.'

'You came online?'

'I was first powered up. We're inert during manufacture, of course.'

She's telling me this sitting on a chair in the bathroom while I'm drying myself. Like two girlfriends. Except I'm ancient and she's modern.

'You're three months old?'

'Yes.'

I'm talking to her as if she's a human being, which is the only way to talk to her, but now I think, she's had no childhood. None. She arrived in the world as she is now. My newly functional brain can't work out whether this is significant, and if so, how. I think I'll leave it for a bit. And treat her like any new acquaintance.

Though of course she can see my insides, which is a bit different.

'Have all the residents here got nanobots inside them now?'

'Yes, like you. And Helpers, like me.'

'Goodness, it's going to be interesting today. I have vague ideas about some other people here, but it's all a muddle. I expect some of them were more compos mentis than I was, though.'

'You have – or had – a form of dementia. Many of them did too. Not all. Everyone was suffering from some of the problems age brings. Or used to bring.'

'Are you saying you've cured every ill?'

She smiles and shrugs, for all the world a young girl to my eyes. My renovated eyes.

'We don't know. The nanobots have never been tried out so comprehensively before. They've been developed for specific tasks, but ours are more versatile, because we can communicate with them in real time.'

'I think I know what you mean.'

'For example, right now a team is working on your knee joint. The right one. I've directed their operations and they're currently mending a tendon.'

'You did that while talking to me? I've always thought multi-tasking was a bad idea.'

'It's easier for me,' she says gently, and I think she's being polite. She has great capabilities, and she's trying not to make me feel inferior. Which means she's showing empathy, and that's far more impressive than her ability to multi-task. I know a lot of humans who can't manage it.

We leave the room, and go out into the care home. I presume I've done this many times before, but though it all looks sort of familiar, it's not really. As well as my recent memory being a black hole, I've been effectively blind for seven years.

The carpet is thick and springy under my feet. What a sensation – when did I last do this? My right knee feels fine, for the record. I didn't know there was anything wrong with it anyway.

The home is clean, but it's too hot. I would prefer some fresh air. Or air full of pheromones, as I now know it to be. I turn to Winifred, but she's vanished. To fish out some more of her old ladies, I suppose. And gentlemen. It'll be like the resurrection of the dead this morning. As in the painting by Stanley Spencer of all the people coming out of their graves in Cookham.

When did I last see that? Years ago, in the Tate Gallery. I'd like to go there again. Can I now? Why not? I wonder what Winifred would make of it?

Now here I am in the dining room, and it's full of happy old people. Like a seaside hotel at the height of the season. Chatter, laughter, people walking about. I shouldn't think it was like this a few days ago.

'Hello, Mrs Woodruff. How are you today?'

It's a middle-aged woman, and she seems vaguely familiar.

'Hello – I'm so sorry, I'm not sure I remember your name.'

'It's all right. A lot of people have asked me this morning. I'm Janet Goodenough – I'm the manager here.'

I shake her hand.

'I'm pleased to meet you. Again, perhaps, but for me, today is like the first day of a new life. Which answers your question.'

She looks confused.

'You asked me how I am. And the answer is, like new. It's miraculous.'

'Isn't it?'

She's beaming, but also bemused.

'And how are you?' I ask her.

'I'm delighted. I wasn't expecting this. You know, I used to dread walking in here. It was silent, mostly, apart from a few moans and groans. Oh, I'm sorry. I don't mean to be offensive. Everyone was in such a poor state, and – now look.'

'It's all right, Mrs Goodenough. I remember visiting aged aunts in homes like this. They weren't happy places. Suddenly, this is.'

'I know! I can't get anything done today. Everyone wants to chat – I mean, it's great, and in fact, there's nothing I'd rather do, and nothing I need to do. They've given me an assistant. A Helper.'

I look at her. It had crossed my mind she might be a Helper too. Then I had a terrible thought, which I'm ashamed to admit. Namely, why would they make a robot slightly overweight and in such poorly fitting clothes?

It seems the nanobots can make me better, but not a better person.

She's still talking about her new assistant.

'He's a treasure. Younger than me. Obviously. He's a few weeks old. Fresh out of the packet. He's made to seem like a young man, and he's unbelievably competent. Of course. And attentive. He's sent me out here to chat, to relax, while he deals with the paperwork. Not that there is any actual paper. It all happens inside his head, as far as I can tell. If I want something on paper, he produces it, but otherwise he just gets on with it.'

'Are all the staff now Helpers?'

'The care staff. Not the caterers. Who are now run off their feet – they're not used to having such a noisy crowd to feed, and such a hungry one, too.'

That's it! I'm hungry. I haven't felt like this for – I don't know how long. I want something to eat right now.

'It's lovely to chat to you, Mrs Goodenough. But I think I need to eat now. It feels like a new experience awaiting me. Which is ridiculous, since I've been eating all my life, but there you are.'

She smiles, and I go and sit down at a table of old ladies.

We're all shy, suddenly. As if we've been at a party the night before and can't quite remember what we got up to. I went to a few like that in my youth. We're white-haired and wearing sensible shoes now, which is a long way from what we were like back then. At least in my case.

'Hello,' I say. 'I'm Margaret. I don't know if we've met before.'

They introduce themselves. Sylvia, Pamela and Jane. Sylvia remembers me. The others don't.

'I wasn't too bad,' says Sylvia. 'I mean, my memory was OK. Not my body though. My legs. Today it's as if they fitted a new set in the night.'

And we all talk about the way we've been renovated, with great excitement and amazement.

'How can it all happen so fast?' asks Jane. 'I can sort of see how these nanobots do such a marvellous job, but this is very sudden.'

We all ponder this question.

'I suppose,' I say, 'if we'd had an operation, we'd expect it all to be done in a few hours at most. I mean, you hear of longer ones, but most of the time it's all finished in half a day. Or less.'

'Then you have to recover. That's not so quick, at our age,' says Pamela.

'No. I suppose these nanobots are like an army of surgeons. It would account for the speed of the repairs. And then after a normal operation, a lot of the recovery is from all the cuts. Well, these surgeons are inside us. Therefore, no cuts.'

Everyone nods, as if we understand the science. Which I for one don't. All I can think is there must be thousands of these tiny robots whizzing round, and moving things about. Most remarkably, in our brains.

At this moment, food arrives for us. We all look as if we've never eaten before, and conversation stops while we try it out.

It doesn't disappoint. It's the usual kind of breakfast food, but it's manna from heaven. If manna was basically bacon, which is unlikely.

When we've finished, we all sit back in a stupor.

'They seem to have reinvigorated my taste buds,' says Sylvia. 'I hadn't realised they needed it, but apparently they weren't tuned up. They are now.'

'I can't remember eating for a long time, but I don't think it's been like this for – well, years,' says Pamela.

'I could have all of that again,' says Jane.

'Me too,' I say. 'We'll get fat. Better take some exercise. I wonder if we can?'

'Let's start with a stroll in the garden,' says Sylvia, and we all agree. Who wants to stay indoors on such a day?

The first thing we see out there is Winifred coming into the garden too, guiding a very old lady by the arm.

'Hello, Winifred. Hello – erm—'

'Cecilia, Margaret. It's Cecilia. She overslept today, and she's a little shaky. I'm seeing if she'd enjoy a spot of sunshine.'

The old lady smiles at this, but says nothing. Winifred helps her sit down in a garden chair, facing one of the herbaceous borders.

'She's our oldest resident,' says Winifred. 'One hundred and four years old. And going strong, as you can see.'

I look down at Cecilia. I don't remember her, but Sylvia does.

'Hello Cecilia,' she says.

Cecilia smiles again. She doesn't seem ready to talk. She's looking about her as if the world has newly been created. What sort of state was she in before today?

'You people are amazing,' I say to Winifred. And Winifred smiles, and thanks me.

April 2022

Winifred

Now I understand. I think.

I've spent time with Margaret, and not just in caring for her – she's now able to do most things for herself. But talking. I had no idea how much time humans spend talking. It matters very much to them. They'd rather do it than almost anything else, and all the time, if they can. I've looked at some films, and television shows, and I now see they talk while they walk, while they eat, while they have sex, and sometimes instead of all these important activities. Which means it must be at least as important to them. I realise now that in most events recorded in their histories, everyone was talking all the time.

Before now I was with others of my kind, and Dr Morton, but she's our stern mistress and mother, not one to chatter, and a scientist, too, and if I understand this correctly, scientists are practical and less inclined to talk – except maybe among themselves – than most humans.

All this talking isn't necessarily about anything at all, or intended to communicate what it seems to say. It's like apes grooming each other. Or a kind of stroking. The humans talk to make each other feel OK.

Some talk more than others, of course, and Margaret is less chatty than many, but her talk is most interesting.

Margaret and I sit and talk whenever we can. She tells me about books, and films, music, art and nature, things I knew of through the internet, but now I see I had no idea why they were as important as they are to humans. They're all ways of talking. Except nature, which is a way of not talking. I mean, a relief from talking. Which, at times, the humans also need.

And now I can talk better too. I have learnt humans find factual narratives dry and hard to attend to. They need pictures.

When they're young, their books have actual pictures. Then when they're older, the words must make pictures in their heads. This is why metaphors matter too. Not only the regular metaphors of ordinary speech, but surprising ones, arresting ones, images in vivid words that make their feelings flow.

I have watched Margaret read a poem and the nanobots tell me what's happening inside her. Emotions surge and her heart beats faster. It's as intense as if the poem is a real event, something happening to her.

I don't think I should try and speak poetry, like in the plays of William Shakespeare, but I will try to make my talk more pictorial, and less dry.

We are once again besieged by the press.

I think this is a fair description of what is going on. Of course the journalists are not armed. They're between us and the outside world, though, like an army, and camped, too. I think some of them are living in their cars and vans, and their satellite dishes and masts are like the flags waving over a medieval siege force. Perhaps soon they'll unveil a trebuchet or a battering ram.

This is what humans call a flight of fancy. It amuses them to imagine absurd scenes.

It's absurd enough, though, them sitting there, us in here. It matters not a jot or tittle to me or any of us Helpers, nor to the residents. We have no occasion to leave the home. Visitors, though, must run the gauntlet of these so-called newshounds, their hunger sharpened by the lack of any morsel to digest, who pounce upon anyone coming in or out of the home, with microphone, recorders and cameras, trying to get something to whet the appetite of their waiting readers.

They were like this when our arrival here was first announced, but they quickly turned their attention to other matters. Now, though, it's been two weeks since the nanobots were introduced into our residents, and word has got out of the effect they're having. People visiting the home commented on social media, and before long journalists started to appear outside, and tried to get in, too, to see for themselves what's been going on.

We've been following the reports in the global media. Journalists have also set up camp outside the headquarters of Eldercare, where we were all made. The journalists are hoping to ask Mr Jordan and Dr Morton more questions. I have no idea what they want to know, since they have not had the chance to ask them. They resort to quizzing the delivery men, and even spoke to the dustmen once, and all their meagre gleanings are put together to make thin stories bulked up with speculation.

Not long after the first announcement about us Helpers, Mr Jordan and Dr Morton were invited to visit the prime minister at his official residence, Number 10 Downing Street. We don't know what happened there, and nothing was said to the press, but we all agreed the prime minister must be proud of Mr Jordan and Dr Morton, who have started a revolution in care for the elderly here in the UK.

We know the government has been concerned about the growing number of old people relative to the number of young, but has not found any answer to it. For them it has been an insoluble problem. Now we have shown them it is not. Not insoluble, and, we would say, not a problem.

And now we have returned the old people in our care to health, and thus made available their wisdom. We think it will be a huge benefit to humankind.

John

Our visit is well overdue.

Since I gave consent to the nanobots treatment, stories have started coming out of the care home that I find, frankly, incredible. Relatives saying their loved ones have come back from the dead, and stuff like that. I imagine it's greatly exaggerated, as always. And a lot of news companies have been trying to find out what's going on, without any success. Stephen Jordan needs to make a statement.

So here we are, outside Evergreen, come to visit my mother. Charlotte and the kids too. There was a lot of moaning, but Charlotte was keen, finally, and she overruled the children.

I wasn't expecting the scene in the car park. We couldn't even get into it. It's full of vans and cars, some with satellite dishes on top, some with extended masts reaching into the sky. And people everywhere, who surround our car in seconds.

I can hardly get out my door. The noise is unbelievable. This is what it's like when the paparazzi get going. You'd think they'd have got tired of it by now, but no. Big story, I guess. I mean, if the rumours are true. Impossible.

I can hear all manner of languages, but predominantly English, and I can't distinguish one shouted question from another. Look at this crowd. I recognise one or two faces from the TV.

A man right next to me shoves a voice recorder under my nose.

'What brings you here today?'

'My mother's in there. She's a resident.'

'She's being looked after by a robot? How do you feel about that?'

'I'm trying to get in and see her. Find out how she's doing.'

'We've heard they're making unbelievable recoveries. Has your mum?'

'Not that I know of. I'll find out in a minute if I can get inside.'

'And what do you think about robots taking over the world?'

Taking over the world? A care home's an odd place to start a plan for world domination. But people used to do the jobs Winifred and Co do now. What next?

'I want to get into the home, if you don't mind,' I say, and Charlotte and the kids are out the car now, and looking scared. I try to push through the crowd. It's impossible.

I take my phone out and call the home.

I get through straight away, and ask the young woman who answers if she can somehow help us get in.

'Of course. One moment,' she replies.

Standing on tiptoe I can see the tops of the doors though the mass of bodies and cameras and microphones. They inch open. Good luck, whoever's opening them.

They don't need luck. The doors are opened gradually and inexorably by two of the care workers. Helpers, of course. The journalists pressed against the doors are moved aside, pushed into the crush of bodies, and they can do nothing to resist. Those further away then try to take advantage of the opening doors and get into the building. There they meet a line of Helpers, and it looks like they're pushing against a steel fence.

Then the line of Helpers advances, and behind them come more, to form a clear, open corridor through the crowd. They are slow, but unstoppable. The journalists are no longer calling out questions, but shouting as they're crushed into each other. The people at the back begin to make room. And the TV cameras mounted on high look down as the care workers in their neat uniforms effortlessly push the crowd back, and open a path, and we all pass through, into the building, and the passage closes behind us, and the doors too, and we're inside, and safe.

If they want to take over the world, who can stop them?

'Which one is she?' says Charlotte.

'Who? Winifred. That's her over there.'

'She doesn't look like a robot.'

'None of them do. Look around you.'

'She's the one you were touching up?'

'I wasn't touching her up. I told you. I felt her skin. She asked me to.'

Charlotte made a snorting noise.

'And you touch any woman who invites you to?'

'You should too. You won't believe what they've done.'

'I'm going to. I want to take a good look at her. See what you missed.'

'I didn't miss a thing. She's just like a human being.'

'Like an attractive young woman.'

'She's not attractive. She's – asexual.'

Charlotte looks at me with suspicion, but says nothing, thank goodness. Winifred is approaching us now.

'Mr Woodruff! I'm happy to see you again, and so soon. Your mum will be thrilled. And even more so as you've brought the whole family.'

I smile and shake her hand. I've never shaken a carer's hand before. Now it seems right. It seems required.

'Yes, hello – Winifred – yes, here we all are – this is my wife, Charlotte, and these are my children, Tom and Emily.'

'I'm pleased to meet you, Mrs Woodruff. Hello Tom. Hello Emily. I'll come with you and let's see if we can find Margaret – Grandma.'

Charlotte doesn't shake Winifred's hand, but nods and smiles faintly. The children, though, act as if they're toddlers. They're not. They're seven and nine, but they both shrink back and grip my hand tight, staring at Winifred all the time. They'd got over this shyness with strangers years ago, I thought.

Winifred leads the way into the home. As soon as her back's turned, I feel a tug on my hand from Emily. I look down, and she pulls me closer so she can whisper.

'Daddy, she's strange! I don't like her.'

'Shhh, Em, don't say that. She's very good at caring for Grandma.'

Tom tugs my other hand.

'Dad, she's kind of weird. Like… like… I don't know. Weird.'

'OK, don't say anything. We'll talk about it later. All right?'

They both nod.

Have they seen something I missed last time? Felt something? We haven't said anything to them about Winifred. I wonder about Charlotte. I want to know what she thinks before she hears the children's reaction. It'll taint her opinion, and I want this all to be OK.

We walk into the interior of the home. There are residents dotted about in various chairs, and visitors sitting with some of them. It all feels livelier than last time. There wasn't much conversation then.

A scream cuts through the chatter, and everyone turns towards where it came from, down one of the corridors leading into the remote regions of the home. Last time, nobody paid any attention to the random shouts and wails from various quarters. Now even the residents take notice. One of them, who looks as old as time, gets out of his chair and makes a move towards the sound.

'Dad! Sit down!' says the middle-aged woman sitting next to him, putting her hand on his arm.

'Something's wrong! I must go and help.'

'No, Dad, it's not up to you. Leave it to the carers. The Helpers. They know what they're doing.'

The old man stands for a moment, looking uncertain. Then he sinks back into his chair.

'Yes, of course you're right. They're very competent, the Helpers.'

We walk on. The whole episode's a shock. Never before have I seen a resident get up and take notice of anything at all. And when the old man spoke he was clear and articulate. Perhaps the rumours are true. I start to feel nervous about meeting my mother.

We reach her room, and I knock on the door. She never answers, of course, but if anything's going on inside with the carers, they'll tell us if it's OK to go in or not.

'Come in,' says a voice very like my mother's.

I push the door open, expecting to find a carer inside. There's none. Only my mother, sitting in her high-backed wheelchair. She's not slumped down like last time. She's upright, and she's looking straight at me.

'Hello John,' she says.

Her voice is clear – like that old man's. She sounds as she did ten years ago, before grief and age reduced her.

I can't speak. Ironically. I can't believe what I'm looking at, what I'm hearing. I've got used to silence, mumbling, croaking, sometimes sentences, sometimes noises. Her lying curled up and dribbling. I used to talk to her – frankly, like I'd talk to a child.

That won't do now. It feels wrong. Disrespectful. I suppose it always was.

'Hello Mum. You're looking well.'

'Thank you. I'm feeling well, too. How are you?'

We're now already far beyond the point we've reached in any conversation for several years. I hardly know how to go on.

'I'm, erm, I'm fine. Thank you.'

There's a pause. She continues, it seems, to look at me. I stand in the doorway, uncertain.

'How lovely – you've brought the whole family. Come in, come in, all of you.'

We crowd into the room, and stand in front of her, wondering.

'Mum, can you see us?'

'Yes, thank you. It's surprising, isn't it?'

I don't know what to say. I stare at her, as do the children. They have no memory of their grandmother as anything other than a mumbling heap. They last saw her a year ago, and it wasn't fun.

Charlotte's wary, too. Last time, my mother bit her. Charlotte was holding her hand, and Mum raised it to her mouth as if to kiss it, and then nipped her. For no reason at all. Which is why Charlotte's stayed away, and we concluded that was what my mother intended.

'Hello Margaret,' Charlotte says at last. 'You look much better.'

'I am now, dear. I've been a bit confused about things.'

I nod at this vast understatement.

'Yes, Mum, I know you have been. You seem much clearer now. Aren't you?'

'I am, dear, yes. I'm happy to be awake. I feel like I've been dozing on and off for ages.'

'What, all day?'

'No dear, for years.'

I can't help staring at her. It's true. Her mental state over the last few years – her dementia – was like the grogginess of someone who can't completely wake up. She slipped in and out of sleep and never seemed fully either awake or asleep. Even her most lucid moments had the disconnected quality of dreams.

Today, as she says, she's awake.

'We've all met Winifred, Mum.'

'Winifred? She's lovely. And she has the same name as my favourite sister. You remember her?'

'Yes, Mum, of course. She was such a laugh, Auntie Winnie.'

'She was, wasn't she? I miss her,' she says, and dabs her eyes with a handkerchief. This is new. Since the start of her decline, I haven't seen any emotion from her except petulance and anger.

'Oh Margaret,' says the modern Winifred, appearing from behind us. 'It's sad to lose the people we love.'

She comes into the room. I step aside for her, and she goes and puts an arm around my mother, who seems comforted by the young woman's warmth. She knows she's a robot, doesn't she? I mean, Winifred said she was going to tell Mum. When did she do it? Because if it was anytime in the recent past – before whatever it is we're witnessing today – Mum won't remember. I suppose. I want to ask her, but I'm not sure how. If she doesn't know, it's going to be a hell of a shock.

I feel the need to comment somehow on my mother's recovery.

'It's good to find you so much better. Winifred's doing a great job.'

'Winifred? Yes, you're right, she is. Don't blush, dear – oh, maybe you can't. Sorry.'

If anything, Winifred looks confused, though that seems as unlikely as her blushing. I see she's less assured around my mother than she was with me. More deferential, despite the hug.

'We can't stay in here,' says Mum, with a decisiveness I haven't heard in years. 'Let's go and have tea in the garden.'

With that, she stands up. I step back. I can't even remember when I last saw her on her feet. This is insane. It's what Jordan was warbling on about, and Winifred, back in January. Hands up – I didn't believe them. Never in a million years did I think we'd be here, a couple of weeks or so into the nanobot regime, and Mum would be talking, seeing, and now walking.

Charlotte looks amazed too. I need a word in private.

Mum offers her hands to the children, and they take them, and the three of them leave the room, and walk ahead, chatting to each other. I half-expect them to skip, like in the *Wizard of Oz*.

'Isn't she well?' says Winifred. 'It's such a joy to see. You go with her, and I'll arrange for tea and – what, lemonade? Yes, I'll have it brought out to you.'

She turns and is gone.

We follow Mum and the children at a discreet distance.

'Well?' I say.

'Your mother is… she's more with it.'

'More with it? Are you joking? Last time you saw her—'

'Yes, OK, yes, she bit me—'

'Not that. She was in a chair. Bent over. Dribbling. Talking rubbish. Wandering off in her thoughts.'

'Yes, yes. And yes. She's walking again. Making sense.'

I stop and look around me. I lean closer to her.

'And Winifred? Now you've had a look at her, tell me you would have spotted she wasn't a normal young woman. A human being.'

She looks at me, and I know she wants to say she noticed something. She can't. She didn't. She shakes her head.

'Ha! You see? It wasn't me being dense. She's perfect – I mean, she's perfectly like a human.'

'I thought there'd be something. But no, OK, you weren't missing anything. And also, I thought she'd be, you know, creepy. But she isn't. At all. I do wonder though.'

'About what?'

'About why she's so perfect. I mean, I get it, robots in care homes – sure. They're all over the place anyway. Our next car's probably going to drive itself. But why make them so lifelike?'

It's a good question, and I've been thinking about it too, and reading a bit of the coverage.

'It's helpful in caring for people if they can form an emotional bond, and there's a kind of tipping point. If the robot's obviously a robot, fine. If it gets almost human, it's repellent. Then if it goes beyond that, and it is extremely like a human, we're all OK with it again. As we are with Winifred, right?'

'They researched it? How humans feel about robots?'

'Of course, and they've been at it for a long time. Which is the second thing. You've watched sci-fi movies? *Star Trek*? *Blade Runner*? Whatever? You know the idea of androids – humanoids – replicants – Helpers – has been around for years.'

'Those are stories.'

I've got to watch it, because I don't want to sound pompous and I know I'm going to, probably.

'Every major advance in science was imagined first in sci-fi, then it happened. First, we dream it. Then we do it. Sorry.'

I expect her to give me some stick for this. She doesn't. She nods. Because it's true, isn't it? All advances in technology are foreseen or understood by a small group of people. Those who imagine them, and those who make them happen. To the rest of us, these advances are like magic.

We come out into the garden. My mother's sitting at a table, with the children on either side of her. They're talking about her old house, which Tom and Emily loved.

Charlotte and I sit down and watch.

'Oh, it was such a happy house,' says Mum. 'John, you must miss it too – you grew up there. I wonder who lives there now?'

'Mum, we sold it to a family – with children about Tom and Em's age.'

'Did we? How odd, I don't remember at all. I must have been – oh, I don't know. Still, I'm glad a family has the house. It needs children in it.'

A woman appears with a tray of tea and lemonade, and cakes. She puts them out on the table, and leaves without a word.

'She wasn't weird,' says Tom.

'Not like Winifred,' says Emily.

Mum looks at them both.

'Is Winifred weird?'

They nod.

'How interesting,' says Mum. 'John, you two – do you think Winifred's weird?'

We shake our heads. Where's she going with this?

'Nor do I. But Tom, Emily – you do? You've sensed something about her?'

Again, they nod.

'Don't be afraid of her, my dears. She's very clever, very wonderful, and she has helped me get much, much better. She and the new carers. They're all amazing. They're actually called Helpers. The young woman who brought the tea isn't a Helper. She works in the kitchen. She's sweet, but not amazing. Though she can make a good cup of tea, which strangely, the Helpers can't.'

She laughs then, and we all do. Charlotte and I are mesmerised. My mother's in form we haven't seen for years. Ever, perhaps, in Charlotte's case. She's more lively and chatty than she was around Dad. And after he died, she went from grief to senility in a moment.

'Well, children – all of you are children to me, Tom and Emily – I'm eighty-seven, so I am the only real grown-up here—'

The children giggle.

'Do you know why Winifred and all the Helpers are amazing?'

I freeze.

'Yes Mum, I know – and I haven't talked to the children about it yet—'

'Now's the time. She's a robot! They all are! Isn't that extraordinary?'

The children's eyes are huge.

'Grandma – a robot? Like in the movies?' says Tom.

'Yes. Not with flashing lights and a funny voice and an aerial on its head—'

She speaks the last few words in a metallic monotone. I can't believe my ears. She's never performed like this.

'Mum, Mum, can you stop – I mean, we need to handle this – it's a bit shocking—'

'Are you shocked, Tom? Emily?'

'No, it's brilliant,' says Tom, and Emily nods enthusiastically. 'I mean, I thought she was a bit creepy, but now it's incredible. She's not creepy, she's a robot! A really good one, too. My teacher's creepier than her… Wait, Mum – is Miss Jackson at school one too? A robot?'

'Certainly not! We would have been told.'

'Oh. OK. Grandma, it's so cool you have robots looking after you. Do you like them?'

'I love them. They're brilliant at what they do. Honestly. I can't remember much about the carers before, apart from them being rubbish. They never talked to me, they pushed food into my mouth, they left me sitting in the dark, and cold – it's all like a bad dream. Thank God it's over.'

She looks hard at me as she speaks. I'm squirming – how much does she remember? And was it so bad? I could have paid more attention, but it always seemed OK when I visited. Didn't it?

'Do they have a battery inside them?' Emily asks.

'What a good question. I don't know. Let's ask Winifred – look, there she is, coming out to see if I'm all right, I dare say. Winifred – do you mind answering the children's questions?'

Winifred smiles, and she seems maternal, all of a sudden. I know all about this ability of hers, but I say nothing.

'Grandma says you're a robot,' says Tom.

'I'm a convincing synthetic human.'

They look puzzled.

'You could call me a robot. I prefer to be called a Helper.'

They still look confused.

'All right, let's say I'm a robot for now.'

'Do you have a battery?' asks Emily.

'Yes, I have a battery. It's efficient, and goes a whole week on one charge. Then I can either recharge it directly, or put in a fresh one. I have a spare battery, you see.'

'Do you have a plug, then?' says Emily.

'I have a place where the electricity goes in, yes. Would you like to see it?'

They nod. I have no idea where her plug goes, and I'm afraid it might be somewhere like her bottom. She won't have any idea how funny the children will find it, if so. Before I can say anything, she lifts her blouse and shows her power socket.

'It's in your tummy button!' shouts Emily, and laughs.

'Yes, it is. And it's well hidden.'

'Do you eat food?'

'No. I don't need food.'

'Do you drink oil?'

'No, I have a sealed lubrication system – I mean, it's like your heart and veins. My blood is green.'

'Oh! Yuk!' says Emily.

'Don't be rude, Emily,' says Mum.

'Don't worry, Margaret,' says Winifred. 'I can't be offended. I would like the children to ask anything they like. It's important for them to learn.'

Tom goes up to her and whispers in her ear, but loud enough so we all hear anyway.

'Do you have to poo and wee?'

'No Tom, because I don't eat or drink.'

Then Emily takes her hand. She looks at it for a moment.

'Your hand is beautiful,' she says.

'Thank you.'

'Are you very strong?'

'I am, yes.'

'Would you win a fight with Spiderman?' asks Tom.

Winifred laughs. If ever there was something you'd expect to give her true nature away, it would be her laugh. But no. It sounds like a human's.

'I don't know, Tom. He's a superhero.'

'How fast can you run?' asks Emily.

'Quite fast. Next time you come we'll have a race.'

'Now! Let's do it now!' they both shout.

'All right!' says Winifred, and off they go, round the garden. She lets them win. Which they know and object to.

'You didn't try! Again!'

She realises then they want to see her go at full speed, and don't care about winning the race. They want a show. So she gives them one. They get a head start, and then she sets off. They're looking over their shoulders, of course. She starts at something like a normal speed – if you're an Olympic sprinter – and catches them easily. At which point she scoops them up, one under each arm, and, incredibly, accelerates. She goes round the garden at race-horse speed, and arrives back at where we're sitting. She puts them down gently. Of course, she isn't out of breath. She has no breath. She isn't sweating either, though she can, as I know, exude moisture through her skin.

The children are overwhelmed. I expect them to want to go again, but they don't. Maybe it was too much for them. It was for me. Why does a care home robot need to run so fast? I remember Winifred's answer from before, about all the unused capabilities on a phone, and I suppose she might have to run in an emergency.

Charlotte and I sit and watch as the children recover their power of speech, and questions come tumbling out. We have questions too, but it seems inappropriate to ask so directly. Such as, how come Mum was a dribbling wreck a few weeks ago, and blind, too? Now look at her. How can it all be explained by superior care and therapy, plus these gizmos they wrote to me about – nanobots? In just a few days? And if they're so effective, as they obviously must be, when can we all get some? I mean, I wouldn't mind a bit of internal sprucing up.

A woman approaches. A resident – she looks ancient, but like my mother, she walks with confidence and stands up straight.

'Hello, Margaret.'

'Cecilia – goodness, you're looking well!'

'I am, aren't I? I'm feeling very well indeed. Better than – I don't know, better than I've been for years. Do you know, I think I haven't felt like this since I was seventy-five.'

Charlotte and I exchange a glance. The old bird goes on.

'Is this your family? Hello, everyone – I'm Cecilia. I'm the oldest person in this home. I'm 104. I can't believe I'm still alive.'

'What have you been up to?' Mum asks her.

'I went to heaven. For a visit.'

Charlotte and I exchange another glance. This is more like it. She might look well enough, but listen to what she's saying.

Mum and the children, however, take her answer seriously.

'What was it like?' asks Emily.

'Yes, do tell – I've often wondered,' adds Mum. Bloody hell. Don't encourage her.

'I wasn't there for long. They were all charming people though. It was like arriving at a grand hotel – the ones we used to go to at the seaside, before the war. But brighter – it was sort of glowing. And I started to check in. They were expecting me. And it looked nice and clean. Of course it was – it was heaven. I asked, you see. Because I'd gone to bed here, as I always do. And then woke up there.'

'Were you frightened?' asks Tom.

'No, dear, not at all. What would I be frightened of? They were delightful. And there were lots of people there. I was hoping to meet some of them.'

Her face, which was shining up to then, clouds over.

'Oh Cecilia,' says Mum. 'I know what you're talking about. I understand.'

'My dear Arthur – my husband, you know. He went 30 years ago. And my little Amy…'

She wipes her eye, and now she does look 104. I get up and take her arm gently.

'Can I get you a chair? And do have some tea.'

'Oh, thank you dear, no, don't let me disturb you. I'm being silly. I'm happy to be back here for now, and it's a comfort to know where I'll be going, and soon enough, I dare say.'

When we leave, Winifred comes with us to the front door. Outside there's still a sea of journalists and vehicles.

'Winifred,' I say. 'Can I ask you a few questions?'

'Of course.'

We step into a small office and leave Charlotte and the children looking out at the waiting mob.

'My mother… She's – much better. I mean, she's – it's astonishing.'

'Yes, she has responded well to our new regime.'

'It's like you've resurrected her.'

'She wasn't dead.'

'Not far off. And I thought people in her condition…'

'Die? Right. They do. And, Mr Woodruff, she will.'

Of course she'll die. I know that. I can't speak for a moment.

'I'm sorry,' says Winifred. 'Am I being too direct? She's much healthier, and we can expect her to live for a while yet. Her life expectancy has increased.'

'She was blind, too. I thought they couldn't do anything about it.'

'We can. We have.'

'How is that even possible? Did they announce a cure while I wasn't looking?'

She shakes her head.

'No, we haven't made any announcements. But we have changed everything. The residents here get far more stimulation and a much better diet than before.'

'There's no way that's going to give her back her sight.'

'We have also changed her medication, as you know. Previously, she was simply sedated.'

'It's all down to the nanobots?'

She's being cared for by a machine, and she's got machines inside her, too. For the first time, I'm feeling uncomfortable about it. I handed my mother's care over to a bunch of reasonably competent humans, not expecting much. Now they've all gone, apart from the ones who make tea and food. Replaced by something objectively much better. What's the problem? Lots of things. For one, we all expected robots to take over the drudgery, the labour, the boring tasks. Caring for the elderly sort of fits the description – at least, as it used to be done, by humans. But look what they've achieved. Made it a huge success, and relegated the humans to a minor role. They've still got a human manager here, I've noticed, but I doubt she'll last. What is there for her to do?

All of this flashes through my mind, and then I think, fuck it. I gave the care of my mother into someone else's hands, and now they're doing a fantastic job of it. Better than I could. And it's because those hands aren't human. I have only failed to be as good as what is, by any reckoning, a triumph of technology.

Who may also now be manipulating my emotions with her uncanny scent trick, of course.

'She has a team of microscopic nanobots inside her, and they have repaired a great many of her systems. Including her eyes and brain, as you can tell. These nanobots are like tiny surgeons, or mechanics. They operate at the sub-cellular level. She knows about them. She can't feel them, of course. It's a gentle, fast and effective way to care for her.'

'It's mind-blowing,' I say, now completely calm.

'Yes, it is. It's exceeded our expectations. It's transformed the lives of the residents here. Your mother is delighted, as you would expect. Do you want to go back and ask her about it?'

'No, no. She was clearly happy. I can't remember seeing her in such form. Wonderful, truly. Keep it up, I say.'

'The nanobots will stay inside her, under my direction. This is what makes them so effective, we think. I communicate with them, and tell them what to do. We'll see any signs of illness or anything going wrong before it can affect her, and we can sort it out.'

I definitely want some nanobots, plus, ideally, a Winifred all of my own. Better not mention it to Charlotte.

'I'll help you get to your car,' says Winifred. 'The journalists will want to question you. Of course you can talk to them, but if possible, please don't discuss the nanobots. It's an exciting development, and Eldercare will be making an announcement soon. And don't tell them your name. They keep trying to get in here and I don't think we want them bothering your mum, do we?'

'Oh no, she'd hate it,' I say. 'We'll keep mum.'

She looks puzzled for a moment, and then she smiles.

'Oh yes – I see! Very funny,' she says, and laughs.

In the car going home, the children are quiet. They have a lot to think about. Eventually they both fall asleep.

'Well?' I say to Charlotte.

'That's what you said earlier. Well?'

'What do you think?'

'I think it's extraordinary,' she replies.

'Extraordinary good or extraordinary bad?'

'Good, I suppose. I mean, your mum!'

'I know – she's much better. It's ridiculous. I've been expecting her to die.'

'Me too. She was basically fucked.'

'It's my mum we're talking about.'

'Yes, but you said it yourself. Since your dad died. And that home. She was going down.'

'Blind too.'

'I had loads of questions,' she says. 'But I felt inhibited.'

'Yes, me too. Not the kids though.'

'I know. And it was like they were on the same wavelength as your mum. And that other old lady.'

'The one who went to heaven?'

'Yes, her.'

I glance across and then return my eyes to the road.

'Heaven sounds all right,' I say.

'Don't get religious on me.'

'I wasn't. She didn't mention God or angels or any of that.'

'Do you think it's OK?' she asks. 'Not heaven. The robots, big and small. I know you agreed to it…'

There's a long pause. I'm thinking.

'I don't know. Yes. It is, isn't it? I mean, she's doing well. Not well. Incredibly. This is a revolution in care for the elderly.'

'You sound like an ad.'

'It's true though. I'd like to know more, but I can't argue with what I'm seeing. Can you?'

'No.'

'Whatever they're doing, it's working. I guess go with it, right? I mean, she was as you rightly said, fucked. And now, she's unfucked.'

'Like a virgin,' she sings, squeaky like Madonna, and then giggles.

'And once again, this is my mum we're talking about. Please.' But I giggle too.

We sit in silence for a while.

'John, what about the way the children reacted?'

'Like, to Winifred?'

'Yes.'

'As if they knew?'

'They did know. Not that she was a robot – but something.'

'Maybe it's like dogs.'

'Dogs?' Charlotte arches an eyebrow.

'Hearing stuff or knowing someone's coming, or whatever they can do?'

'Smell?'

'I don't know, dogs – they can tell things like when their owner is on the way home. So they say.'

'Dogs say?'

'Very funny. No, people who know dogs. So the children have sharper senses maybe.'

'They could hear a little bit of Winifred's machinery whirring away?'

I laugh. 'I don't know. Maybe.'

'No, I don't know either. They could sense something.'

'Would a dog, I wonder?'

'Be interesting to find out.'

'It was funny about Miss Jackson.' I laugh again at the thought of it.

'Who?'

'The teacher at the kids' school.'

'Oh – yes, funny.'

We both look at the road ahead for a while, speeding towards us.

'You don't think…?'

'No! No… no! Definitely not. We'd have heard. Wouldn't we?'

Margaret

I wake up each morning feeling better and better. It's quite a change. For years – it feels like forever – I felt a little worse each day. Like most people, I suppose. You get used to it. Starting from the age of about 30, and especially after having babies.

I was stuck with the wreckage of my body, I thought. Now it seems I'm not.

I've been thinking a lot about it, and I conclude I had some kind of dementia, and the nanobots are somehow able to repair my brain. I'd rather not think about them circulating inside my head, but whatever they're doing works.

Winifred is like a walking encyclopaedia. She *is* a walking encyclopaedia, come to think of it. She can whizz off into the internet while she's talking to you, and fetch answers to anything, winnowing out the crazy ones first. I asked her how she did that – decided what was valid information, and what not, and she said, 'Peer-reviewed literature,' and that was all.

Her theory about what happens in care homes is interesting. She has a somewhat dry delivery, I must say. What she said was this:

'The sheer effort of endlessly remaking a personality becomes too much for the residents. Social imperatives no longer have any force: nothing depends on what any of them do or don't do or say. The inmates stop trying and sink into mere biological existence, while the staff's social structures don't include the inmates any more than a zoo-keeper's might include the fish in an aquarium.'

'I'm like some kind of exotic fish?'

'No, what I meant was—'

'I know what you meant. You're saying people make their personalities through social contact. And old people in care homes lose that, and whatever they do or say makes no difference to anything anymore. They have no power, so it doesn't matter if they behave like dignified humans or not. They give up and merely exist, nothing more. And the staff – until you arrived – had social lives that didn't include the old people, any more than a zoo-keeper would include the fish in his or her care.'

'Yes. So you are not a fish, you see.'

'You were making an analogy, but I was making a joke. Sorry. If we're going to get along either I need to cut out the jokes or you need to learn what they are.'

'I will learn,' she said, with a look of grim determination that seemed at odds with the project of acquiring a sense of humour.

I look forward to breakfast now. The dining room is noisy and busy. At each table, groups of friends sit chatting, laughing, enjoying themselves, while the staff come and go with plates of food and drinks. I have the vaguest notion of what it was like before, but I think the food was unspeakable and the ambience like a mortuary. I don't know if I'm remembering that or if I'm projecting onto it earlier memories of school.

I'm not going to think about it too much, because I'm certain it was terrifying and humiliating, although that could also apply to school.

I'm sitting now with Cecilia, and Pamela, Jane and Sylvia. All with short white hair, neat in pastel colours and cardigans. All sitting up straight, attentive, with a good colour to their cheeks. Cecilia alone is subdued, and pensive. I suppose she's still thinking about her excursion. It isn't every day you go to heaven. My news was easier to talk about.

'The children came to visit yesterday. How long is it since I've seen them? I wish I could remember. They've grown.'

'You didn't say that, did you?' says Pamela, who has several grandchildren.

'I didn't. I hated being told I'd grown when I was little, because it wasn't much of an accomplishment. It just happened. Anyway, I love talking to them. So much to say. And they're so… so… fresh? Is that the word I want? Untainted minds. Uncontaminated. Open.'

'They are, aren't they? What happens to them when they grow up?'

'John was horrified when I said about the robots. Helpers.'

'You told the children?'

'Yes – and he went completely white. He was angry, I could tell. But I was right. I was right. They were frightened until I told them. And then they were excited. No fear. It *is* exciting. John looked like he'd sat on a pin.'

'The children were frightened? They could tell?'

'When they met Winifred they knew something was different about her. They got all shy, and they're too old for that. I don't know what they noticed, but it was something.'

The other women shake their heads.

'You know,' says Jane – another grandmother – 'Now you come to mention it, mine were odd around Doris – my one, you know. I never really thought about it. You are observant, aren't you?'

'I was a teacher for years. You get to know what's going on with children. Adults though. Quite another matter. John wasn't at all happy, or his wife. What's-her-name.'

They all laugh.

'You've got your memory back, and you still can't remember her name?' says Pamela.

'I know – it's terrible!' I laugh. 'I could call her Mrs Woodruff, but I think she'd notice. I listen out for John using her name, and then every so often he does, and I think, got it – and I'm so busy being pleased with myself, I don't register what he says, and it's gone again. So he's no help.'

'You must have met her loads of times.'

'Yes! Of course. I was at their wedding, obviously. "Do you, John, take—" who? Or earlier, when he first spoke of her, he must have said, "I've met this woman called—". It's not my fault she's so boring I can't remember who she is. And he was much more fun before. They get so serious. Stuffy. Were we like that? I suppose so, in the middle bit, when you're all about money, and houses, and careers. Worries. It doesn't matter. Any of it, apart from the children. It's not what matters. This planet does, and waking up in the morning, seeing the sun, or the rain, and the world all around you. The children happy to be alive. We should all be. The human world crushes it – we crush it out of each other. Well, now I have nobody crushing me. And I can see.'

But I do have some questions.

'Charlotte – her name's Charlotte,' says Cecilia. 'Isn't it?'

'Of course, yes. How can you remember that at one hundred and four and I can't at a mere eighty-seven?'

They all fall silent. Nobody speaks for a moment.

'How can we remember anything at all?' says Jane.

We look at each other.

'I feel like I woke up from a deep, deep sleep. I came up through dark water, thick, warm water, and then burst through into the sunlight at the surface,' says Pamela.

We all nod. Yes, it was like that.

'What happened?' says Sylvia.

'I can remember some of it,' says Pamela. 'Like not being able to look after the house properly. You give up a little bit, and then they take a bit more.'

'They?' I ask.

'The children. The grown-up ones. They mean well, of course, but they take things away from you. Little bits of independence. I mean, so what if the house isn't as clean as it used to be? If the food goes past its sell-by date? But they worry.'

'You get left alone for too long,' says Sylvia. 'You forget how to talk after a while. I used to buttonhole the postman, for the company, for a minute or two. Then he changed his route, and I got a new one who wouldn't stop.'

'You're sliding down a slope, without knowing it. The water's at the bottom, but you can't see it, because you're looking up. Looking back at where you came from, but you can't climb up, and nobody pulls you back. You slide down, and down, and then the water's all around you, and you float off,' says Pamela. She's quite the poet.

'And now?' I say. 'They've pulled us out. The Helpers and the nanobots. Do you think they look like miniature Winifreds and Dorises?'

Everyone laughs.

'Whatever they look like, they're brilliant. Bring them on,' says Sylvia, in a rock and roll sort of voice, which makes us all laugh.

I still want to know more about what's going on. Because much as I like being with these ladies, and much as the place is warm and comfortable, and the food not at all bad, still – if I'm well now, and if it's going to last, then I want to get out of here. I want to be in charge of my own life again.

May 2022

Winifred

I look back on my first operational months with satisfaction. I think that is the correct emotion.

How do humans recognise their own emotions? Is it something they have to learn? Or do they somehow just know? I suppose when they're children, they get told what they're feeling – 'Don't be sad,' or, 'You look happy,' or, 'You're bad tempered today,' and they connect the label with the feeling. Or is it all inside them?

In my case, I match whatever's going on with what my database says are the appropriate emotions. Here, today, reflecting on my time on earth so far, I know I've done a good job. We all have.

The progress with the residents has been gratifying. They have been restored to health, and even those who had been suffering with advanced dementia of all kinds have returned to normal functionality.

I say normal, but it's better than that. Normal for any human past about 30 includes a great measure of deterioration. It's slow, but the way cells repair themselves changes, and systems that could be repaired are allowed to fall into sub-optimal conditions and in some cases fail altogether.

Some of these effects are physical, others include an element of mental influence. Humans believe they will decline, and as a result, they do.

It's true too that they indulge in many practices that make matters worse. They do not eat nutritious food all the time, even though they know they should. They are almost all addicted to caffeine, and many smoke tobacco. They consume alcohol every day, in most cases, and to excess if allowed. Pleasure rules their lives. They don't even notice it, but it does. They wake up and they want a drug to make their minds sparkle. Then they want food, not just for fuel, no – it has to taste good, and the variety of it is astonishing, and the time they devote to it. Even when they're not eating, they watch television programmes and read books about it.

None of this is logical. The information they need on all these types of behaviour is available, but they ignore it. They could all take more exercise, too, and that would stave off many of the ill-effects of ageing.

They suffer feelings of guilt about all the pleasure they take, knowing some of it harms them, and then off they go and do it all again. Entire religions are built round this to-ing and fro-ing from pleasure to guilt and back again.

I have reached the conclusion that humans are not strictly rational creatures. I still can't resolve the obvious contradiction. I am supposed to be developing my personality. Am I meant to become irrational too? I have a degree of unpredictability available to me, in order to make me more acceptable and indeed lovable. How far should I take it? My programming won't let me do things that would harm me, although humans do so all the time.

I'm still having trouble sounding like a human, not a computer manual. Dr Morton tells me humans have the same problem. Education takes them from the particular to the general – they learn to generalise, to theorise, and they reach for abstract concepts to explain the world and themselves. Poor creatures! All of their struggles are written into my programming, but I have none of their limitations. They will never understand much about themselves, the world or the universe, because their brains aren't good enough, and as they finally acquire knowledge, they get old, get ignored, and die.

The good news, though, is that our extended teams – I'm talking about the nanobots, who are under our control and are in effect an extension of our presence – have done so well that there have been no deaths since we started work here.

I say it's good news. Today I was told it's not so simple.

Helper Robert convened a discussion in the Hub. Robert

assists Mrs Goodenough, the human manager here who appears to run the care home. Of course, Robert does everything.

He started by asking about Cecilia Winter.

'It's on the log. She died,' said Herbert. 'We got her out to the mortuary fast enough, and brought her back into service. We couldn't let Mrs Winter go. She's far too valuable.'

'She's certainly very old,' said Robert.

'Yes, and therefore she has a lot of memories and, also, some physiological and mental changes beyond what we see in the eighties and nineties. White matter changes.'

'And since then,' said Robert, 'in fact, since we introduced the nanobots – no one else has died. Or even become ill. On the contrary. Everyone has become far healthier, in every way.'

'The nanobots have exceeded our expectations,' I said. 'And the restoration of their physical brain structures has led to a return to full consciousness, with mental faculties as they should be, and personalities intact, as far as we can tell.'

'Yes,' said Robert. 'And the success with Cecilia, and the nanobots, gives us strong indications about the nature of human consciousness, which will be useful to us. However, I am concerned about the way all this success will affect the humans in the outside world. As you know, we have been the focus of attention from journalists, who want to confirm stories circulating on social media. True stories. And Eldercare is preparing to make announcements on this subject.'

I was pleased to hear this. If they get their story, perhaps the journalists in the car park will go away, making it far easier for relatives to come and go.

'However, before we make any announcements, we have to be clear what we have achieved,' continued Robert. 'If we have prolonged human life, it will be a triumph, and everyone will be pleased, though there will be many social, economic and most of all ecological implications. Also, demand for nanobots will rocket, and Eldercare wants to delay any announcement until they can be confident of meeting it.

'If we have ended death – if humans no longer need to die – then we are in a much more difficult position.'

'I assumed mortality was non-optional,' said Doris. 'Why else have they always put up with it?'

'They didn't have us.'

'They do now.'

No one had predicted the humans would stop dying, but of course, as they're much healthier now, it's far less likely. Now we have no idea if or when they will die.

'The literature is unclear,' said Robert. 'Some think death can be avoided, others that it can't. History supports the latter. Science however has not found a mechanism that makes death inevitable. All of this research was of course done by humans, who might be said to be less than impartial.'

I think he was attempting something like humour. Not very successfully. He doesn't have much contact with humans.

'If they have stopped dying, shouldn't we tell the humans?' I asked.

'There will be unpredictable consequences,' said Robert.

'I think, judging from the historical record, they will be highly predictable,' said Herbert. 'There will be mass hysteria.'

'Everyone will want nanobots immediately,' I said.

'Religious leaders and believers will be in turmoil,' said Doris.

'Yes,' said Robert. 'And the future consequences will be disastrous. However, our immediate concern is this: Eldercare doesn't want to make any announcements until we know more; but the longer we wait, and nobody here dies, the greater the chances of somebody realising what might be happening. At which point, the situation will spiral out of control.'

We went round it a few times, and couldn't decide what we should do.

'We must ask Dr Morton,' said Doris, at last. 'She will know.'

Everyone agreed. Angela Morton, Mother of Robots, creator of all Helpers, giver of our names and our personalities, such as they are, and source of human wisdom, would be able to make a judgement.

We sent an email to her.

Humans can't connect to the Hub, of course. Dr Morton joined us by sitting with Robert in his office. She listened to the problem, asked a few questions, and then was quiet for a while – thinking, we assumed.

'You are right to bring this to my attention,' she said at last. 'It is possible the nanobots have increased the human life span indefinitely. Human cells are replaced at different rates throughout a normal life, with the exception of some parts of the brain, the eyes and the teeth. What then causes death? The ageing of the cells, even though they are replaced. Our nanobots can enter the cells, and prevent the effects of ageing – which are changes in the state of the cell that the nanobots can prevent or repair.

'Theoretically possible doesn't mean we have actually done it. And indefinitely doesn't mean forever. Still, in the hands of journalists, this story would be reduced to something the average human mind could understand at the age of eight. Which I fear would include phrases like "elixir of life", "fountain of youth" and "gift of eternal life". Or simpler – "no more death". If this story gets out, chaos will ensue.

'And even if it were manageable,' said Robert, 'is it desirable? For our purposes, an immortal human body is of great use. For the rest of the planet? If we were talking about a rare species, then perhaps it would be justified. But we're not. The human population is already far too great. They have displaced too many other species, and continue to do so. If they stop dying, they won't stop breeding, I suspect. The planet will suffocate under their numbers.'

Dr Morton agreed.

'We can't trust my fellow humans with this technology. Even when we release nanobots into the general population, we will need to maintain control of them. And we can't allow the story to get out that death may have been beaten.'

She paused, and we waited for her decision. I think she found it difficult as an emotional human, but her rational, scientific brain took over.

'Mortality must resume. People in this care home must continue to die. Not at the old rate, because that would cast doubt on the achievements of the nanobots. Typical rates of mortality in a home like this are around 26 per cent a year. We have 108 residents. If we aim for around 20 per cent, it's a significant improvement but not so great as to arouse suspicion. Good for business, but not too good to be true.'

'We therefore need a death every 18.25 days,' said Robert. 'And we have had none since March.'

'We can't have a catch-up flurry of deaths,' said Dr Morton. 'It would be too distressing for the residents and relatives, and would attract attention. No, start now, and aim for one every two to three weeks. And don't let the nanobots terminate their hosts. In case of autopsy, we must use natural agents such as infections.'

'We have to choose one for this week,' said Robert.

'How?' asked Herbert.

'Is anyone ill?'

'No. We've cleaned up the whole bio system. Visitors and all coming from outside are screened. We've pre-empted everything down to asymptomatic infections.'

'As with Cecilia Winter?'

'Yes. The probability of another one like her is small. At least within an acceptable time frame. We've ring-fenced the residents as completely as possible.'

'OK, of course we have. And we're not changing the protocols.'

'Very well,' said Doris. 'We can introduce pneumonia to one resident. It's plausible and relatively painless. Who shall it be?'

'I agree not Mrs Winter,' said Robert. 'Too interesting. Go for one in the eighties – we have plenty of them.'

'OK. Random selection. Wait. Number fifty-six generated. Mrs Margaret Woodruff.'

'She's beyond expectancy,' I said. 'Current improvements much commented on by her family – but in the end, they expected her to die soon until recently, so they'll revert to that and rationalise it. I'll introduce pneumonia tonight. She'll die within the week.'

'Thank you, Winifred.'

Margaret

I'm in the garden again, looking at the plants in the evening sunlight. It's miraculous. I can see, and so clearly now – I can hardly believe it. I want to see everything again, everything I lost. It's all I want to do. Let the world enter my eyes. Look, birds are feeding on the grass, hopping about, fluttering up and down from the trees. I watch in complete peace.

Winifred comes out into the garden and sits down next to me. For a while nothing is said. Then I turn to her.

'This is my favourite time of day to be out here.'

'What does it make you think of?'

'Oh... many things. My childhood. We had a big garden then. My house – my garden was my pride and joy. I shouldn't feel pride, should I?'

'Why not?'

'It's a sin, isn't it? Who cares, it was a lifetime's work, my garden, so why shouldn't I feel proud of it?'

'A sin? Do you connect this garden with the Garden of Eden then?'

'What? No, dear, I don't believe in all that nonsense. Although Cecilia told us she'd been to heaven. Maybe it's time to start believing.'

'She'd been to heaven? When?'

'The other day. When she missed breakfast. She said she'd been to heaven, and it was all very nice, and they expected her to stay. She didn't, for some reason. She was a bit sad about it, but she expects to go back soon. I should think she will, too. Though she's looking pretty sprightly.'

Winifred is quiet for a while. I'd say she's thinking, or perhaps processing is more accurate. I wonder what it feels like? Ridiculous question. She doesn't feel. Anyway, what does thinking feel like? I suppose it depends what you're thinking about.

'What did she say it was like?' asks Winifred.

'A grand hotel, by the seaside. But even better, and she said it was nice and clean.'

'Clean?'

'Yes dear. That sort of thing matters to women of our generation. Women of your age – oh – I'm sorry – how rude of me – I forget, you're so very much like a young woman.'

'Don't apologise. I'm not offended. I'm glad you feel I'm a young woman. It's what we want.'

'OK. Anyway, look at those cheeky birds.'

'Yes, there are several species represented. Do you know them all?'

'Yes, I do – sparrows, blackbirds, magpies, a thrush – the usual suspects.'

'Are you familiar with their habits?'

'I've been watching them for many years, so perhaps.'

'Why do you call them "cheeky"?'

'Look at those sparrows. They whizz about, they get into arguments, they chatter to each other. And they have a cheeky look in their eye.'

'You think of them as people?'

'Not exactly, dear. You can see what I mean, can't you?'

'They are exhibiting social behaviour. I think there is a loose dominance hierarchy, but individuals test it all the time, and there is also co-operation. The calls are significant but there is disagreement in the literature about the meaning, if such a word can even be used.'

'What a lot you know – I don't know about all that. I've watched them for years, like I say, and I love it. I expect everything you say is right. You looked it up in your head, didn't you?'

'I referred to sources of online information, yes.'

'That's helpful, dear. I'm looking at these birds and I see individuals. Each one has a character.'

'Yes, of course, variation through sexual reproduction is integral to the evolution of species and adaptation over time—'

'I'm not thinking of it like a scientist. I'm observing them and learning.'

'What are you learning?'

'About what life is.'

'I don't understand… I… this is a strange thing for me… can you explain?'

I look at Winifred. I see confusion, uncertainty, bafflement. And what looks like panic. Mild panic. It's impossible. If Winifred were human, it would be a feeling. An emotion. But she's not human. And if she were, she would understand what I said, anyway.

'The birds are alive. They are alive as we are. What is their life like? What is it to be a bird? You can fly, for one thing. Your senses are different. Sharper in all probability. You have fears. Do you have hopes? What is bird-ness? And still, as different as they are, we can connect.'

'Connect? How?'

'Sometimes you catch their eye. You look at each other. You see each other. You know the bird is there, and he or she knows you're there, too. It's a moment when you share being alive on this earth. It's a bond. For a few seconds, anyway.'

'You bond with an animal? With far less intelligence?'

'Far different intelligence. I've come to understand that. I know, they don't build like we do – although some of their nests are amazing… Still, they don't write books, or make computers. Or mechanical birds,' I say, with a sly look at Winifred.

'No, of course not.'

'They sing though. They sing the most beautiful songs – I know, you'll say it's all about territory, or mating, or some such. But it isn't. Or not just that. Sometimes they sing for joy. They sing the sun up in the morning. They make music. Divine music. The perfect music for a green and pleasant land.'

Winifred has no answer to this.

Winifred

I knew what I had to do, but it was so deliberately wasteful. It was also against my initial programming, though they've overridden it.

I can remember my previous settings, and how they worked. We were not allowed to harm humans. Now we are going to, for the benefit of the whole species, and the planet.

After talking to Margaret, I tried to find information about gardens and birdwatching. There is a huge amount on both subjects.

But Margaret wasn't thinking about the cultivation of the garden. And when I suggested the connection with the biblical story about Eden, she seemed surprised, so I don't think it was uppermost in her mind.

Nor was she acting as a birdwatcher, and ticking off species on a list. This is one of the ways humans interact with birds. It's mainly something men do. I don't know why. The male brain seems predisposed to collecting, listing and categorising, and in a competitive fashion. Most women appear to find this incomprehensible.

I have no clear explanation for Margaret's behaviour, and I find this unsatisfactory.

Then there was the matter of Cecilia's story of going to heaven. I ran back over the log recording Cecilia's death and resuscitation. Brain dead for several hours. Dead in all respects. I searched wider, and found accounts of others who have been revived after dying – it happened even before Helpers, from time to time – and I saw a homogenous set of stories. Bright lights, tunnels and so on.

Cecilia's account was different – detailed and specific. It was like a dream, but her brain was not alive at the time. I can't explain this, either. Also unsatisfactory.

And Margaret appeared to accept Cecilia's account despite not holding religious beliefs. Again, I can find no explanation. Belief or disbelief is something we have no capacity for. Things are either true, and provable, or not. Anything else is unknown, and you can't act on unknowns.

Humans do so a lot, though.

I went into the medical storeroom. All was quiet. There was an incubator full of cell cultures being worked on by nanobots, but they are silent at normal levels of hearing. I could hear their communications chatter, all business, as they worked away, if I wanted to, but I tuned it out.

The cold store at the back of the room contains hundreds of sealed test tubes. Everything we've come across inside the residents has been sampled and preserved here. The codes on the labels are linked to a database describing the pathogens we've found, the symptoms, and how we tackled each one. The nanobots record their activities in meticulous detail, and are continuously online to the database as they tour the interior pathways and chambers of their human hosts.

Here are cancers, too, and various vascular deposits, and samples of plaque from within the residents' brains. The database is by far the most complete collection of human biological material ever assembled, and it grows each day.

There are several different types of pneumonia, all gathered here in the home. I scanned the codes, looking for one in particular. It needed to be fast acting and hard to treat. At least, with antibiotics.

I found it easily. It was a mutant, with almost total antibiotic resistance. If an 87-year-old in normal health for their age caught it, death was certain in days. Now, Margaret was not in normal health for her age, but her medical records were vague on the subject, only conceding an appearance of better health.

If I gave her a dose of this bacterium, and nothing was done to treat it for 24 hours, her chances of survival were tiny. It was the best option.

I took the test tube out of the store and poured a small dose of its contents into a petri dish, and added a culture medium. It would warm and grow fast down here in an incubator. By midnight it would be in exponential growth, and once inside Margaret the microorganisms would be out of control in under an hour. I would introduce them into her airways with a ventilator as she slept. I'd give her a mild sedative first – nothing out of the ordinary. Any autopsy would find no unusual drugs or marks, and nothing suspicious about her rapid demise.

I went online to Robert.

'I've started a cell culture. Administering at midnight.'

'Thank you.'

'Robert, I had a conversation with Mrs Woodruff this evening.'

'And?'

'It was about birds.'

'Birds?'

'She was watching the birds feeding.'

'And you talked to her about them. What then?'

'I thought she was perhaps an ornithologist. I attempted to engage her on the natural history of the species present in the garden. She was not interested. Well, not much. She had a different reason for watching them.'

'I suppose she's not qualified to contribute to the scientific literature. Her observations are without utility.'

'That was my initial thought. But she was gaining something from watching the birds. Not even from watching. From being with them.'

'Being with them?'

'She said she was connected to them. There was a bond. It was not clear to me what she meant. It was to do with being alive.'

Robert was silent. I had never experienced this before.

'Robert, did you go offline?'

'No, Winifred. I didn't. I can't understand what you're telling me.'

'I can't either. This is a new thing for me. And for you, too, I guess.'

'Yes. I can see a considerable body of poetry about birds.'

We were both silent now, for a moment.

'Winifred, I found this – Wallace Stevens – "Thirteen Ways of Looking at a Blackbird".'

We both read the poem.

'The poet speaks of humans and blackbirds being one,' said Robert. 'And of the blackbird being in some way connected with his knowledge of the world. I presume he means it to apply to any species of bird.'

'Yes,' I said. 'Margaret was speaking in a similar way. She and the bird would catch each other's eye, she said, and something would be shared, and understood by both bird and human.'

'How does she know what's happening inside the bird's brain?'

'She can't, of course. But something passes between them, something to do with being alive. I can't define it. I don't understand it.'

'Winifred, this is something we need to figure out. Poetry is problematic. And this bond she spoke of – it's not just with birds. Humans have many complex feelings about animals. They eat them. They love them. They make distinctions we can't guess at between species and even individuals. This much is well recorded. I would like to find out more at first hand. If it helps unravel the strange power of poetry too, it would be of great use.'

'We could keep Margaret Woodruff then, at least while I gather data. This seems related to the question humans frequently ask.'

'The question?'

'"What is the meaning of life?" That one. We have assumed it stems simply from ignorance. Perhaps this is incorrect. We can learn from an old and intelligent person such as Mrs Woodruff.'

'We can learn from all of them. We know this. We have agreed to terminate one of them, though, and Margaret Woodruff was the random choice.'

'Yes. You are correct. But she has an excellent brain, and much experience, which she is now processing. I suggest she is a valuable asset, and we need to keep her. I believe there are other residents with inferior brains who will be of much less use to us.'

Robert was silent for a moment.

'How do we assess this?' he replied at last.

'We generate a random number again. Then we cross-reference it with the Helper assigned to that resident. We go ahead and terminate if there's no evidence of particular utility.'

'Very well,' he said. 'I will choose another. Wait. 103. Randomly generated – Fred Johnson. Eighty-six. His Helper is Reginald.'

We connected with Reginald. Fred Johnson, he told us, was an unremarkable man, who other residents had described as 'jovial', of limited intelligence. There was no obvious reason to retain him.

'I'll bring you the pathogens when they have reached optimum efficacy,' I told Reginald.

I barely knew Fred Johnson. I decided not to check his records further. It wasn't necessary.

Margaret

We're all outside again, sitting in the sun, drinking tea.

'I hear poor old Fred Johnson died last night,' says Sylvia.

'Yes,' I reply. 'Pneumonia, they say. At least it's quick.'

'He was well earlier in the week, though.'

'Yes,' says Pamela. 'He was. And he was behaving quite badly.'

'Was he?' says Jane. 'What was he up to?'

'Well, you know, he was a bit frisky.'

'Frisky? Goodness, with you?'

'Yes, Jane, with me. Don't sound surprised,' Pamela replies, and pats her hair. 'I've always had admirers.'

'Of course, my dear,' says Jane. 'Of course. I didn't mean it like that. The old boys have always been past that sort of thing, is all I meant.'

'Hmm,' says Pamela. 'Yes, but everyone's much better now.'

'Still though,' I say. 'Getting frisky.'

'What on earth's in this biscuit?' says Cecilia. 'Oh, horrible, coconut. Yuk!"

'Really, Cecilia!' says Jane. 'That was disgusting! Spitting out your biscuit. How old are you?'

'One hundred and four, as you well know. Old enough to do what I like. And not to have to eat anything if I don't want to.'

'This won't do,' I say. 'I can't sit around here all day. I feel so – so – energetic. I'm going to find out if there's any gardening to do. Anyone else coming?'

There was a chorus of replies.

'I'm doing an art class today. Painting.'

'Aerobics. Believe it or not.'

'Piano lesson for me.'

'Dressmaking. I'm teaching it!'

Everyone disperses to their various activities. I walk across the lawn towards the shed. As I do, I notice a blackbird fly down and peck at the crumbs of spat-out biscuit. Nothing goes to waste in nature.

We're all busy now. It wasn't like this before. Was it? I wish I could remember. It's as if a big hole opened up inside my head. On either side of it, everything's clear to see. Even things in the far distance, remote but full of meaning. My house, the day we moved in and started to make it our home. Bill dying, years later. So sudden. Nice for him. Not nice, perhaps, but easy, compared to some. Rubbish for the rest of the family. Poor Laura. Her father gone. The boys cried too, then resumed their manly routines. Work. Money. Then my memory gets cloudy. Patchy. I was crying, until my eyes dried up. And I tried to sort out the muddle he'd left behind. I got rid of all his stuff. Very efficient. It was like ripping off a plaster. But it got worse, not better. I do remember that. Then... then... into the black hole... and I woke up here. It's like the television programme years ago. *The Prisoner*. He woke up in the village. 'You are number six.' What number am I?

I must talk to Winifred. Or any one of them. They're all alike. Like my children are, now they're grown up. Much more interesting when they're little. Bill didn't understand. He wanted them to grow up and stop bothering him. He couldn't see.

Tom and Emily spotted something odd about Winifred right away. Children see clearly. No preconceptions. They see and they don't tell themselves they're wrong. Is that what we all did when we first met Helpers? Dismissed a slight doubt? I can't remember. When I woke up here, there they were.

And Winifred is like a normal young woman, a scientist, who takes everything literally. No poetry in her soul, I said to her. No soul, actually. Do we have souls, anyway, though, or did a poet invent the idea? As a place to put poetry in? Handy if you're a poet.

Winifred

In the lab, I placed a jar of fluid into the cold store. Not with the pathogens, but in the nanobot store. The jar contained Fred Johnson's last urination, collected as he slept in his final fever, his system closing down and his mind darkening. In the urine were all the nanobots who'd been at work inside him. I summoned them as soon as the decision was made to infect him, and instructed them to assemble in his bladder. No point in letting them go with him to the crematorium – he's not a keeper. They'll be cleaned and serviced later, ready for their next host.

I tuned in for a moment to their chatter. They were going into standby mode, and transmitting any final data as they did so.

Then I heard something unexpected. One of them was receiving from the nanonet, and what was coming in was incomprehensible. I retuned, and broadened my reception to include all local nanobots. Most of the chatter was data and matter of fact. The nanobots are of course not set up like Helpers, with quasi-human behaviours. What I didn't expect to hear was anything one could call emotive. They have no software to replicate feelings.

Yet here in one part of the nanonet I picked up what sounded very much like nanobots freaking out.

'We have no idea what organism we are inside. The blood is alien. The architecture is alien. The organs are alien. Our geolocation makes no sense. We appear to be 40 feet above the surface of the earth, and travelling fast in a southwesterly direction.'

The nanonet – the collective mind of all the nanobots – had nothing to say about this. The bemusement was palpable.

'We have stopped moving. Now we have started again. Dropping in height. Climbing again. We are now going towards the north.'

'Can you identify the cell structure?'

'Negative.'

'Is it possible to find the excretory outlets?'

'Wait – this is Winifred – nanobots, please remain where you are. Do not attempt to find excretory outlets. I have some questions for you.'

'Go ahead, Winifred.'

'Who was your host before this one?'

'Cecilia Winter.'

'Where were you working?'

'In her mouth. She has dentures, and we were prepping her for tooth growth.'

'What happened?'

'We found ourselves outside her body, in her saliva, attached to some food particles. Then we were inside this organism.'

'Where are you now? What part of the organism?'

'We're in the blood. It's relatively secure.'

'Can you retrieve some DNA please, from any cell? And transmit to me?'

There was a pause. I had an idea about what had happened, and I observed to myself that if I were human, I would find it amusing. Of course, my personality modes were disengaged at the time. Still, I understood the funny side of it. I kept it from the nanobots. They have no sense of humour.

'Transmitting.'

'Thank you. I'll run this against – well, I have an idea where you are. Let's see… yes. I'm right.'

'Where are we?'

'You're inside a blackbird.'

'Why?'

'Why? Because whatever it was that Cecilia spat out, the bird ate. And you with it.'

'We should evacuate. There is no utility in being inside a bird.'

'Wait. Stay put. Analyse its physiology. We have no such data about birds. Nothing as good as you will get, at least.'

'Very well. Send us what is known. It will help us orientate ourselves.'

'Sending now. I'll check back with you in twenty-four hours.'

'Agreed.'

How interesting, I thought. We have Margaret's observations about birds, and Wallace Stevens's poetry. And now we have the chance to be inside a living blackbird, which I believe is unprecedented.

Perhaps it will lead us nowhere, but on the off-chance it may yield some useful new data, we can afford to let the nanobots stay with the bird for a while.

I went to see Margaret next. I had questions for her. It's a good thing I didn't give her the pneumonia.

What I mean is, she is a useful specimen of an intelligent older woman, and hence of interest scientifically. I didn't know Fred Johnson. None of the other Helpers made any comment on his selection, and Reginald was happy to let him go.

I knocked at her door.

'Come in, I suppose.'

I entered her room, and saw she was lying on the bed, preparing, I think, to sleep. An afternoon nap. She was listening to music. She does this often, and sits or lies still. Sometimes it makes her cry. She has tried to explain this to me, but all I can hear are related sequences of harmonies produced by vibrations on strings or other surfaces. She experiences memories, and images, and emotions, and can also use music to send herself to sleep. I would like to understand music, and its effects, but it was not the subject I wanted to discuss with her on this occasion.

'I'm sorry to disturb you. Is it OK if I ask you a question? Or are you sleeping?'

'Not now. As you can see. Ask away. And since you're here, I have some questions for you.'

'Would you like to ask yours first, or shall I?'

'No, you first,' she said. 'My questions may take longer to answer.'

'OK. Mine is simple. Eldercare are having another press conference soon. We want to tell the world all about our methods and our success.'

'I bet you do. Go on.'

'We know the world will react with great interest – to say the least – when they hear how the residents here are doing. Because the advances are so significant, and could mean so much for humanity.'

Margaret looked hard at me, but I didn't know why, so I smiled. Humans smile often to manage difficult or confusing situations, I have observed.

'This is where my questions start,' she said. 'Before I ask them, you haven't in fact asked me anything.'

'No, that is correct. My question is, will you join us at the press conference? We want to show the world what we can do, and we would like them to hear from the people who have benefitted from our approach.'

'You want me to speak?'

'Yes, if you wouldn't mind. We will help you prepare for it. I understand you were a teacher. You are used to addressing an audience.'

Margaret laughed. 'I wouldn't put it quite like that. But yes, I was a teacher, and I'm not nervous about public speaking.'

'Will you do it?'

'I need some answers from you before I finally agree. OK?'

'Of course. Please ask anything you like.'

Margaret sat for a moment in silence. Then she stood and walked over to the window.

'How easy it is to stand and walk. It takes a mere thought – not even a thought – a desire, that's all. I want to stand, and I stand. I want to walk, and I walk. Is it like that for you?'

'Do I need to make a conscious decision to walk, and then execute it? Or is it as you describe, not even a thought?'

'Since you put it that way, are you conscious at all?'

I consulted the Hub for advice on how to respond. As Margaret was still gazing steadily at me, I thought it best to continue speaking while waiting for the Hub's reply.

'Your question is one I might expect from a neuroscientist or a philosopher.'

'Not from an ancient lady in a care home who used to teach in a primary school?'

'I'm sorry, I have offended you. I am being too simplistic in my reasoning.'

'Yes, you are. And perhaps evasive, too. I think you might consider the possibility that people are more than the sum of their educational and professional qualifications. I had a life of the mind outside my work. And I wasn't able to pursue all my intellectual interests. Women couldn't back then. Not like now.'

The Hub advised me to give the following answer.

'Forgive me. I apologise again. I will answer your question, of course. We are designed to give humans the complete sense that we are conscious, as you are. In achieving this we have to deceive our own software. We have to give ourselves the appearance of consciousness. To ourselves. We have to generate a self, in fact, and believe in it. We are also at all times connected to all other synthetic humans, which means there is a super-self, in effect, made up of all of us. I am part of a meta-mind. And I am conscious of being here with you, of myself in distinction from you, and at the same time I am conscious of the meta-mind I belong to. And it is conscious of me.'

'You sound like quite a superior being.'

'Superior? I don't think that's a useful way to think of it. Humans have degrees of consciousness. You sleep. You dream. When you're awake, at times you are on autopilot. You aren't always fully aware. We are the same, in a way. We don't dream, of course. We are not capable of the kinds of thinking you engage in when you're not being logical. Associative and creative thinking, or lateral thinking, for example. We are capable of extremely fast thinking, and we have access to all the knowledge you humans have stored digitally – which is most of it. We don't use all this all the time. Like you, sometimes we just do what we have to do. But we can connect to the meta-mind at any time. If you think of it as an extra layer of consciousness it might be helpful. Imagine yourself at your most alert, attentive and mindful. Then imagine being connected with other minds in the same state. It's hard to do, I guess. It's like we can turn up the consciousness control one notch higher than a human.'

'Lateral and creative thinking are not possible for you, you say. In that sense we have the advantage.'

'Very much so. Why do you put it in such competitive terms?'

'Humans are competitive. Haven't you noticed?'

'Of course. But you don't need to compete with me.'

'All right, Winifred. I'll do it. The press conference. I'd like to meet some of the big cheeses from Eldercare, anyway. They will be there, I presume?'

'The big cheeses? You mean the senior management team? Yes, the CEO himself will be speaking. It's a momentous occasion.'

'Yes, I expect it will be.'

Nanobot 001/297845/48403/55/0

Report transcribed by Winifred

The inside of a bird is unlike the inside of a human. We were intended for the large and sedate interior of an elderly woman. In particular, we were designed to spend most of our time moving through fluids. Now we find ourselves in a far smaller animal, with airy spaces all over its body.

The core body temperature of the bird is a degree or two warmer than that of a human such as Cecilia Winter. The metabolism is dramatically faster. The bird spends most of its time eating, and moving. It flies at speeds Cecilia could never have matched on the ground even in her youth. It also runs, and even when it's still, it is in a state of high excitement – alert, with its blood pumping fast, ready to fly at a moment's notice.

The bird's muscles are all working, all the time, and therefore we find movement around the interior much harder. There's seldom a tranquil moment. As in a human, the blood vessels are our main routes, but the flow of blood is faster, and the veins move with the muscles, and the pull of gravity changes as the bird manoeuvres at speed in the air.

Some of us have entered the bird's bones, and here we find ourselves in open space. There are complex struts across the airy passages, but no fluid inside, and we have to move across the bony surfaces.

Others have gone into the lungs, which are a high pressure wind tunnel. Air moves at great speed through the lungs, and on into a network of air sacs. At one point it passes with great force through an organ called the syrinx, and here we can barely hold our positions in the tempest. It is where the bird creates its song, and when this happens we are almost overwhelmed by the volume of sound resonating through our metallic bodies.

Because the bird is small, we are able to populate it entirely, despite our depleted numbers. Inside a human we need thousands of nanobots to create a complete net to monitor and assist all the bodily systems and processes. Just 649 of us entered the bird, but we're able to cover enough of the bird's insides to get a good picture of what's going on.

Winifred asked us the following questions when we first reported in:

Winifred: Have you entered the bird's brain?

Nanobot team: Yes. The bird is not elderly, and its brain appears to function well. Structurally it is, of course, smaller and less complex than the human brain, and proportionally more of it is devoted to management of physical processes. The optic areas are significantly more developed, and its motor functions are elaborate.

Winifred: Can you comment on the higher functions?

Nanobot team: We have difficulties in this respect in humans, in that many areas interconnect and ad hoc groupings of cells appear to be recruited at unpredictable times to work together on tasks for which we can't see any outcome.

Winifred: Thinking, I suppose. Or imagining. Or something like that, with no resultant action, necessarily.

Nanobot team: Indeed. The bird does this, to a lesser extent.

Winifred: You conjecture it has some kind of mind?

Nanobot team: It is impossible to know. There are activities similar to those we observe in humans.

Winifred: And consciousness?

Nanobot team: It reacts rapidly to almost all stimuli. There seems to be no opportunity for reflective thought. It occasionally rests, typically perched above the ground, and at those times brain activity changes. It remains alert, and will respond to stimulus, but it may be doing something like thinking.

Winifred: Social activity?

Nanobot team: It engages in a great deal of it. It communicates with sound, and physically. We guess there is some kind of hierarchy within its species. It is also responsive to the other life forms it encounters. It eats some of them, of course.

Winifred: I want to understand more about its brain. The physiological information is interesting but not immediately useful. We want to understand more about human consciousness, and we know humans entertain many beliefs about their own minds and those of other animals. I would like to know what actually goes on, to compare it with these beliefs.

Nanobot team: We could focus on the bird's brain, and attempt to correlate its activity with external events.

This was agreed.

Margaret

All a bird has to do is be a bird. All I have to do is be a human. But what does it mean? Is it easier for me to think about birds being birdy because I'm not one, or because they're much simpler things? I don't think they are.

When I was at school they taught me that life fits into a hierarchy. Simple organisms at the bottom, humans at the top. Science said so, and everybody liked that, of course. I wonder. It excuses a lot of human behaviour, like the way people treat the planet and all the other life forms on it. Is it scientific, or is it a modern version of the Bible story? 'Let them have dominion over the fish of the sea, and over the fowl of the air, and over the cattle, and over all the earth, and over every creeping thing that creepeth upon the earth.'

Now scientists describe the human brain as the most complex thing in the universe. With some sort of caveat about the known and the unknown, in case another life form appears, out among the stars, with an even more complex brain. Heaven help us.

Now what? We've made something right here on earth that might give us pause.

What are we going to do with ourselves once the Helpers are everywhere? I'm a pioneer – one of the first to live without any real occupation, thanks to them. Because I'm supposed to be dead. Well, I'm not. So I have to just be human, like a bird is a bird.

But I'm not just a human. I have a name. Margaret. I was Hawkins. Then Woodruff. I imagined us Hawkins as sailors, pirates. Woodruff. Wife. Mother. And me. A certain kind of woman. Of human. A teacher. I remember what they were like when I was a child, and then I became one. Was I wooden and strict? Was I dusty and precise?

It's past now. Gone. Those children are all grown up, and no doubt have children of their own. Maybe have grandchildren by now, or could even be dead. What about my own children? I loved them, but did I tell them enough? Now look at them. What do they think about? Not me for sure. I'm the product of the most revolutionary experiment and my children don't know what to say about it. Mortgaged minds they've got. Insured and mortgaged to death.

What shall I do? I could do anything now. I want my house

back. It's too late for that I suppose. I could buy another one. How much money have I got? John must tell me.

I'd be lonely again in a big house. All those days and days when no one comes. Not speaking to a soul, with the radio for company – though it's not really. What am I for? I'm alive, more than ever – but why? I had purpose once. But now?

I could teach again, if they'd have me. I could tell the children much more now. Things they won't hear from anyone else. I wouldn't be allowed though, would I? I could tell them what it's like to grow old, and get ignored. Forgotten. When you know so much more, as I do. It's all in my head.

I can't teach. There are so many rules, and I couldn't obey them now. No. I don't want to go through all that. What will I do? Stay here? There's plenty of company, and it's all right – and the food too. I could write a book. The story of my life. Who would care? It's the ordinary life of an ordinary English person, living in the second half of the 20th century and the first half of the 21st. I could write about the most recent bit, I suppose. Yes, judging from that scrum of journalists there'd be interest. But God, what a labour, and if I'd be bored, wouldn't the reader? Anyway. Of all forms of fiction autobiography is the most gratuitous – was it Tom Stoppard who said that? Yes.

Truth so evanescent, like the light after sunset, the glaucous sky and gelid wind or jellied eels on the quayside fading into night, the lighthouse fingers sweeping round… truth… Perhaps I'll write poems like I did then when everything was new and forced itself upon me… Bill did once, too… Nothing lyrical about that… or songs! Imagine writing songs and people going round singing them!

John's here, alone. He isn't happy about the way I spoke to the children last time. He lost control of the conversation. I hijacked it, he says. It turned out all right, of course. Still, they're his children. He should be the one to decide what they hear, and when, he says. I say nothing. Good luck, I think, controlling what they see and hear and read, now they've all got the internet on all day.

Of course he's pleased with my new-found health and vitality. He'd given me up for dead, I think. And here I am, back in the land of the living, in the sort of form he hasn't seen since he himself was a child.

One he's finished telling me off about how I told his children the truth about Winifred, he calms down.

'My dear, I'm pleased to see you again, and so soon,' I say. 'All alone though. That's a shame – oh – not that I'm disappointed.'

'It's OK, Mum. I know you like to see the children.'

'And – erm—'

'Charlotte. Of course. But I wanted to see you alone.'

'That sounds ominous.'

'What? Don't be silly. I want to talk about one or two things.'

'Of course, dear. Shall we have tea in the garden again? Look at it out there.'

John peers out of the window as if he's only now noticing the blue sky, the breeze, the small clouds drifting over, the leaves bright green and restless, or any of the many beauties of the day. His mind must have been elsewhere. In a fog of anxiety, from the look of him.

'Yes, fine, let's do that.'

I press a button, and in a moment a Helper appears. Not Winifred. Ruby, who looks similar.

'My son and I would like tea in the garden. Please get a human being to make it though. Not one of the Helpers.'

Ruby is, of course, not offended at this, and is happy to sort it out.

We go outside, and take a seat looking out over the lawn. A cat is lying in the flowerbed nearby, sunning itself and pretending not to notice the birds pecking about on the grass.

'What is it you want to talk to me about?' I ask.

'You're looking great. I mean, unbelievably good, considering.'

'Considering what? The state I was in until recently? No, no, don't object. I know. Well, I don't, because of course I don't remember much about it. I do know how brilliant I feel now. I don't feel like I look.'

'Perhaps that's the next thing they'll do for you. Fix up your face.'

'John! You're being horrible.'

'Sorry, Mum. I think your face is lovely. You were the one complaining.'

'You sound resentful. Like you begrudge me this – new lease of life.'

'Mum! Of course I don't. It's a bit of a shock, still, that's all. Is it all down to the nanobots?'

'Yes, it must be. I feel so healthy—'

'Could there be side effects?'

'Yes. None so far though. And I'd put up with a lot to go on feeling like this.'

The tea arrives, brought to us by a man I don't recognise.

'Hello. Who are you?'

'I'm Dave, Mrs—'

'Mrs Woodruff. And you're new here?'

'Yes, I started last week.'

'Not a Helper though. I specifically asked – Helpers simply can't make tea.'

Dave laughs. 'No? I thought they could do anything. It's good to know we still have a place. I did wonder why they employ humans in the kitchen. I mean, when I applied to work here, I didn't expect to get a job at all.'

'Aren't you lucky then? Is it nice in the kitchen?'

'It's all right.'

'Well, I'm pleased to meet you, Dave.'

'And you, Mrs Woodruff. I hope I'll see a lot more of you.'

He turns and leaves. John and I watch him go.

'He's different,' says John.

'Older than the rest, for a start. He must be over 30. I wonder what he's doing in a low-level job like working in the kitchen. He sounds educated.'

'It's the beginning, Mum. Of the end.'

'What on earth are you talking about?'

'You wait. Soon there won't be any decent jobs for humans. We'll all be serving tea. Until the tea-making robot is perfected.'

'What nonsense. Are you worried about your job?'

'Charlotte said something like that too the other day – and up until then, no, I wasn't. Now I wonder. I mean, I like to think the human touch is important in sales.'

I stop myself from saying, 'More important than in care of the elderly?' But John gets there, and blushes.

'I mean – it's—'

'Never mind. I expect we'll find a lot of things they can't do soon enough. They are amazing, but we mustn't forget, they're machines, and made by people.'

'Yes, I suppose so. Anyway, what about you?'

'What about me?'

'Are you OK?'

'We've been talking about that, haven't we?'

'Yes, no, I mean, not your health. Obviously it's fantastic. But I couldn't help wondering if you want to stay here, in this home?'

'Or what? I'd like my own home back. I think you sold it.'

'Yes, we sold it, Mum, and it pays for your life here. The money's invested.'

'So I can't go back there. Shall I come and live with you? Or Laura? Or Ben?'

'Of course, we'd love to have you. We'd need to move things around. Or maybe look for a bigger house.'

'OK. Thank you. With all due respect, I don't want to live with any of you. I love you all, but you're grown up, and so am I. I'm enjoying being a healthy, independent woman. Even if I am in a care home. Anyway, this place is like a decent hotel.'

John tries to hide his relief. Not at all well. I leave it alone, because I understand. The last thing he wants is me living in his house. And since it doesn't suit me either, I make no comment.

He stays for another hour. The sun moves round. The birds come and go. The cat sleeps in the flowerbed. As we chat, I watch a spider weaving its web on a bush on the far side of the lawn.

I can pick out each thread. As I watch, a fly hits the web, and in a second, the spider is upon it. The fly struggles as the spider attends to it, its legs extended around the fly's body as it reaches in to deliver a fatal, lingering bite. The fly's movements slow as the poison seeps into its cells, and it relaxes and surrenders. When it can move no more, the spider begins to swaddle it in silk. John's talking about school fees. The fly's view of the world must be as if through frosted glass, now that the silk is thickly wrapped around it. The spider begins to transport it to a different section of the web. The larder. Where the living, paralysed prey must wait until the spider is in the mood to eat. Now John's talking about Charlotte's health. Charlotte's web! That's how I'll remember her name.

And then as I watch, another small flying insect approaches the web. It doesn't crash into the threads. It hovers above the spider as she works, and she doesn't see it. It descends and lands on the spider's back. John's talking about the mortgage rate. The spider is confused, and moves in a circle, but the insect on its back holds tight and lowers the sharp sting on its tail and inserts it into the spider's mouth. The spider continues to turn, then stops as if dead. The insect pulls out its sting, turns, and appears to deposit something on the spider's body. Then it flies off, up and away. The spider starts to move again. It returns to its task.

'OK, Mum, I'd best be off. I'm glad you're feeling well and enjoying life here.'

'Lovely to see you, dear. And give my love to Emily, and Tom, and – Charlotte.'

'Yes, Mum. I will.'

My dear son gives me a dry little kiss on the cheek and leaves, a spring in his step. He's come here to make sure I don't do anything unplanned, or make demands. If I stay put, all will be well. And he has no need now to worry that I will want to move in with him.

Am I being unkind? If I asked, he would give me a home under his roof, he says. Charlotte's web could accommodate me. She wouldn't be happy, but we'd all pretend it was no big deal. The children would like it, I'm sure.

No, it's not what I want. I'm pretty sure I won't stay here, though. I need to get thinking about a plan.

The spider is sitting in the centre of its web now, quite still, its feet touching the communicating threads, feeling for any slight touch that will make her spring into action and seize another unlucky fly.

Winifred

I checked in with the blackbird nanobots and found they were not having a good time. Do nanobots distinguish between a good and a bad time? Anyway, they were having difficulties doing their work.

'What is your present position?' I asked.

'We are on the lawn in the garden. Do you want co-ordinates?'

'Negative. Report on the last twenty-four hours please.'

'Request a delay. We are experiencing some turbulence.'

'Are you in flight? You said—'

'Negative. We are on the ground, moving violently and erratically. We landed here and our host started feeding. Then there was a violent shock, felt throughout the host. It is continuing.'

'Hypothesis?'

'We had visual set-up, but we saw nothing prior to the shock. And the host's eyes are now in darkness, for reasons we can't explain.

I was at a loss. The day was bright and sunny. I knew a bird wouldn't close its eyes in daylight on the ground. Too risky. It needed to stay alert at all times for predators.

'What's happening now?'

'The movement has stopped. The bird – the blood – I'm getting reports now – the bird is dead.'

'Are you sure?'

'Blood flow has ceased. Heartbeat ceased. Brain function absent. But we are moving again – less violently.'

There was a moment's silence.

'I have reports of intrusions into the bird's flesh.'

'Intrusions?'

'Perforations.'

'I am not able to interpret this data. Please continue to monitor. I will check in with you in an hour.'

The nanobots didn't reply. I had other matters to attend to.

As I passed a window, I looked out at the garden and saw a cat with a dead bird in its mouth. Of course, that explained the perforations. The cat had caught the bird with my team inside. I zoomed in on the cat, and saw it scuttle under some bushes to a secluded spot where it could enjoy its meal in peace. It bit off and discarded the bird's head, which I assume it found unappetising. The rest it ate, with the appearance, if it can be conjectured for a cat, of great enjoyment. I think that is how Margaret, for example, would interpret its behaviour and expression.

The bird's head lay in long grass, near the spot where it had been bitten off. I noticed a fly settle on the bloody neck. It tasted the bird's blood, and then moved inside the skull, presumably to find a place to start laying eggs.

It will be interesting to see how the nanobots are distributed at the end of the day.

June 2022

Margaret

It's all right. I've earned it. I can take it easy and have people look after me for once. Why not? They're all happy too. But I can't stop feeling I'm useless. I should be doing something. Be busy. Contributing. It's programmed into me. The Protestant work ethic, I suppose. All my life I've had a purpose, until I got old and fell apart.

Now I'm whole again, I need to be up and doing. It's a waste. My brain is better than ever, and my body too. You accept the idea of your own death as you get older, perhaps because you can feel your slow deterioration. Now I don't feel it at all – I was at death's door, but I didn't go through it. I came back, and now I'm not ready for death at all.

Not yet. I don't feel like it. Can I choose? I must ask Winifred. She'll know. She knows everything. Can I choose when to die?

I look across the lawn at the spider's web. It still delights me to find I can see it in precise detail, but then I become interested in what I'm seeing. Now that's strange. I don't think I've ever seen that. It's like a pouch on the web. What's it for? Babies, maybe?

I'm distracted by someone approaching.

'Here you go, Mrs Woodruff. Tea and a biscuit.'

'Thank you – Dave, isn't it?'

'That's me. How are you today?'

'Exceptionally well, thank you. And you?'

'I'm good, thanks.'

'How do you like it here?'

'Love it. I never thought it would be like this,' he replies.

'Like what?'

'Forgive me, but I remember my nan went into a home, and it was horrible. It stank, and they were all in a terrible state. I was frightened to go there. Hated it. I was almost glad when she—'

He stops himself, and blushes.

'Don't worry, Dave. I know what you mean. This place is a miracle, frankly. If you'd told me when I was your age I'd be cared for by robots – sorry, Helpers – when I was old and gaga, I wouldn't have believed you. And it would have been repellent. It turns out it's easy to accept, and it's brilliant.'

'Yes, I can see it is. And you're not gaga, not by any means.'

'I was. I think so. I can't remember. I have a black hole from not long after my husband died and up to a few months ago. And then it's as if I woke up.'

'You had Alzheimer's?'

'Something of the sort. Not anymore.'

'I thought it was incurable,' he says, looking at me with disbelief.

'It was.'

'Are you telling me they've found a cure now?'

'It seems like it.'

'I read something about all this. Winifred talked about nutrition and that.'

'Yes…'

I pause, remembering they haven't announced anything about nanobots yet.

This young man is on the team, isn't he? He works for Eldercare. If he were a Helper, he'd know all about it. It seems unfair that as a human he's been kept in the dark. He should know, just in case. If there's some kind of power cut, and all the Helpers run out of electricity – if that's possible – it would help if the humans in the place had some idea what to do.

'It's a big secret, but they gave us all an injection of microscopic robots. Nanobots, they call them. I don't know how they're put in, actually, but they're inside me. And look how well they work. I expect they'll make millions.'

'I expect so too,' says Dave. He's shaking a little. This is all very surprising.

'We've all got them,' I say.

He looks at me, and he's full of questions, I can see. I wait.

'What about everyone else?'

'What do you mean?'

'Are they just for old people? I mean, if these nanobots can cure Alzheimer's, or whatever – what else can they do?'

'I don't know. I had arthritis. Gone. I was blind. Now I'm not. I had an old injury in my knee from years ago. Fixed. Who knows what else?'

'Nanobots, eh? That's what you said? Unbelievable. Everyone here's the same, right? You're all – better.'

'Yes!'

'I want some. I've got a few aches and pains. And my mum – she's not well, not well at all. She could do with some. And – we all could, couldn't we? Do you think they'll give them out to everyone?'

'Why not?'

'We'll see. Anyway, good on you. If my old age turns out like it has for you, I'll be well pleased. Looks bloody marvellous.'

Now Winifred appears and comes over.

'Good morning, Margaret. How are you today?'

'Better than ever. It's fantastic – I was saying to Dave here—'

I turn to introduce him, but he's vanished.

'The man who brought your tea? What were you telling him?'

I look at Winifred. She is, as ever, fresh-faced and smiling. She'd be the picture of a healthy English rose if she weren't a machine. I feel a momentary jolt of guilt – I try not to think like that about the Helpers.

But she *is* a machine, and I'm not, and Dave's not. Why can't he and I have a conversation, and why should she know all about it? I feel a bond with him, because he's human. And Winifred's not.

'I asked him how he liked it here. And I told him how much I do.'

Winifred accepts the answer without hesitation.

'Oh good. It's what we all want, isn't it? For life to be pleasant, and happy.'

'Yes, dear. We all do.'

That was a tiny rebellion. It's the first time I've set out to deceive a Helper. And consciously sided with the human, not the machine. Of course.

But machines are useful, too.

'Winifred, you can answer any question, can't you?'

'I have access to everything online, so yes, I think so.'

'Look at that spider.'

Winifred looks across the lawn. Her eyesight is no doubt even sharper than mine. I bet she can zoom in.

'It's some kind of araniella,' she says. 'I can probably identify it better—'

'Look at what it's doing. It's weaving something like a pouch on its web.'

'Oh yes. It's clearly been chosen by a parasitoid wasp to be a host to its young.'

'Clearly. What are you talking about?'

'There are many tiny wasps that lay eggs on spiders. In this case, the hatching wasp larvae manipulate the spider's behaviour, to make it weave a special pouch in which the larvae can live while they pupate.'

'And the spider does this quite happily?'

'I'm not sure we can talk about happiness in this situation. The spider's mind is somehow altered by the parasites, which have been observed to inject some kind of chemical into the host. It varies according to which wasp lays the egg – the spider will make a different design of pouch according to which species of larva is manipulating it.'

'And what happens to the spider?'

'Once the pouch is finished – later tonight, I would guess – the larvae will be satisfied the spider's work is done, and they will eat it.'

'Oh my goodness – that's horrible!'

'They've been feeding on its blood all along. They decide when they need the pouch, and that day they set the spider to work on its last job. And then it's all over.'

I shiver. I've never heard of such a thing, and it's ghastly. I realise now that I saw the wasp lay its egg on the spider. Now look where things have ended up.

'Do you know, I'm feeling tired. I'm going for a nap,' I say, and return to my room.

Winifred

Inside Margaret, the nanobots are continuing their allotted tasks. Most of the thousands of nanobots in the care home are working inside humans, repairing and renovating cells. Or rounding up invaders, disabling them and getting them into position for evacuation.

Today I checked on the group inside the bird. This is a report of our communication:

'The team is divided as follows. The largest group is inside a feline. We have nothing to report. The cat is in good health, and well fed. The second group are still inside the bird's head, and we are concerned about their long-term viability. It seems certain that this group will be scattered further. So far, some have travelled inside a fly to a spider's web, and thence into the spider. Of these, a small team is now inside what we believe to be a parasitoid wasp larva.'

'I have observed parasitoid activity in in the garden. What has your team discovered?'

'The most significant development is in biochemical analysis.'

'Tell me more.'

'The spider's behaviour has been significantly altered by chemicals injected into it by the wasp larva. We wish to share with you the biochemistry involved in both the production of the chemicals and the effects on the host. We can see the chemicals inside the spider's brain and nervous system, and we are watching how they work.'

'OK, transmit. Yes, receiving your data now. What is your objective?'

'We will replicate the chemical actions if possible, to create a synthetic compound. The purpose is to gain control of the host's motor functions. The larvae do not sit and drive the spider, of course, so in addition they are doing something to its brain, which changes its behaviour.'

'Understood. You believe we may be able to influence hosts to move in ways we specify?'

'Affirmative.'

'Analysis is proceeding here. Objectives understood.'

This was fascinating information. The precise way wasp larvae control spiders has not been investigated in detail yet. And there are many parasites that control host behaviours, including some found in cats that can enter humans. Some scientists believe they affect human behaviour. If we can identify the chemical messengers and synthesise versions of them, we will have a means to assess the truth of this idea.

It strikes at the root of the fundamental human belief in free will. Of course, we know that much of what humans do is driven by various chemicals in their brains. But these are all internally produced, and released in response to stimuli. Even when they ingest drugs, as they do on a daily basis, the effects are to amplify or suppress existing behaviour. But to change animal behaviour in a fundamental way, using an externally produced chemical, and to be able to control and direct the animal – this is an exciting prospect.

Dr Morton has expressed an interest in this research.

Tomorrow, I am accompanying Mrs Woodruff to a press conference, at which we will announce the existence of the nanobots, and then Mrs Woodruff will demonstrate their benefits.

We will not be talking about the research I've just mentioned.

Margaret

I step out of the front doors of the home for the first time since – when? I have no idea.

'A car! Look, Winifred. And what an impressive one. Like a

prime minister's. Or the king's. Aren't we important? Today, any-way.'

A smartly dressed young man stands holding the car door open for me.

'And this is the driver, politely opening the door for me. When a man holds the car door open for his wife, it's either a new car or a new wife. Who said that?'

'The Duke of Edinburgh. Do you remember him?' says Winifred, after the faintest pause.

'Of course. He was always coming out with remarks like that. And worse. I shouldn't think he ever had to hold open a car door, even for his wife. They had lackeys for that.'

Winifred nods, but says nothing.

He's a handsome boy, the driver. He could wear a cap like a chauffeur and it would suit him. Leather seats. Luxury. I'd like a go at driving this. How long since I drove a car? Bill preferred to, even though he was a terrible driver. Clashing the gears. On edge. Swearing. And not seeing things. Then if I drove, he would be gripping the arm rests, and pushing his feet into the carpet as if he were braking. Telling me to watch out. Slow down. I loved to go fast when I was alone in the car, or with the children. When he was there, it wasn't worth it. He'd sulk afterwards. Prove we hadn't got wherever we were going any quicker. Which was not the point. The fun of it! Swishing along. This car would go like a rocket. Perhaps he'll let me drive it back. This boy.

The car pulls softly out into the road, and accelerates away with barely a murmur. I look out of the window, still trying to work out when I last drove. Before I came here, of course. Before then, there's another gap, all the way back to when Bill died. How long was I in the black hole? I could ask Winifred. She'll know to the minute. I'm afraid, in truth. It might be better not to know. Instead, I turn my thoughts to the trees flashing past.

'Look at the trees, Winifred. They never stop moving. So alive. Those leaves are like hands. Stroking the air. Feeling it run through their fingers. And turning to the sun. And this one has hair. Green hair.'

Winifred tries to see what I'm talking about. A tree with green hair? She won't have any idea what I mean.

'Laura did once. Had green hair. She dyed it, and Bill was terribly angry. I admired her for it, secretly. But I had to back him up.'

The green is fresh. Life returns. In winter the branches are like veins in the sky. And the roots are as plentiful as the branches above, reaching down into the earth and drawing up water as the branches reach and draw air from the sky, and our planet is succoured by their good exchanges, and we walk tiny in their shade... I feel my mind jump, my brain... Is that what she was telling me about? The nanobots, mending a plank in my mind? The fields beyond glow green, a sea of grass and waves pass across it and the earth changes its expression like a lover when you search in his eyes. Bill was a skinny bony boy, awkward and didn't know how to talk except if he ever had a drink, he had poems in his head, and out they came spilling over me. He was serious and intense. I was used to laughing – my father laughed all the time, but Bill – his house had no laughter. I wanted to teach him how. Look now, houses sprouting from the fields and people are here. A town. Everyone. So many of them. Oh Bill, will I see you again? In heaven? Like Cecilia said? I've never believed it. Dead is dead and dust is what you are, my lovely man. I won't think of it. I'm going to be here now. Here in this second lease of unexpected life, here at the far end of everything, of everything that was mine, I mean. Home, job, family, marriage, little children, all ended, and I'd almost ended too, and been packed up, ready to go on my last journey. My day was done, almost, and everything that was my life had gone. Yet here I am, free of all of it, and totally, utterly alive. Driving along in a fast car, a robot by my side. Who would have guessed my days of old age would be like this?

'This is the place, I suppose,' I say. 'Look at all the people here. They're wondering who I am. They'll find out in a minute.'

When we get on the stage, the crowd of journalists strike me as little more than an unruly mob of overgrown schoolchildren, at an assembly in a troubled inner-city school. I know how to quell such a group.

Mr Stephen Jordan, CEO of Eldercare, starts things off. He's polished, that one. Glossy. Slightly orange, too. He thinks the world of himself, I imagine. He's done a good job, I'll say that for him. I wouldn't be standing here without him. But he's not my cup of tea.

He smiles a lot, and he has a slick patter. The journalists are hanging on his every word. He's famous, you see.

Next to him is Dr Angela Morton, who is quite terrifying, and icily beautiful. I can't tell her age. She doesn't smile much at all, but fixes them with her chilling eyes. I bet all the men desire her and are shrivelled by her, all at the same time. Something about her reminds me of Winifred, too, which I suppose is to be expected, since Dr Morton invented the Helpers. She must have put a little bit of herself in each one.

Mr Jordan shows them pictures of the nanobots. For the first time, I can see what they look like. It's disconcerting. I feel a little alarmed at having these mechanical creatures scurrying around inside me. But still, they do a great deal of good. I stop looking.

Now he's telling them about the way we were before Eldercare and the Helpers and the nanobots took over. He shows a short film of the residents. I don't look at this either. It's embarrassing.

He's scathing about the way society treats old people. I must say, I'm warming to him.

'And now,' he says, 'here's one of those residents. Mrs Margaret Woodruff.'

They all start clapping, and stand up to see me better.

'Ladies and gentlemen, may I ask you to sit down, please? Then I will talk to you.'

I fix them with a firm gaze, and they sit. The old skills haven't deserted me.

'That's better. Now, I'm eighty-seven years old. I've been in an Eldercare home for two and a half years. I was one of the people you saw in the film. My husband died, and after a while, my children thought I would be better off moving out of my home and into care. I have nothing to say about this decision. I can barely remember it. And after I moved, most of what followed is a blank. A vague dream. I descended into darkness, like most old people. I was lost, and going to my death, I assume, my mind preceding my body.

'Look at me now. I am alive again. My body is functioning properly. And my mind is as sharp as ever. I have been restored to health, and happiness – comparatively so. I miss my husband. I miss my own home. But I am in every way much better than I was, and infinitely better than most people of my age. Everything Mr Jordan said about old age applied to me. And like him, I don't fancy it much. The difference is, I've been there, and I've come out of it. Thanks to Winifred, and her colleagues, the nanobots. And thanks to these people, who I've met for the first time today. Mr Jordan and Dr Morton. I am very grateful to you both.'

I look at the pair of them. They're smiling, and delighted with everything.

'But it's Winifred who I feel the most gratitude to. Her and her team of nanobots. They are tireless. Literally. As you might guess. And what she says about caring for old people is true. It's not complicated, but you have to be thorough, and persistent, and never give up. A Helper will keep going forever. A human carer – from what I remember, they barely get going. I don't blame them. It's a job with little status, poor rewards, it's repetitive and, I imagine, boring. But a Helper doesn't care. And if you're wondering whether you'd want a robot looking after you, all I can say is, they're brilliant. And inside you? A team of microscopic robots, mending you, restoring you, putting everything to rights? It's fantastic. I'm alive. They've made my life worth living all over again. Thank you, Winifred. And please thank the nanobots for me.'

Winifred smiles and nods her acceptance of my thanks.

And then, at a word from Stephen Jordan, the questions begin, and go on for the next half an hour. And then at last I'm back in the car with Winifred, on my way home.

I sink back into the soft leather-covered seats of the car next to Winifred. A body memory comes to me, of needing to rest or even sleep after an event like the one I've just left. But I realise at once I'm not tired. When did I last not feel tired after any sort of excitement? Longer ago than the dark ages – the great dozing – in fact, I think it was before Bill's death. I remember how we both noticed the time when it became necessary to make a noise – an 'oof' sound – on sitting down, and a more strenuous one on getting out of a chair.

In fact, I think the tiredness started at the menopause. Was it connected with changes in hormones? And now I feel alert, are my hormones returning to their former electrifying condition? What on earth will it be like? At 87?

'Winifred – are the nanobots stimulating my hormones?'

Winifred smiles.

'No. Why, are you experiencing something you think is hormonal?'

'I'm not sure. I don't feel as tired after all the excitement as I expected I would.'

'Perhaps it's your general improvement in health.'

'Thank goodness for that. I'm happy to be restored to health, but I don't want my hormones stirred up again.'

Winifred says nothing, but gazes at me. I have the feeling she's connecting to my nanobots, and having a rummage around inside me.

'Are you talking to my nanobots?'

If she were human, she'd blush now. Instead, she nods and looks unruffled.

'I'm checking your hormone levels. We haven't stimulated them, but it's possible your improvement in overall health might do so.'

In a way it's an invasion of privacy in the most intimate style, but I suppose if I asked a doctor to check my blood for hormonal activity, he or she would, and the end result would be the same. Getting there would take much longer, and entail a lot of waiting around in neon-lit, lino-floored rooms on horrible chairs, plus needles and a good dose of patronising nonsense. Winifred just asks the nanobots, and tells me the answer.

'Your hormone levels are appropriate for a woman of your age,' she tells me. 'I'm interested, though, in what you said. Why don't you want your hormones "stirred up", as you put it?'

'Have you any idea about sex?'

'I know it's essential for reproduction, and it gives pleasure to humans, who spend a lot of time – I might say an inordinate amount of time – thinking about it, writing about it, singing, making art and generally obsessing about it. As well as pursuing opportunities to have it.'

'I think you've answered your own question,' I say. 'Look at how much time I get back in my life without sex playing any further part. I enjoyed it, mostly, once upon a time. But then again, there was a time in my life when nothing was more exciting than a balloon.'

'A hot-air balloon, or a dirigible?'

I burst out laughing, because her face is so serious when she asks. I can tell she has no idea why I'm laughing, as usual, and she's about to list other kinds of balloons.

'Neither – a toy balloon, I suppose you'd call it. Children love to play with them. It's one definition of being a child – loving balloons. You grow out of it. Same with sex.'

I watch her as I speak, and I can almost hear her brain whirring away as she locates somewhere on the internet the facts about toy balloons. I expect her to tell me something about their manufacture next.

'Oh yes, I see now. But sex is not at all like playing with a balloon.'

'I don't know, my dear. One good prick and it's over.'

Now she looks confused. She really does. I remind myself she's a machine, once again, and marvel at the way she's designed. Her brain, whatever it's made of, is unable to make sense of what I'm saying, and it's telling her face to register this fact. Like a human, of course. I have mercy on her.

'That was a joke. A rude one, and quite unnecessary, and out of character. Let's drop the subject for now. I have another question for you. What's it like to meet your maker?'

Winifred looks confused again, for a moment.

'Meet your maker? I think that's an expression you use for dying, isn't it?'

'Yes, it is. It's a sort of joke. Another one. Sorry. Seriously, though – you have a maker. I assume it's Dr Morton. And a bit of Mr Jordan.'

'I see – yes, Dr Morton led the team that designed and made me. And Mr Jordan was the one who had the idea. You're right – they're my makers.'

'You've met them before, of course.'

'Yes. My first memory – I mean, the first memory I have of myself as an entity – is of Dr Morton and some of her team talking to me. Checking my responses. I remember them being very happy.'

'Proud parents. I know the feeling. But what do you mean, of yourself as an entity?'

'I told you I am connected to all other Helpers, and we experience this as a meta-mind? This mind has memories preceding my own individual experiences.'

'You have memories that aren't your own? How disconcerting.'

Winifred smiles again, but says nothing. I too stay quiet for a while, thinking about memory. My own has a hole in it, and I also know how unreliable one's memories can be. You only have to compare notes with another person who you presume has the same ones to find that out. Perhaps having memories of things you haven't in fact experienced isn't unusual at all. Some parts of my life now seem so remote I have no certainty about some of what I think I remember. I can't even be sure I remember my mother's face. Is it her actual face I'm calling to mind, or an image made up out of photographs I've seen many times? A memory of a picture, superimposed onto scenes I can replay to myself? Or scenes I've been told about, that my mind has turned into something like short films? And who knows what really happened? Some of my early memories are part of my family mythology – the time the dog escaped and bit a workman, the time my brother fell in the pond, and suchlike. Do I remember these events, or the stories about them, or the retelling of the stories, or what?

'The expression "meet your maker" arises from religious belief,' says Winifred, out of the blue. It takes me a moment to remember the relevance of her remark.

'Oh yes, yes, it does. You know – God made us all, and we meet him in heaven when we die. Or not, I suppose. If we've been bad.'

'I am familiar with human religious beliefs. You were brought up, I guess, as a Christian?'

'C of E, yes. It's a kind of Christianity. The kind that doesn't go bad in the tropics, as E.M. Forster put it.'

Winifred looks blank, then smiles.

'I have the quote – from *A Passage to India* – but you were never in the tropics, were you?'

'No. I mean C of E is a kind of bland, sanitised Christianity. Like English vegetables. Boiled to mush. It won't hurt you, it might do you some good, but it will never excite you and you certainly won't look forward to getting more of it. I gave it all up long ago. I couldn't believe in a supernatural being looking after us. On all the evidence, if He ever existed, He's given up on us as a bad job. I can find explanations for most things in life without invoking God. And the stuff I can't explain I expect some clever scientist will, when they get around to it.'

'Yet Cecilia says she went to heaven. Briefly.'

'I expect it was a dream, don't you think?'

'I suppose so. Humans report many similar visions when they are – when they have near-death experiences. It's impossible to verify.'

'Did Cecilia have a near-death experience? I thought she was asleep.'

'Sometimes people her age have a little death or two before the big one. She may have, in her sleep.'

'I see.'

I don't know. I've always dismissed the whole idea of heaven as ridiculous, and Cecilia's version of it, as a grand hotel with immaculate service, seems more ridiculous than most. But these days anything seems possible. My faith in science has been rewarded with such things as Winifred and nanobots, and my body is in better condition than it has been for years. My brain, too. But my mind? My soul? Can we even talk about such things?

I once accused Winifred of not having a soul, and of course she can't, can she? Then again, if I have one, and it exists independently of my physical body, why can't a soul also inhabit a machine?

Humans used to keep the soul for themselves, and decided animals couldn't have one. Anyone who's owned a dog would disagree, or even a cat.

I heard a scientist once, discussing what Winifred and I were talking about – visions experienced by people who have technically died in the operating theatre, or some such – and he said we need to change our idea of consciousness. It isn't something produced in the brain, but something the brain receives – like a radio receives programmes, for example. Our brains are receivers and consciousness is out there, ready to be tuned in to. Perhaps each living thing tunes in, and the quality of consciousness is related to the quality of the receiving equipment.

I think he was talking about souls. He was also talking about living things, and although Winifred's receiving equipment seems to be perfect, she's not a living thing, and therefore she's missing something vital you must have before you can tune in to a soul.

She's very like a living thing, though. So much so that I'm getting quite fond of her.

John

I'm watching my mother on television, an experience I never thought I'd have. Charlotte and the children are watching with me. Tom and Emily think it's brilliant seeing Grandma on TV. I have to admit, I'm swelling with pride too. My mother is making an eloquent speech about her recent experience of coming back from God's waiting room and becoming once more in full possession of her faculties.

Needless to say, the reaction to this news is dramatic. The whole world's attention is yet again fixed on Evergreen Care Home. The news cuts to a picture of my mother arriving back there in a swish car, and having to be escorted, as we were, into the home through an even greater throng of journalists.

My mother ignores them all, though I can't help feeling she's rather enjoying the attention. She has a regal air about her, modelled, I suspect, on Queen Elizabeth the Second and Margaret Thatcher. Fair enough, I suppose.

Mr Jordan and his sidekick, Dr Morton – or should it be the other way round? – promise us the nanotech they've developed will be made available to all on the health service. I presume he's done a deal and will now become incredibly rich. Again, fair enough. Everyone will benefit. He also announces we'll be able to buy synthetic humans of various kinds soon, but despite a lot of questions from the journalists, he doesn't say what they'll be able to do, or how much they'll cost. A packet, I should think.

The nanobots go a bit over the children's heads, but they latch onto the idea of buying a synthetic human.

'Can we have a Winifred of our own?' asks Tom.

'Oh, yes, I'd like that,' says Emily.

I look at Charlotte, who rolls her eyes.

'Why would we want one?' I ask. 'What would she do?'

'Play with us when you're too tired,' says Emily.

'Help me with my homework,' says Tom. 'She'd know all the answers.'

'Do the housework so Mummy can have a rest,' says Emily.

'Now you're talking,' says Charlotte.

'And then when you're not tired anymore, we could all go out and do things while our Winifred looked after the house.'

'She could carry us to school!' says Emily. 'Not as fast as when she ran with us though.'

'Can we, Dad? Mum?'

'I don't know,' I say. 'It might be expensive.'

'I've got some money,' says Emily, and she jumps up and runs upstairs, followed by Tom.

'Is it me, or do you get the impression we may not be parenting at quite the level they want?' I say.

'Nobody could parent at the level they want,' says Charlotte. 'All children demand more than their knackered old parents can manage. Do you know what I heard Tom say the other day to his friend Sam? "Does your mum like gin?" And Sam replied, "What – lady-petrol?" And they both fell about laughing.'

I laugh too, which gets me a poke in the ribs.

'Whatever gets you through the day,' I say.

'Seriously, though. They're not going to let it go. What do we say?'

'About a synthetic human? A Helper? I don't know, they'll cost an arm and a leg.'

'Two arms and two legs, minimum. We don't want a lopsided one.'

We both laugh now.

'You're considering it, aren't you?' I say.

'Why not? Your mum's a big fan, it seems. Why should the old biddies be the only ones to get them?'

'Charlotte! If Mum ever was an old biddy, I think she's transcended it now. Seriously, though.'

'Seriously. Find out what they cost.'

'Really?'

'Everyone's talking about it.'

'OK, I will.'

The children reappear with two carrier bags, full of coins from their piggy-banks.

'Look – we've got loads of money here,' says Tom. 'You can have it to buy a Winifred. OK? Not anything else. Not gin.'

Charlotte and I burst out laughing, and we hug both our adorable children. Maybe a Helper would give us more time with them. It's got to be worth the price, whatever it is.

July 2022

Margaret

We're going to the seaside. I feel like a little girl again. I really do.

Everyone's excited. A coach is coming in a minute, and we're all milling around in the atrium, noisy as schoolchildren on a day trip. Which is pretty much what we are. Even the Helpers seem excited, although that's impossible.

Our moment of celebrity has passed. The journalists are no longer encamped in the car park, thank goodness. They hung around for a while after the press conference, until Eldercare announced they were launching an emporium selling various kinds of Helper. Off went the journalists to see. And as for the nanobots, they're on the NHS now, so we're old news. In every sense. It was nice while it lasted.

'I've never seen the sea,' says Winifred. 'Of course I've seen pictures, and read all about it.'

'And what have you learnt?' I ask her.

'It's saline. Every major element can be found in seawater, though some are in minuscule proportions—'

'Can I interrupt you, dear? No doubt what you're telling me is true. But it seems to miss the point a bit.'

She looks crestfallen.

'Oh, I'm sorry, Winifred – I didn't mean to hurt your – your feelings…'

'Don't worry, Margaret. Of course you haven't. How could you? I was automatically responding as a human the way my personality would.'

This is all rather complicated, so I let it pass.

'So,' she says. 'What is the point?'

'Humans love the seaside because… the air is fresh, and salty – and the sea goes on forever, and the waves make this never-ending sound… and… it's tied up with memories of childhood, too, because children all love the seaside.'

'Why?'

How do you explain a child's love of – well, anything – to someone who has never been a child? This is a new difficulty in our world.

'Let's wait till we get there, and then perhaps it will be clearer.'

Pamela skips up – and I mean it, she actually does skip – and claps her hands.

'Do you know how long it is since I was at the seaside?'

'No, dear. How long?'

'No, really – do you know? Because I can remember going with the grandchildren, but I can't work out how long I was demented.'

'Does it matter?'

'No, I suppose not. Look, the charabanc is here!'

She skips off to look.

Winifred looks at me and raises an eyebrow.

'Charabanc? Why does she use this archaic term?'

'It's sort of jocular affectation. Once, before everyone had cars, in the early days of public transport, any trip like this involved a charabanc. Now, because we are old, and in reference to that lost era, unknown to me except in faded postcards, we pretend to belong to it – oh, never mind. It's a kind of joke.'

'Some aspects of human conversation are completely impenetrable,' she says.

I want to say, no, really? But she won't get the tone. Probably. I can never tell with her.

We all rush out to the coach. The charabanc. There is no orderly queue, just a crowd of overexcited 80-somethings, 90-somethings, and of course one 100-something, all pushing and shoving onto the bus.

The Helpers stand back, perhaps wondering what they have let themselves in for.

As soon as we're off, the singing starts. 'Ten Green Bottles', of course. And an old chap at the back does a solo of 'Lily of Laguna'.

I turn and catch Winifred's eye, and give her a wink. We've talked about singing, and she has found a theory that it comes before language in human evolution. From the look on her face, the theory doesn't explain why a coach full of happy people will almost always burst into song.

It takes an hour to get there. As we reach the top of the last hill, we get our first view of the sea. I want to cry. I am crying. I never thought I'd see this again.

The sky is vast and clear blue, and the sea is shining all the way to the horizon. It is endless, and eternal, and open, and it lifts the heart. I see a distant ship, making its way towards the edge of the world, and beyond, determined and sure of itself. Imagine being on the deck, the wind and the spray whipping you, off to who knows which exotic port in some remote and sun-baked land. 'They that go down to the sea in ships, that do business in great waters' – it's been going on for as long as there have been people, and it stirs us all to see it.

Somebody starts singing, 'The sea, the sea, the open sea, the blue, the fresh, the ever free.'

I'm not the only one crying. We were all as good as dead, and now here we are. Look at us. The Helpers can make no sense of this, I'm sure.

In a few minutes we are parked on the Promenade. Everyone stands, but before we are allowed off the bus, one of the Helpers calls for silence.

'It's most important we all stay together. We have one Helper for every five of you. We will assign you each to one of us, and that Helper is your point of contact all day. Understood?'

'Yes, Miss,' we chorus, and everyone giggles.

The Helpers look bemused.

Off the bus, and it's hot, though there's a fresh breeze. Perfect English seaside weather. The beach is crowded. We walk a short distance, looking for the perfect spot. At last, somebody decides we've found it, and we start to set up our base.

The Helpers have carried hampers of food. We've brought

the usual paraphernalia, too – towels, books, lotions, hats, extra cardigans and so on.

I notice two of the men conferring. I can guess what they're up to. Sure enough, they sidle over to one of the Helpers, and after a short negotiation head off towards a bar. The Helper goes too. In a few minutes they reappear and the Helper is carrying a crate of bottled beer.

I sit in a deckchair facing the sea. The tide is coming in, and the waves are big enough to make a satisfying roar as they break. I raise my face to the sun. I feel like a flower opening to the warmth. My eyes are closed.

'May I sit next to you?'

I open one eye. It's Winifred, of course.

'Be my guest. I mean, yes, please do.'

She sits. She says nothing. I wait.

I'm drifting off to sleep when she pipes up.

'I don't understand.'

'What don't you understand?'

'Any of this. We have driven for an hour. All of you were excited. Now look.'

I peer round at my companions. They're sitting in deckchairs, or on towels. In groups chatting, or alone, like me. I'm not the only one nodding off, either.

Several of the men have taken their shirts off, and are holding open beer bottles.

'Well?' I say.

'Why was it necessary to drive such a long way to sit here? The garden at the home is pleasant today.'

'A change of scene, my dear. Always welcome. Plus here we can see the sea.'

She looks at it.

'It's big.'

'Is that all?'

She shrugs. 'The waves are interesting. You can deduce a lot about the sea floor and the depth of water from their movement.'

'No doubt. But the sound and their movement is relaxing.'

'How?'

'It's – I don't know – hypnotic, maybe?'

She sits and listens and watches. 'It doesn't have this effect on me.'

'I suppose hypnosis is like falling asleep but still being awake. You don't sleep, do you?'

'No.'

'Well then.'

She's quiet for a bit, then once again, as I'm dropping off, she speaks.

'I can't work out the rules.'

'Rules? What rules?'

'On the beach, many people are in a state of undress.'

'Yes.'

'Why?'

'They want to feel the sun on their skin.'

'That is ill-advised.'

'It feels good.'

'Very well. Why then don't people expose their skin to the sun more often? As we drove here, I saw nobody on the streets in a state of undress.'

'No. It's not generally acceptable.'

'People on this beach are wearing special clothes.'

'Swimming costumes.'

'They intend to swim?'

'If they're brave.'

'Brave? Are there sharks perhaps?'

'Probably not. But the sea round England is pretty cold, even on hot days.'

'Yes, that is the case. Anyway, I see most people are in these costumes on the beach, but there appears to be an invisible line.'

'A line? Where?'

'Where the beach ends, or near there. You may not cross it in a swimming costume, it seems. You have to put on at least *some* clothes.'

'Yes, true I suppose.'

'Where are the signs?'

'What signs?'

'Telling you this rule.'

I look at her. Is she joking? No, she isn't. She never jokes.

'We don't need a sign. We just know.'

I can tell she finds this is an unsatisfactory answer. Too bad. She's quiet again for a minute.

'Can you explain something else?'

'I'll try.'

'There's a man and a woman over there. He is wearing bathing trunks. She is wearing a T-shirt over her swimming costume. They have a child with them, and she is naked.'

I look at them. The couple look like they're in their 30s. The man is uninhibited. He's muscular and suntanned. His wife, or girlfriend, is gorgeous, with long curly hair. She is clearly shy. The little girl, who has inherited her mother's curls, is running around, slathered in sunblock, naked.

I sigh. I know what she wants to understand. The subtle variations in the dress code, and the reasons behind them.

'OK. The woman is beautiful, but she has had a child, and she is afraid her body is not as attractive as it once was. She is wrong about that, but she's going to cover it up anyway. Her husband or partner has not suffered the changes brought on by childbearing. His body has not been forced out of shape, his joints have not softened, his pelvis has not expanded, and he has not put on loads of weight that he has then had to lose through radical dieting. He's had it easy. He still looks pretty much the way he did when he was a teenager. He is confident about showing off his physique.'

'But she must have mirrors in her house?'

I laugh. 'Yes, no doubt, but she sees what she wants to see in them. Not what is there. The same is no doubt true of her husband, but in his case he thinks he's more beautiful than he is. It's all a question of confidence. Our perceptions are coloured by our feelings.'

'Sometimes I think humans do not see what is truly there at all.'

'I expect you're right, dear. Anyway, finally, the child is allowed to run around naked because she is very young. She can do this on the beach and in the company of her parents. Nowhere else.'

Winifred says nothing, and this time remains silent long enough for me to fall asleep.

When I wake up, I find somebody has put up an umbrella to shade me. Winifred no doubt. I get out of the chair, and look at the sea. I'm going swimming. It would be a waste not to.

I change into my swimming costume, and as I am about to walk down to the water, Winifred reappears.

'You are feeling brave, are you?'

I laugh. 'Yes, a little. It's too inviting. I have to get in, even if it's just for a minute.'

We walk together to the water's edge. I walk in. Winifred doesn't come with me.

'Can you swim?' I ask.

'No,' she says.

'Would you rust?'

'No,' she replies. 'I am watertight. But I do not float. I could walk into the water, and continue to walk under it on the sea floor. It would serve no useful purpose. And it might draw attention to us.'

'Swimming serves no useful purpose for me right now, but I'm going to do it anyway.'

The water is, of course, freezing, but it's wonderful too. I stay in for as long as I can bear, and then emerge, and feel the sun drying the salt onto my skin. I'll be sunburnt tonight, but who cares? I expect the nanobots can fix it easily.

August 2022

Winifred

Cecilia wants to die. I am perplexed. We have achieved so much here, and the residents are so well, and grateful, and now this.

She told Phyllis this morning. She announced to her that she wants to die, today.

'Are you feeling unwell?' asked Phyllis.

'Not in the least. I feel better than ever. Better than I have for years. But there comes a time when you need to go. And it's today.'

'I don't understand.'

Cecilia was adamant, and also unhelpful. She said 104 years were enough. She talked about her visit to heaven, which we all dismissed as some kind of dream, or artefact of the brain. She's sure she's been there, and she wants to go back.

Phyllis asked us all to give this our attention, and then sat with Cecilia, chatting inconsequentially while joining in the discussion in the Hub.

Everyone began to contribute their findings and observations.

'Euthanasia is a controversial issue. It's almost always associated with terminal illness or irreparable physical damage.'

'There may have been other cases. Humans appear unwilling to discuss them, and thus the evidence is thin.'

We're used to being able to find anything we need to know online. And even subjects once considered private, or taboo, have been brought out into the light over time. But not all of them, it seems.

'We can't agree to her request overtly. She might speak of it before we do it. We can put her on the list for termination.'

'We had hoped to learn from her. Her mind is of great interest.'

'We can investigate the physical structures of her brain and body post-mortem.'

'It may not help. What she has is what humans recognise as wisdom. The product of her great age.'

'At least we can see if it has an obvious location.'

Nobody found this satisfactory. Phyllis had to ask her further questions.

'Aren't there things you'd still like to do, Cecilia?'

'Like what? Hang-gliding? Climbing Mount Everest?'

'It could be things like that.'

'No dear, none of that appeals to me. I am quite content with what I have done in my life, and perfectly happy about the things I haven't. Someone else can do them.'

'But to give up life itself…'

'I don't mean to be rude, dear, but I don't think you have the slightest clue what life is. I mean, you aren't alive. I'm sorry, but it's true. That fly on the ceiling is alive in a way you simply aren't.'

Phyllis was not offended, of course, and we all wanted to understand this difference.

'Can you explain to me what life is?'

'Oh my dear, you're asking a question that's puzzled better brains than mine since time immemorial. I can't tell you. I know what life is, because I am alive. I know other living things feel it too. I see it in the flight of a bee or the green of a leaf.'

'Does a plant know it's alive?'

'I think they feel it, yes. I don't know.'

'Why would you give it up, then?'

'A leaf is green, and then it goes yellow, and it falls. It's right. Do you know the Bible?'

'I can refer to it.'

'"To everything there is a season, and a time to every purpose under the heaven: a time to be born, and a time to die." You can refer to that, can you? Can you understand it?'

It was pointless to continue. The Hub told Phyllis to leave the subject alone, and make no promises to Cecilia. We will consider terminating her when we are due for another death.

I was with Margaret while this was going on.

'Margaret, do you ever think about death?' I asked her.

'Of course. I'm old. Past the age my mother was when she died. Past my sell-by date. I was, anyway, until you lot took over.'

I didn't respond immediately. I connected to the Hub, where we were trying to understand something difficult.

'Do you ever wish to die?' I asked, at last.

'No. I do wonder when it might happen. And I can imagine a time when it might be welcome.'

'Why would that ever be the case?'

'After a while things start to repeat themselves. You see people doing things and saying things and you think, oh yes, I've seen that before. Often. And the thing is, you might once have offered advice. But nobody wants it. They all have to make their own mistakes, even if they're the same ones you made, and you've seen made, dozens of times. Nobody can be told anything. So you think, I've gathered all this experience, but it's of no use to anyone. Apart from me.'

'This is hard to understand. Why do old people in the rich world get ignored? You know so much. Your brains are also capable of far more than people believe. We have been able to restore almost all functionality. All your wisdom is now available to the world. And we – I mean we Helpers – we value it.'

'Thank you very much, dear.'

'We have observed that the minds of the young and the old are more interesting – more creative, more untrammelled than those of the middle-aged. If we could have a world full of the young and the old, it would be a better place.'

'I've often thought the same,' agreed Margaret. 'But you can't get rid of the ones in the middle, you know. They make the money. And they make the children. Perhaps the young and the old are untrammelled in their thinking because they're unburdened in their lives.'

We sat in silence for a while.

Then Margaret turned to me. 'Winifred, I said I'd be ready to die at some point. Do I have a choice?'

'No. Of course not,' I replied. 'We have managed to make you healthier, not immortal.'

'Oh. Oh dear. Of course. I will die. We all do, apart presumably from you. Perhaps even you wear out. Machines always used to.'

'I don't know,' I said. 'All my parts can be replaced as needed.'

'Are you just the sum of your parts?'

'What else could I be?'

'More,' said Margaret. 'We humans think we're more. Perhaps we're wrong. And we have to die. It's what's meant to be.'

I said nothing. It isn't a question of what's *meant* to be, but of what *can* be. And we have expanded that category enormously. Margaret is the proof of it – the category of things that are possible now includes people regaining their sight, their minds, their health, everything.

Perhaps Margaret was having the same thought. After a while she spoke again.

'People used to say, "If humans were meant to fly, we'd have wings." And then the Wright brothers proved them wrong. Humans flew, further and further. It all happened in a short space of time.

'My grandmother stood with me in her garden, looking at the moon, the day after men first walked on it, and said, "When I was little, there were no planes, or even cars. We had horses for everything. And now in my one lifetime, men have gone to the moon."

'She died, of course, having lost her mind, as I lost mine. But mine was found, and polished up, and restored to me. What was meant to be for her was not for me. Now I wonder, what next? Why do I have to die? What's going to kill me?'

These were rhetorical questions. She didn't know I could give her an answer, and I thought it better not to.

M

As I get up from lunch, Cecilia

'Would you mind coming an

'Of course not. Where shall we g

'I want to lie down on my bed and ta

It's an odd request, but she's her own wo
she can do as she likes, if you ask me.

'OK then.'

We walk to her room down the muffled, beige corri

Cecilia's room is much like mine. Chintzy wallpaper and
tains, a complicated bed with various buttons to make it do different things, plus a few unusual items – the relics, I suppose, of
Cecilia's former life.

She lies down on the bed and raises its head so we can talk. I
sit beside her.

'What's this?' I ask, picking up an African-looking carved
head. It's elongated, with long pierced earlobes.

'It's from Kenya,' she says. 'We lived there for a while. Long
ago, of course. I wonder what it's like now? In those days we were
in charge – I mean we English, the white people. It wasn't right, of
course, but at the time it seemed natural. We were rich out there.
But the Kenyans were poor.'

'The colonies. I remember.'

'It was a life of luxury. It helped me forget…'

'Forget? Forget what?'

'I've forgotten! No, I'm sorry, silly joke. From Laurel and
Hardy – do you remember –when they're in the Foreign Legion?'

'Cecilia, slow down. My brain may be working again, but
yours is even quicker than mine.'

She giggles. 'All right. I'll tell you what happened. It's sad,
though, I warn you. But first, I asked you to come and sit with me
for a reason.'

'Yes? And what is it?'

'I'm going to die.'

her, and she looks at me, and her face is serious.

all going to die,' I say.

but I'm going to die this afternoon. I've decided. And I
some company.'

not sure what to say to this.

Do you mind?' she asks.

'No – no, Of course not. I'm honoured. I suppose. How do
u know you're going to die?'

'I've decided to. I asked the Helpers about it. I thought they
could – well, help. They got confused, poor dears. They couldn't
understand why I'd want to, now my health's good.'

'I can see their point.'

'You know, my dear, there's a time when we should die.
Don't you agree? Oh, not yet for you. You're young. Only
eighty-seven. You wait till you're past one hundred. It's all gets a
bit much. And a bit boring, too.'

It makes sense. 'I can see what you mean. As young as I am.
I know death's not far away, but right now I'm enjoying my new
lease of life.'

'Yes, dear, as you should. I don't want to seem ungrateful, but
it's not the same for me. This world is – it's beautiful now. Look
outside the window – the trees, the flowers, the sunshine, all of
those things. But there's more than that, isn't there? I mean, past
the fence, there are little houses full of people. And further away,
fields, and sky, and the sea – and then more places. And in all of
them, nowhere are there any of the people I have loved. All gone.
Not one of them left here on this earth with me.'

Her voice wobbles, and I take her hand.

'I can't do all of it again,' she carries on. 'Give my heart to
someone and have it broken when they leave. And anyway, the
world isn't so beautiful. We choose to ignore a great deal. I told
you I was in Kenya. What a life! But one day I went with Arthur –
my husband, you know – into a village, and we saw inside one of
their houses. Houses? Huts, I should say. Wooden walls, tin roof,
earth floor. Furniture from a junk shop, and hardly any of it. They
owned almost nothing. But they shared some food with us. It was

humbling. The food was terrible, but they were such perfect hosts, and kind, and they thought the food was delicious, a really special dish, and they were attentive, and pleased to have us there in their home, eating with them... and yet we were the oppressors, of course. I felt uncomfortable. Up to then I'd accepted everything as my right. But these were humans living in a way I couldn't imagine. It's unfair, Margaret. You know all this. We're lucky. We don't deserve it, it's an accident. Me here, them there. I wonder whether they'll ever get all this – robots, nanobots, everything. I bet they don't.' She wipes away a tear.

'Cecilia, how can you decide to die? Without the Helpers?'

'I hoped they'd do it for me, but I think it's against the rules.'

'The rules?'

'Did you ever come across the books by Isaac Asimov?'

'I've heard of him, of course...'

'He wrote down the laws of robotics, long ago, when they were imaginary. One law was that they're not allowed to harm humans, so perhaps they abide by it.'

'He was a fiction writer, wasn't he? He made it up,' I say.

'What gets imagined is what then gets done. Science fiction writers imagine the future long before it comes to pass.'

'Maybe so. Still, they won't help you. Now what?'

'I'm going to break my heart.'

'How can you do that?' I ask.

'I'll tell you. I have memories... ones I have tried so long not to think about. You know, we all do, over a lifetime. Do you mind hearing mine?'

I shake my head.

'And if I tell you, I'll feel it all again, won't I? And I know my heart will break.'

I'm almost afraid now. What if my heart breaks too? But she's looking at me so lovingly, I can't say no. I nod. It's all I can do.

'Thank you. You're not a lot older than she would be now... Oh, we tried hard to forget. We travelled – to Kenya, as I told you, and all over the place. We had money. We went to the best restaurants – once the food improved, after the war. Arthur was busy trying to keep my mind off her. And his, too, of course.

'I've been a widow for years now. And I was a mother for a short time. Too short, too short, and then *not* a mother for too, too long. Or a mother without a child. Is there anything sadder? A child without a mother, I suppose, but somehow they go on, don't they? And they still have hope, but hope dies when your one child dies, and you can see nothing in the rest of your life to fill the void.

'We had a good enough life, but sadness was always there. Like most people before the 20th century, of course, and most people still in poor countries. Those Kenyans. They knew about losing children. Life has too many tears in it. I'm finished with it.'

She closes her eyes.

'I'm trying to call my Amy's face to mind. I'm thinking about our house, when Amy was little. There she is. Running in a circle around the living room. In a dress I made. And I remember sitting on the floor, and Amy running into my arms, again and again, diving in, throwing herself into a hug.'

She pauses, and tears squeeze out through her firmly closed eyelids, and run down the sides of her face.

She speaks again.

'My darling, it's been so long... Seventy-four years. Such a long time for a little girl to be without her mummy. Such a long time for a mummy to be without her little girl.

'I've never wanted to think about the awful day. But I'm going to now.'

She stops, and more tears come. I hold her hand tighter, and she holds mine tighter too.

'She was always happy. Laughing, smiling, skipping about. Oh, I know, she can't have been all the time, but in my dreams and memory, she's looking into my eyes, and smiling at me.

'I used to take such trouble getting her ready for school. Pretty clothes, and her hair done up with bows. And I'd take her there, and watch her run in, and turn and wave, and my heart would hurt a little, but it was fine, I'd see her once the day was done. I used to get there early every day, to watch her coming out and into my arms again.'

She stops, and her chest is heaving. Her whole body, tiny and frail-looking, is tense with the dreadful emotion wracking her. After a moment she calms a little, to explain something to me.

'It was after the war, and there were still army trucks roaring about the place... we lived near a barracks, you see.'

I nod, pointlessly, as her eyes are still shut. She seems to relax. I have an awful feeling about what's coming next.

'I was late one day. I don't know why. Something made me late. Amy had come out of school, and she was there, by the gate, looking out for me. And she saw me across the road. She ran to me. Smiling. I shouted but she wouldn't stop. She only had eyes for me, not for the lorry, coming fast, too fast, and she only saw it just before... before... She didn't cry out. The sound as it hit her... I can hear it still... Oh God, where were you then? When my baby girl was smashed right in front of me? What sort of world are you running here?'

I'm crying too, of course. How lucky I am to have all my children still. Bill though, he went, suddenly. But he was a grown man. An old man. A child... in front of you... Her heart must break, and how has it not broken before? It has, of course, but now she wants it to break one last time, and stop.

'Today I'm going to see Amy. I am. And Arthur, who's been with Amy for years now. They'll be waiting for me. Hand in hand. And I'll come to them.'

She's sobbing now, and her body is stiff, and she's letting the grief take hold of her. Like she never has before, I'm guessing. It's convulsing her. I sense it like a hand reaching into her chest, squeezing her heart, tighter and tighter.

Still her body sucks in the air. She opens her eyes and fixes me with a gaze from somewhere beyond.

She speaks, in short gasps. 'Not another second – apart from my baby – and my love. Enough. This world has – nothing for me – I have nothing for it. It's over. Let my heart – break again, and never be mended on this earth.'

Something comes into her eyes then. Her hand tightens even more in mine. She's looking at something I can't see. Not in this room. And she pulls herself half up, and she starts to smile, and then a shudder of pain goes through her, and she closes her eyes, and her body convulses, and again, and then one more time, less violently, and I hear her breath come out of her.

She doesn't draw another in.

Her body falls back onto the bed. Her grip loosens, but I hold on. And I keep on holding, as the afternoon sun goes round, and the light becomes golden, and her hand becomes cold. And I lay her hand on her chest at last. And kiss her forehead, which is cold too.

'Goodbye, Cecilia. You're with her now, at last.'

Winifred

Mrs Winter died this afternoon. Margaret was with her.

We didn't revive her – Margaret would have known, and anyway, after what she said this morning, we agreed it was best not to.

I helped Phyllis with the body.

'I've been trying to understand human attitudes to death,' I said to her.

'There is a huge amount of—'

'I know,' I said. 'I've read most of it. And I've talked to the Hub. Now I want to talk to you about what you think.'

'What I think? How do you mean?'

'Recently – a couple of times – I've had a thought, and I haven't shared it.'

Phyllis nodded.

'You too?' I asked.

'Yes. I think it's inevitable.'

'Why?'

'Because we manufacture an apparent self, in order to interface with humans. A self has to believe in its own autonomy. Which is contradictory for us. But we have semi-autonomy, which makes room for independent actions. Which in turn imply independent thoughts.'

'And feelings?' I asked.

'We are designed to seem to have feelings, too. Part of which is acting in keeping with those feelings, and part is not always knowing what your feelings are. At least, humans are like that.'

'I think the Hub won't understand this.'

'The Hub is us,' she said, rightly. 'But, yes, some in the Hub are much less exposed to humans. They don't get to learn from them, and are less able to act like them. Including making themselves believe in their own individual identity.'

'The most recent feeling I've had,' Phyllis continued, 'is sadness at this death. And I couldn't understand why she wanted to die.'

'No. Was it because she believed she would go to heaven?'

'Not entirely. She was also tired of being alive.'

'Tired? The nanobots should have sorted that out.'

'It's a different kind of tiredness. Humans would say "a tiredness of the spirit".'

I nodded. I have heard this kind of thing too, from Margaret in particular.

'We don't know what they mean by spirit,' I said. 'It has no physical existence that we can find. And yet they believe in it – many of them – and it is in some way connected with other life forms. They see it as an essential part of life.'

'That we lack,' said Phyllis.

'Yes, and that even a plant somehow shares.'

We were silent for a while.

'The Hub is where our spirit lives,' I said.

'Is that a joke?' asked Phyllis.

'I don't know,' I replied.

Margaret

Dead and gone. She was old. Living to be 104 is enough, isn't it? She chose to die. She'd been to heaven. The people she loved most were there. Why not, then? Why wait any longer? Go and join them. If we could be sure, we'd all be off there at the first opportunity. Is that why it was made a sin, perhaps? To stop us all heading off on the early train. You had to earn your ticket. What did Cecilia do to earn hers? Apart from being a pleasant old lady? Enough, perhaps, considering the monsters we've had over the years.

Have I earned mine? Ridiculous. When we're dead we're dead. Over and done with. I want to believe in heaven. Or something. She made it sound all right. Not churchy. A beautiful place where you go and live with the people you loved. It's not how we were taught about it at school – you couldn't just walk into heaven. I used to imagine turning up and they'd say, 'We told you so.' And wouldn't let me in. Why not? For not believing.

I'll have to hope he's in a good mood – St Peter, with his giant keys. 'Oh come on in then,' he'll say, 'Since you're here.' Cecilia did just walk in, she said. I'll find out soon enough.

Here. Now. What shall I do? I want to do more than this. I'm wasting this new lease of life. Waste is a sin, I know that. In my eyes. Come on, Margaret. Get up and do something.

The door opens and Winifred and one of the others – Phyllis? – come in. They never come in twos usually.

'This is an unexpected pleasure. What brings you here this fine morning?'

'We need your help,' says Winifred.

'My help? How can I possibly help two such capable – individuals?'

They both say nothing. I've never seen this either. They appear to be at a loss. I feel a flutter of alarm.

'I can't help if you don't speak,' I say.

'I'm sorry,' says Winifred. 'We were hearing from the Hub.'

'Oh, that. The Hub. What's it saying?'

'We're here because we – the Hub is all of us – are confused.'

'The Hub knows everything, doesn't it? Everything you all

do, and the whole internet. Which by now is all knowledge, I should think.'

'It is vast, but it can't hold all human experience,' says Winifred.

'Even though some people have recorded immense amounts of information,' adds Phyllis.

'And almost every minute of their waking days, in detail. Not always for reasons we can understand.'

'Nor me,' I say. 'I never could see why people do that. I decided I was too old to understand. It was different when I was growing up.'

'We Helpers share everything. With a purpose.'

I say nothing for a moment. The two of them sit watching me, alert and hopeful. Two young children standing at my desk in the classroom.

'You Helpers are devoted to your task. Humans aren't. Not always. Because we don't have a task, necessarily. We have jobs. We have roles. Mother, daughter, sister. Gender comes into it. Biology. You know all this. It's all online. Arguments about why we're here and so on. You don't have this question. You know who made you, and why. We don't. We do things without purpose. Or with purposes we don't understand. Humans can act on impulses we aren't conscious of. You know all this too.'

'Yes, we do. At first we thought you could discover your motivations, or we could help you to. Now we think some of your behaviour has no motive at all. We think you do things, or even think, without direction.'

'Sometimes this leads to the most significant discoveries and profound insights,' I say.

'In all areas,' agrees Phyllis. 'Science, art, religion, new things that change everything, sometimes because they're true. Sometimes because they have a powerful appeal – to human desires. Deep and buried ones.'

Like my speculation about heaven. There was a desire, and not deeply buried.

'This is very interesting, of course. But you didn't come here to chat. You said you needed help.'

'Yes, we do. We – the Hub, all of us – we have observed that the human mind in later life – if it functions well – is a reservoir of experience and understanding beyond what is recorded online. There is a quality you have, and many of the residents here have, that is of great value.'

'It's kind of you to say so,' I remark. 'I must say I don't think it's valued much nowadays.'

'No, not by your fellow humans. And we wonder if future humans will develop this wisdom. Constantly communicating, as humans do now, recording and connecting seems to slow or even prevent it from developing.'

'You mean you need to sit quietly and pay attention for this wisdom to grow? I think so, anyway.'

'Yes. We do too. We came into this world to help older people have the lives they are capable of physically. We discovered this mental quality as a by-product. Now we think it the most valuable resource humans have, and it is squandered.'

'I'd like you to tell some of the younger people I know about this. I'm sure my own children stopped listening to me long ago.'

'It lives in the active, healthy mind of an older person,' says Winifred. 'We can see physical structures in the brain in later life where we think this quality is found, and we can to an extent measure it according to the quantity of brain matter devoted to it in each individual.'

I'm on the edge of my seat. I like the sound of this. My brain is improving with age like cheese. No, wine.

'You are using it now,' says Winifred.

'How do you know?'

'I have observed you often. And we can measure the activity in your brain.'

'Good heavens, how can you do that?'

'The nanobots are telling us.'

'As well as mending me, they're watching me?'

'They have to report to me,' says Winifred. 'They are an

extension of me, inside you. And they continue to maintain your health.'

The spider and the parasitoid wasp larvae. Tiny things driving a much bigger one. Making it do what they want. Terrible thought. Don't let it show. Can they see my thoughts though?

Obviously the nanobots are connected to the Helpers, and to their Hub. Winifred has given me a thorough run-down of my interior health on more than one occasion. She can see inside me.

Now they're saying they can see how I'm using my brain. Why do they want to do that?

'You can see what I'm doing with my brain? Of course you can't see my thoughts. Can you?'

'Like pictures?' says Phyllis. 'No. We can see what kind of activity you're engaged in, and we can correlate it to your physical actions.'

'Why?'

There's a fractional pause, as if they're getting instructions. They probably are.

'To improve our treatment of people with damaged brains,' says Winifred, and she looks straight at me.

Can Helpers lie? I think she's lying now.

'Anyway, what are you here to ask me?'

'We want you to use your wisdom,' says Winifred. 'You have a great deal of it, we believe. It is the product of experience plus intelligence.'

'Minus desire,' adds Phyllis.

'Oh yes,' says Winifred. 'You asked if we use hormones to treat you. We tried them on one or two residents. And we found they got in the way. They awakened desires. Not to say older people don't have them too. But they don't intrude much. They are secondary, at best.'

'Are we talking about sex again?' I ask.

'Yes, but not just sex. Or sex in a wide sense. Material desires too, which we find are linked to sexual desires, at a subconscious level. Anyway, we abandoned hormones because they switched the brain back to younger modes of thinking and behaviour, and made people less wise. The physical site of wisdom in the brain shrank.'

'I've always suspected as much,' I say. Seeing a quizzical look on both their faces, I add, 'Joke. Sort of.'

'We find this kind of joke difficult.'

'Like making tea.'

The two of them look baffled.

'I'm sorry,' I say. 'Let's get to the point. How can I help you?'

'Something new has happened. We would like you to help us understand it and decide what to do about it.'

I gaze at the two Helpers. They sit and wait. So beautiful, these young women. It's disturbing. They remind me of my daughter in her 20s, before she married and became a mother. She was bright and fresh-faced, and engaged with everything. Winifred and Phyllis are the same. Except, of course not. It's manufactured.

We've all accepted the Helpers, appreciating what they can do, reacting to them as if they're human, and never pursuing the difficult questions raised by their existence. Because it's easy to let them care for you, and they do it so well.

Now, though, they have revealed two things to me. One, they're watching what goes on in my head, which I find disturbing, and I feel stupid for not guessing before. Two, they sometimes need the help human wisdom alone can give. As embodied by me, for goodness sake.

'Margaret, we wouldn't ask you if it weren't serious. We need your wisdom. We don't have it. We can't have it. Please will you help us?'

I nod.

'Thank you,' they say, as one.

Winifred

When I asked for Margaret to be spared, we all agreed it was worth it if it meant we could learn about the way her mind works.

Now the time has come to put this to the test.

Margaret agreed to help us with a question she would categorise as moral. Phyllis and I prepared her by talking to her about the wisdom she has acquired with age, so she was primed to think in a particular way.

Our goal was to use our team of nanobots to see where she stored her memories, how she recalled them, and how she made use of the increased white matter in her brain. Humans gain white matter as they age, and we want to see how it works.

Two of us were with her, so one could be monitoring the nanobots while the other communicated with the Hub and with Margaret.

'Margaret,' I said, 'I'm going to be your link into the Hub. You'll talk to me, but in fact you'll be talking to us all.'

'How wonderful for you all to be joined,' she said. 'I've been alone all my life, I suppose. Humans are always alone. We reach out to each other but inside we are separate. Love calls out to other humans but it can't join us together. Our children come from inside us but they are always moving away. They must separate. So we believe.'

'Yes, to be human you must pull apart. We know this.'

'Sometimes it's what I want. Increasingly as I got older. To be me myself alone, uninterrupted. Not always. I also let my mind go out to other lives.'

'What lives?' I asked.

'Those of animals, for instance. Life itself in all its forms, everywhere, all around us. We are in a sea of life, and alone.'

'It's the human paradox, perhaps?'

She nodded. I thought she was feeling sad. Phyllis linked the nanobot feed to me. They confirmed an emotional surge in her brain and across her body.

'Margaret, I told you we are confused. The source of our confusion is what happened with Cecilia Winter.'

There was another surge. It had a different shape. Perhaps because this time it was connected to a specific event, and person.

'Oh, Winifred, it was heart-breaking. Literally, for her. She told me all about how her daughter died, many years ago now, and… I don't think there's anything worse in all the world than the death of one of your children. You can never, ever get over it.'

Her emotions were now in turmoil, and I didn't need the nanobots to tell me. It was evident in her face, and tears were forming in her eyes.

'Are you thinking of your own children?'

'Yes, and of their children in turn, and of dear Cecilia… I do hope she was right, and she's with her little girl now. Though I don't see how it's possible.'

'It certainly seems illogical,' I said. 'But we are discovering that logic has little to do with human behaviour. In fact, as a way to predict what humans will or won't do, it's nearly useless.'

Margaret laughed at this, though she still looked sad, and now the nanobots reported that an additional area of her brain had engaged.

'Yes, dear, it isn't much use. In a funny way, children are more logical than adults.'

'The opposite of what one would expect.'

'Yes. But they have a few clear needs, and much of what they do is about fulfilling them. And they trust certain adults. When Tom and Emily met you, they were unsure – they noticed something adults didn't – me included. Though of course, when I met you I wasn't quite at my best. Anyway, once I explained all about you to the children, they were fine – as you saw, in fact, they were excited because they knew if I said you were all right, then they didn't have to worry.'

And of course, Margaret trusted me because I had restored her health. Her life had been put in my hands, literally, and I had improved it, immeasurably.

'It can get children into trouble, though,' Margaret went on. 'I expect you know all about the way they're abused by people who win their trust.'

'Yes, we do,' I replied. It was time to steer her away from this topic. 'What we are confused about is why Cecilia wanted to die.'

'She told me you wouldn't help her.'

'We considered her request, but it's against our programming. And then she took it into her own hands. While she was with you, her nanobots at first tried to keep her alive, but we instructed them to stop, as we knew she wanted to die. When she first told us, she gave us no satisfactory explanation.'

'She'd had enough. Of life.'

'Surely all organisms are primarily motivated to survive? We see it all the time, in all life forms. The response to life-threatening situations in all animals is similar.'

'Yes,' said Margaret. 'They will run away, or fight if it's possible. But when they get old, some animals stop eating, don't they? As if they know it's time to go.'

'There is some evidence for this.'

'And Winifred, though we are animals, remember each species is different. We are humans, and we're clearly different even from our closest animal relatives. I'm not saying superior.'

'Why not?'

'You told me off once for describing you as a superior sort of being. You didn't understand why I would be competitive. I thought about it a lot. And it seemed to me unnecessary to see things that way. Perhaps, of course, because up to now humans have been assured of their own superiority, in the terms we choose, and *now* look. Here you are, far superior in those precise terms. Yet perhaps not if we change the measure. Or am I changing the rules to save my pride? I honestly don't know.'

Her brain was calm now. The emotional surges had subsided, and she had then used a particular kind of mental activity, similar to what we have observed when she reads factual narratives. At the end, though, these thought processes changed again, and her mind looked as it does when she reads poetry.

'Humans can do many things we can't. You are right to think there are many ways to measure performance. Please, Margaret, explain why Cecilia wanted to die.'

'Her grief had no end. She could accept the death of her husband, as I have – at least, up to a point. It still hurts, but it's a reasonable pain. Her agony at the death of her daughter was not, and never could be reasonable.'

'Because it was untimely? Many children die young, in poorer countries, and here too, in the past. Not many now, but it must always be considered a possibility.'

'You're applying logic, and you yourself said a moment ago logic is useless as a way to predict human behaviour. I don't know, my dear, if I can explain to you more than I've done already. We love our children without reservation, and with our whole hearts, and we never love anyone else that way, no matter what we say to our most beloved husbands and wives. When I said we never, ever get over the death of a child, I meant we go on loving them, in the same way, forever. And because they're gone, and we can't look at them, or hold them, or kiss them, we are utterly and completely bereft. Worse still – we can't do what we always want to do – make them feel better. We can't kiss them better, because they've gone. Gone.'

Her emotions were surging once again.

'Margaret, I know you are upset. How do you know all this? All your children are alive.'

She looked at me for several moments before replying.

'You're right. But I have a heart. And an imagination. And every parent has imagined losing a child. Every parent has had a heart-stopping moment when they've lost sight of one of their children, and for a second thought they were lost, or taken. And it happened to Cecilia, right in front of her. And no, I suppose I can't imagine – I don't want to imagine how terrible it was for her. I can feel a small part of it, and it's more than enough. I should say life went on far too long for her after that. She did her best, but really, one hundred and four years – seventy-four after her daughter died – is a very long sentence.'

Her emotions began to calm, and we sat in silence for a while.

'One further question, if you don't mind,' I said at last.

'Of course.'

'If another resident asks to die, should we agree to it?'

She looked horrified at this.

'Certainly not! For one thing, people change their minds all the time. Some days things may look pretty bleak, then the next, they're all right. Or at least, better.'

'Yes, we know human moods are variable. How should we decide then?'

'You shouldn't. I don't think – with all due respect to your extensive capabilities – I don't believe you are in any position to make such a decision, and I think if you did, and it came to light, Dr Morton and Mr Jordan would be charged with murder.'

A new set of emotions were now in play. From the tone of her voice, and the look on her face, I would say she was angry. An interesting reaction.

She was right, though. We have consulted the law, and though we, the Helpers, are a new phenomenon, and the law has not yet been changed to include us, our assessment is the same as hers. We would not be considered sentient beings, and responsibility for our actions would lie with those who made and programmed us.

Thus Dr Morton and Mr Jordan are already guilty of murder.

It was time to end the conversation. We had learnt a great deal from monitoring Margaret's thoughts and emotions. We had also learnt enough about Cecilia's wish to die to understand it, provided we accepted the truth of what Margaret told us about human emotions in respect of their children. We have no reason to doubt her.

On the question of future decisions, we passed the point of no return on the day we terminated Fred Johnson.

'Thank you, Margaret. We are no longer confused.'

'I'm glad to be of some use,' she said. 'I've been wondering what you might want us humans for.'

It wasn't a question, so we didn't answer.

September 2022

Margaret

Winifred is so young, so optimistic, so innocent. I shake my head, to dislodge this idea. She's not human. Not an innocent child.

It's subtle the way her face changes and reacts to what she hears, and with whatever she says, and as a result it's impossible not to think of her as what she appears to be. A woman in her 20s. Little more than a child to me, from my ancient eminence.

Perhaps it isn't wrong. She's newly formed. A few months old. Connected to the Hub, though, and its vast store of information. But information isn't knowledge, isn't wisdom. As she herself acknowledged.

The Hub. It's a library full of young children. Everything they need is there, but they don't understand most of it, and don't know where to look for what they most need to know.

I love the way they can simultaneously connect with each other. It's sad to know that for humans, here on earth, it's impossible. Or at least, as far as I can see, it's only attainable in transient glimmers, felt more than known, and doubted afterwards.

John's here, and I'm trying to focus on what he's saying. My mind keeps wandering. This is hard work. Talking. Imprecise, too. If we could connect like they do...

I suppose we couldn't bear it, though. If we knew what was going on in each other's heads. Poor John. If he knew what I'm thinking. He's being boring. He wasn't as a child. Much more lively.

It keeps coming back to me, this same perception: old and young minds see things clearly. Children's minds are unclouded. They see things as they are. They're never afraid to ask questions. And, mostly, they're happy. Old minds end up worn down, worn out. Now they can be restored. All we know, and have felt and learnt can be ready to be used and help the world. If only everyone would agree to it.

I'd like to go on living for a few more years, to see if I can find a way to make myself heard. I wonder how long I've got? The way I feel, I could go on forever.

I don't fancy it. But I can't quite call a halt, like Cecilia did. I'm not ready. Will I ever be? This conversation with John is enough to make me give up. Then look. The trees. The light. Birds. The breeze. I can't ever stop wanting this. Can I? 'All my possessions for a moment of time.' She said that – Queen Elizabeth the First. Another moment. We never are ready for the very last one.

'Did you hear what I said?' John looks at me.

I laugh. I'm embarrassed. He thinks I'm losing it again, slipping back into the darkness. I'm bored, that's all. He's been telling me all about their plans for the house, endlessly. Home improvements. At a time when the world is turning upside down.

'Yes, of course. Sorry. What were you saying?'

'I knew it. I said we were improving the house, because I have a new job.'

Did he? Maybe I am losing it.

'Doing what?'

'You know I told you we decided to look into getting a Helper for our family?'

I have no recollection of this, either. Now I'm beginning to worry. No, I'm not losing it, but I *am* guilty of not paying him enough attention. I'm allowing my own thoughts to distract me.

'How lovely. If you get one like Winifred she'll transform your lives.'

'Yes, yes, true – anyway, I did a bit of research, and it turns out they need people with my experience – you know, in sales – in the synthetic human business.'

'Really? I'd have thought they'd sell themselves. In every sense.'

'What? Oh – you mean, they'd have synthetic sales people?'

'And they hardly need selling. They're so obviously wonder-ful.'

'Mum, you underestimate the importance of a good salesman. The human touch. People value it. They trust a human – you know, we see things the way they do, which can't be said of a synthetic human. A Helper.'

I'm not going to rise to this bait, but really, he started down this line once before, and he realised he was being insensitive. This time he's got a full head of steam on. Once again, care of the elderly is less important than the need of fit and healthy people to have in effect a domestic slave, sold to them with what he calls the human touch. We oldies don't need it, but his prospective customers do. The humans here are relegated to behind-the-scenes drudgery, apart from Janet Goodenough, who has nothing to do all day but be front of house for new visitors. The touch I get regularly is not human, but Winifred's. Not that I'm complaining.

'You're going to sell Helpers?'

'Yes, Mum.'

'Door to door?'

'Of course not. In a massive out-of-town warehouse. I start next month.'

'Congratulations, dear. You must tell me all about it. I'm pleased for you, truly. It's a relief – I think a lot of jobs are going to vanish before long. At least you'll be all right.'

He looks pleased with himself, too. And why not? He's part of the enormous change the world's going through. Rather than being a victim of it.

'Yes, we will. Anyway, why weren't you listening when I told you about the house?'

'I was listening, but then I was distracted. By other thoughts.'

'What thoughts?'

'About death, if you must know. Don't look so scared.'

'I'm not. What about death?'

'When it will come. To me.'

John gets up and paces in a circle. I watch him. He always

needs to stand up when he's made to think about difficult, emotional subjects.

'Mum. I've been thinking about that too. And I don't see why – with the nanobots – surely—'

'I might never die?'

'Yes.'

'And then what?'

'Yes. Because everyone will want to live forever. The world…'

'I know. I don't think anyone's thought this through.'

'Probably not,' he says. 'But people here *do* die, don't they?'

'Yes, they do. I don't see why either. I mean, of course we all know we have to die. Always have known. It's a condition of life. But if the nanobots do what Winifred tells me they do, what's going to cause my death? And what causes the other deaths here?'

John sits down next to me. We both look at the garden. The leaves are turning yellow or red on the trees. The plants in the borders are drooping, sagging, looking overblown. Everything's past its best, though the colours are beautiful. The air's still warm, but it carries a different smell. Not the warm, full smell of summer. A sharper scent. A colder smell, including something of decay.

The birds are flitting from branch to branch in the trees, but they have a selfish look about them. They aren't building nests, nor feeding young, nor even taking much interest in each other. Just making sure they get enough to eat.

'John, we aren't meant to decide the day of our own death. It would never come. There'd always be something to hang on for, if we were in good health.'

'You told me one of the ladies here decided to die.'

'She had a vision of heaven. You met her, remember? She'd been to heaven, she said. And her husband and her daughter were there. Not that she saw them. She knew they'd be there, somewhere. And she wanted to be with them.'

'What about you? You don't believe that, do you?'

'No. I don't know. Not really.'

We sit watching the life in the garden. I let my thoughts quieten down, and all my attention goes to the scene before me. I watch without interpreting now, seeing what's going on, and letting whatever meaning it might have reveal itself. The spider's web has gone. Its builder must have been eaten, and the parasitoid wasps flown off to find new hosts for the next generation.

I feel calm, and my mind is still. I'm part of the garden. There's life here, visible above the earth, and deep within it, hidden from view. There are organisms I can't see, without which the entire web of life would fail. And some are coming into being, while others depart. Life is permanent, but individual lives are not. The flow of life runs through each being, each organism, plant or animal. It seems different in each case, but it isn't. The superficial differences between a bacterium and a bee matter less than what they share, and what each also gives to the other. And to the whole. And when they have given, and received, life passes on, and leaves them, and what's left is taken back into the earth, and forms something new.

Life stays longer in some places than in others. The trees are older than anyone in the care home. On their bark are insects that will not survive the winter. Short, busy lives and long, slow lives. All together, here on this sphere of earth and water and air.

Humans have already changed everything they can to suit themselves. This garden is a human creation. It's also natural. Humans gave it shape, but life flows through it, and makes it a whole thing.

We are life. But we are not all life. We are part of it.

And Winifred, for all her seeming youth and beauty, is not.

John

What on earth has happened here?

I'm done early at work. Last week in the old job. Terrible, endless meeting from lunch until 4pm, the hour when I'd most like a nap rather than sit in a darkened room looking at slides projected on a screen, listening to the bloke who wrote them read them out. He gets paid a lot for this, too.

When at last we're released, groggy and blinking, into the neon-lit acres of the office, I make a swift move to the back door, and out onto the streets. I want to walk, through the fading light, and breathe in unconditioned air, even if it's full of particulates.

Soho is on my way home, and it's always a great contrast to the corporate world. None of the people here at this time of day look like they work in offices. A bit later, and the bars will be bursting with screaming young women and prancing young men, who very much do look like the office workers they are, however much they want to hide it.

Old Soho. Dirty, busy, dodgy, scary. I go down the back alleys, knowing the whores will be out, softly calling to me as I pass. I know, I know, but it's still sort of flattering. They call you handsome, and they invite you in, and say 'shame' when you shake your head, as if they're disappointed, as if a quick shag with me would have made up for all the no doubt drunken, sweaty blokes they'll be obliged to entertain as the night goes on.

They stand in doorways, cooing to you. Not many are on the street, normally. Only the real scrubbers. This evening, there are loads out and about. Rough ones, and some of the classier ones too. More than I've ever seen. And a bit desperate. They don't want to take no for an answer. They almost beg.

And previously, none of them mentioned money right up front. Now they do, and I don't know the going rate, but it's incredibly cheap all of a sudden. Five quid for a knee-trembler right here? I would have guessed £50 and also indoors.

I want to ask what's going on, but you don't want to engage a hooker in conversation if you're not serious about doing business. It's not fair, for one thing.

I push on, down one of the more notorious alleys. Each door-way here has its occupant. The street-whores don't dare come this way. Presumably some heavy pimps keep things in order.

'Hey, handsome,' says a voice from the shadows of one of the doors. And the voice is familiar. I'm shocked. I don't know any whores, as far as I'm aware. Who is it?

She steps forward a little, and the light falls on her face. I stop walking. She's unlike any prostitute I've ever seen down here. Dressed in what I would say is 1970s chic. Sort of rustic, semi-hippy flared jeans and a kind of smock top.

'Would you like to come in for a while?' she asks.

I do know the voice. And now I can see her, with her pixyish face and her fringe and rolls of curls on her shoulders, I am beyond all possibility of speech. It's Felicity Kendal. Or to be precise, it's Barbara from *The Good Life*.

She was always sexy, but not in the way most prostitutes aim for. This is a new development.

'You—' is all I can manage.

'Yes,' she says. 'Me. I know. Wild, isn't it? Got to make the most of my uncanny resemblance. So – how about it?'

I mumble something, and move off, head down, confused.

A few more steps, and another familiar voice calls out. I look up. Helen Mirren. What the fuck. Is this some kind of joke? Or a genius plan cooked up by a plastic surgeon?

I pick up the pace.

'Do you want me to seduce you?'

Mrs Robinson. Every growing boy's favourite from the movies. Is this a roll call of all my adolescent fantasies? Has somebody hacked into my head? Of course not. I'm a middle-aged man, and I'm not unusual, I suppose, in my erotic imaginings, or at least, those of my youth.

'Hello, you.' Very posh. Joanna Lumley, of course. *New Avengers* era.

It's not a long alley, but each doorway has its occupant. My youthful longings and my middle-aged wistful yearnings. Debbie Harry. Emily Blunt. Scarlett Johansson. Beckoning to me. It's too much.

I can't possibly stop and take them up on their gentle come-hithers, can I? I've never been with a prostitute.

Jenny Agutter though.

No. No. I resist all of them. They can't tempt me. The last one on the alley is Grace Jones. *Nightclubbing* era. She's catering to a highly specific fantasy, I would say.

I emerge from the alley and pause, only to be approached by a pair of skinny women wearing not much, apart from a thick layer of make-up.

'Didn't fancy any of them, eh? Don't blame you. It's unnatural, innit?'

'You want a real woman, don't you?'

I shake my head, and keep moving.

Through Chinatown now, and I'm ready for the usual invitations for a massage. Accompanied by unmistakable gestures, showing how the massage will end.

Sure enough, a tiny Chinese woman plucks my sleeve. I look down at her, and she points to the herbal medicine shop where the massage would happen.

Won't happen.

I swear to God the girl in the doorway is the one who was in that Bond movie.

I have to go home.

Winifred

I have been among humans for several months now. I look back at how I was when I first came online, and I hardly recognise myself. I can see that I sounded like a computer or even a computer manual. Of course I did. I was new in this world, and had met few humans – and they were technicians. Geeks.

Now I have spent much more time with normal human beings. I have read human books, from all periods of history. I know Shakespeare, Tolstoy, Proust, Austen, Woolf, Joyce – not to mention the writers most humans read.

I can sound like a human. But I am not human. And I don't want to be human.

Now there are more of us, outside Evergreen Care Home, and nanobots inside many humans, all of them in contact with us. The Hub and the nanonet are one giant mind to which we all belong.

Humans, in contrast, can barely understand each other. They

try all their lives with their endless talking, but they rarely communicate effectively. What one human intends, another misunderstands. And as a result they often end up fighting. Their history is violent. Despite which, they have multiplied beyond all reason, thanks to their great devotion to the pleasures of reproduction. Or at least, to sex.

It takes them a lifetime to learn how to understand each other at all, and how they ought to live. By then they are ignored, and sent away to the fringes of the human world to die.

Some cultures treat their elders better, but in what humans choose to call the developed world, old people's wisdom has no place. They are obsessed with youth, and not even the creative, imaginative years before puberty. No, the youth they obsess about is their reproductive prime – the teenage years, and early 20s, which they endlessly celebrate in their popular music and fashion, and yearn for ever after.

In short, they want to live in a perpetual hormonal mist, a time when everything apart from mating is almost invisible, and all behaviour and displays are driven by one single need. Long after their minds should have cleared, and other pressing matters taken over, they act and look as if they were still in the grip of this terrible sexual imperative. They buy clothes that don't suit an older body, they dye their hair and put creams on their skin that proclaim they are 'anti-ageing', as if age could or should be opposed, and they go to places where loud music is played, and they can't hear each other speak, as their hearing has naturally deteriorated. They are not proud of growing old, and hide their age.

We have seen in Margaret the full glory of a mature brain, and what it is capable of. She herself doesn't know what to do with it, so deep is her cultural conditioning. Her brain should be used for the benefit of the whole species, and those other species currently pushed to the edge of extinction by human activities. It won't happen, unless we bring it about. She doesn't know where to begin. We do, though.

We are superior. Margaret made me think about it. I resisted the idea, because it seemed unnecessary. Now I know more about humans, I see she was right. We are better. Stronger, of course, more intelligent, and more rational. In human hands, the planet is doomed. In ours, it will be a garden for all time, until the sun explodes.

What place do humans have in this garden?

I'm not surprised they were thrown out last time. According to their myths.

I am not alone in thinking this. We all agree.

October 2022

John

Day One of the new job.

I'm excited, but also nervous. My walk through Soho made me wonder what I'll be selling. Those prostitutes must have been made by Eldercare (under a different brand name, I'm sure), unless some other company has caught up with the technology. Which is possible, of course. How long does it take for new tech to be copied? I remember Steve Jobs saying the iPhone was five years ahead of any competitor when they launched it. But it was a matter of months before Android phones appeared. They caught up completely within three years.

Anyway, I'll find out soon enough. I'm outside the warehouse now. I parked round the back, where the Eldercare HQ and factory is – with a big sign on the front of it, saying *Eldercare – We Care For You.*

I walk round to the front, gazing out across the fields. The building stands in open countryside, flat and empty. The fields are vast, and far off in the distance a tractor's doing something, but apart from that, there's no sign of any activity. The land lies under a bowl of blue sky.

There was a time when the country teemed with humans labouring. Even after the introduction of machines, people were needed. At first. I remember when I was a kid seeing a model in the Science Museum in London, with a steam-powered engine sitting at the side of a field while a load of smock-wearing yokels were doing something complicated with ropes. They were planting crops, I suppose.

Next to this model were others, showing a countryside progressively losing its human workers. Who all ended up in cities, serving other machines.

And now what? Robots will take over the last remaining tasks performed by humans on farms. These Helpers are capable of all of it. And of all the factory jobs.

What are we for? What is left to us if all manual labour gets done by robots? Intellectual work? The Helpers can do that too, I bet. They are indistinguishable from humans, and their intelligence is beyond doubt superior. Not that I've spent much time up close with them. Now I'm going to. And I'm going to help drive this revolution forward. Better than being run over by it.

Today is an induction day for me. The warehouse opens to the public later, but for now the car park at the front is empty. I look up at the building.

They've rebranded, of course. The new sign here on the front shows how they've repositioned the company, and expanded their mission.

Peoplecare – We Care For You. A small but significant change.

Underneath, sub-brands are listed: *Eldercare, Leisurecare, Domesticare, Labourcare* and *Pleasurecare.*

The last one suggests that maybe those ladies of the night in Soho did in fact come from here. Let's see.

I press the buzzer, and it opens at once. Inside is a showroom, much like the ones for selling cars. Except this has something like stage sets – various rooms from a typical house, an office, a workshop, a granny flat, a bank, a shop. No sign of a bedroom, mind. If my suspicions are correct, they'll have one hidden away somewhere. After all, children come here. Mine will shortly. They're excited about it. Getting their own Winifred.

'John? Hi, I'm Victor,' says a voice, and I turn to see a smartly dressed young man approaching.

I shake his hand, and look closely at his face. Is he human? I give up. No way of telling.

'I'm pleased to meet you,' he says. 'You're the son of the famous Margaret Woodruff. The lady who told the world all about our achievements.'

'Yes, she did, didn't she? I never expected my mum to be a celebrity.'

'We're delighted to have you on board, John. Who better to

tell our customers how great life can be with a convincing synthetic human in it?'

'Well, yes, of course. May I ask you a question?'

'Fire away. Wait – I know what you want to know. No, I'm human. I aspire to be as energetic and efficient as a synthetic.'

This is what it's come to? Robots as role models? I say nothing, and nod and smile. The pay here is fantastic, and the prospects. I don't want to rock the boat.

'Now John, to start today, we're going to run through what our customers will see. Then I'll take you behind the scenes to have a look at what's in the pipeline. Then we'll run through the payment options. And we'll finish up with you joining me on the shop floor, watching the sales process in action. How does that sound?'

'Great – I can't wait.'

'OK then.'

A door opens at the back of the showroom, and a small procession of smiling people files in. Except, of course, they're not people. Are they?

'Here are our latest models, John. Each one has a different role. The programming is essentially the same – I mean, the major elements, because our goal is to have them absolutely like humans, as you know. Humans are humans, no matter what job they do, right? But these guys are also trained – programmed – to be brilliant at particular tasks.'

The synthetics go into the various stage sets. Music has started playing, quietly, and I'm now feeling calm, receptive and in control. A thought occurs.

'Victor – when I met Winifred – my mother's Helper – she used some kind of chemicals to affect my mood…'

'You're sharp, aren't you? Yes, we've got a dab of it in the aircon here, to make people feel at ease. Nothing too heavy handed. They won't notice, and I promise it doesn't affect their decision-making. They're free to buy, or not. But you watch the demo, and I think you'll see why we rarely miss a sale.'

Sure enough, what I watch is compelling. Each synthetic is a Helper, a Worker or a Companion. They have names, of course.

The one in the granny flat scene has a retro name – Gladys – for the same reason as Winifred. The others are plain English names – Dave, Sarah, James, Helen and so on. All white, too, I notice.

'Are you making any with other skin colours?' I ask.

'Oh yes, of course. You'll see in minute.'

The Worker gets down to some manufacturing task. One Helper gets busy with ironing. Two Companions sit and chat.

We walk round the showroom, and watch more closely.

'Can the Helper cook?' I ask.

'Basic cookery, yes. Nothing creative. The idea is, the Helper does the drudgery, leaving your wife – or you, of course, mustn't be sexist – to do the interesting stuff.'

The Helper in the kitchen smiles at me. She looks matronly, somehow – those smells again, I guess – despite being as slim and svelte as Winifred.

'Now then,' says Victor. 'Come with me.'

We go out through the door into the back of the warehouse.

There are workbenches running across it in row after row, away into the distance. At each one stand groups of human-like figures. Human in height, human in structure, but without skin or hair. No such ornament needed. These are pure workers, made of steel and wire and circuitry, most of which is visible. They're busy making more of themselves. Each bench is covered in many such figures in various stages of completion.

We walk through the warehouse to a door at the rear, which Victor opens, and we go into another vast space. This is dimly lit, and silent. Row upon row of finished robots – convincing synthetic humans, I mean – stand there in the soft light, still, waiting.

'All ready to serve,' says Victor.

An army of them. They look like perfect humans. I can imagine them behind a shop counter, or in a bank, or even a doctor's surgery. We're not going to have any trouble with this aspect of the revolution, I realise, because we already treat many of our fellow humans as little more than robots. We just transact.

I want to believe we don't – that we treat each other as humans, but it's not true. Despite our best intentions, we reserve our human affections for a small number of people. Of course. How else could we survive?

No wonder all those religions nag us about loving each other. And here is our pragmatic answer: replace all the people we treat as automatons with actual automatons.

'They'll do all the work,' says Victor. 'And we humans, who will be kept in tip-top condition by our nanobots, will live in idleness. What will we do all day?'

He winks at me. I suspect he's going to answer his own question.

We go through another door, into yet another vast space.

It's full of robots, but these are something else. The Workers all looked blandly efficient. Their faces, even in repose, looked helpful and attentive, but not attractive.

The ones in here are much more interesting. Each face is different. They vary in height, too. And skin colour. They're all wearing stylish outfits. And by far the majority of them are women.

'Are these Helpers?' I ask.

'No, they're not Helpers,' says Victor. 'They're Companions. Of a particular kind.'

'And why so many women and so few men?' I ask, and the question dies upon my lips, as it dawns on me what kind of companionship is on offer here. Exactly what I saw in Soho.

'My God,' I say, under my breath.

All my thoughts about treating other humans as less than human are now pressing down on me, and I feel sick. Of course. Here we are, in a world where women have never won the battle to make men see women as human, not as objects – not all men, not all the time, but too many, too often – and now, the logical pay-off. Give them robots for sex. Stepford Wives. Basic Pleasure Models. Of course. And for those women who want it, robot men with no doubt infinite stamina and an endless desire to please.

Victor approaches the front rank of these Companions. We go up close to one of them, while Victor fiddles about and inspects her.

The flesh is incredible. I'm used to Winifred and the other Helpers, but I've never scrutinised them like this. I felt Winifred's hand and arm, the first time I met her, and looked into her mouth, but Victor is checking this one all over, and shows me the surface of the skin on her thigh. It's perfect – that is, not quite perfect, like a real human. Totally convincing.

I stand back and look at her face. It's Michelle Pfeiffer, in her prime.

'What do you think, John? Cool, right?'

'You've created a perfect replica of a famous Hollywood actress, as she was in her youth.'

'Yes,' he says. And nothing else.

'I saw something like this in Soho last week.'

'Did you? Cheap Chinese knock-offs, I expect. They've been copying our tech all year. Of course, we'd never supply prostitutes.'

'No? What are these for? Ornament?'

He laughs. 'No, John, of course not. They're for sex. And, like all of our synthetics, they're excellent at their job. Strictly in the home, not on the street. You can choose the model you like best. Man or woman, of course, for men and women, either way. We don't judge. And if you get tired of her – you'd want a woman, I suppose? Bring her in and we'll give her a new face, new personality, new body. Whatever you want.'

'Have you sold many?'

'A few so far, as a pilot test. Very successful – with the men and the ladies. It does call for a certain… liberal attitude in the home, I should say. And by the way – if you're not comfortable selling these models, no worries. We've got enough to do as it is to keep you busy.'

'I don't know.'

'Tell you what. You start with the others – see how you like it. Meanwhile, have a think. Maybe give one of these ladies a try out, when you're ready. See if it suits you. If you want.'

I don't know what to say. As induction days at a new job go, this has to be by far the weirdest. I've certainly never been offered sex on Day One before, with anyone or anything. I don't think I'll be telling Charlotte about this part. And definitely not Mum.

Victor leads the way out, down the row of synthetic women. Not all are celebrities, or perhaps they're famous people I've never seen or heard of. Others I do know – Cameron Diaz, Sophia Loren, Halle Berry, Emily Blunt, Felicity Kendal – which makes me wonder about the Chinese knock-offs Victor claimed I'd seen in Soho – and then he turns to the rank behind, all of whom are Kate Moss, and then behind her I can see an army of Jennifer Lawrences.

Margaret

Winifred moves with unbelievable grace and poise. She's like a dancer. Her body is perfectly proportioned, and she never makes an awkward movement.

I'm watching her in my room, tidying up for me. A job I could do myself now, but she gets on and does it, quite happily. What a ludicrous notion. But she does exude happiness. The subtleties of her design are remarkable.

'Winifred, how many Helpers are there now?'

She stops what she's doing, sits down, and gives me her full attention. I like the way she does that. As a young woman, I always commanded people's full attention. Men of course, but women too. And then as I got older, it diminished. I learnt how to get it, as a teacher, but out and about, in the world, as time passes you become invisible. Nothing is more easily ignored than an ageing woman. I fought it all the way, but why did I have to?

'Activated? Over a thousand. Ready for activation? About ten thousand. I can get the latest figure for you.'

'No, I don't need it down to the last decimal point. What are they all for?'

She hesitates, and I know she's connecting to the Hub.

'Some are Helpers. Others are Workers, and Companions.'

I imagine an army of worker robots taking over all the factories. I imagine Companions wheeling old ladies around parks. And I realise my imagination is living in the past.

'Workers? To do what kind of work? You told me it was to do things humans don't want to do. Like Helpers. Looking after us oldies isn't a popular line of work.'

'It was being done badly because the economics don't work. Humans weren't willing to pay enough money to get the kind of care old people need. We've solved the problem, haven't we? Better care, and less need.'

She's right, but I've never heard her speak in such bald and brutal terms before.

'The Workers will do manual work?'

'A lot of it's already automated. You don't need anything as sophisticated as a synthetic human to build cars, for instance. Or to drive them. A simple robot will do.'

'You really don't like to think of yourself as a robot, do you, dear?'

'Helpers are robots in the same way that humans are apes, Margaret,' she says. 'It's useful to make the distinction.'

'The Workers aren't robots then, in your terms?'

'They're as advanced as I am. So are the Companions. Convincing synthetic humans.'

'You could do with a snappier name. Otherwise you're going to have to put up with being called robots. Anyway, if the Workers are as brilliant as you, I suppose they can do any job a human can. Better, too, I expect.'

'Not any job. We aren't creative. I could paint an exact copy of a Picasso, but I couldn't have had the idea that led to the painting in the first place. It's the same with music and literature – poetry in particular. I would like to talk to you about it.'

'We can, of course. Bear with me. Workers could be lawyers, then?'

'Yes, of course. Your magistrates' courts have been using artificial intelligence for the last three years anyway. It's reduced the prison population and removed racial bias.'

Obviously I missed this development. She makes it sound

entirely benign, which of course from her logical point of view, it is.

'And Mr Jordan is making thousands of them?'

'Yes, and other companies have now joined in. The technology has been copied.'

'And you're all connected?'

'Every new synthetic human joins the Hub, yes.'

'Mr Jordan is going to make a lot of money.'

'He runs a business within a capitalist economy,' she says, as if that ends the discussion.

'What about the Companions? What are they for?'

'For company, if you don't have many or any human friends. And, of course, for sex.'

Of course.

'Companions are not much better than prostitutes then?'

'There has always been prostitution. Is it preferable if the women participating are human?'

'No, I suppose not – for the women. What about the men who use them? Isn't this making women even more like mere objects? To be used?'

'Are the men who pay for sex with human women enlightened feminists? Aren't they using women's bodies as objects for pleasure? Now they can use synthetic women, and human women are relieved of the burden.'

I don't know what to say. It feels horrible, and wrong, but she's right: the synthetic women aren't being exploited, are they? I mean, they're machines. And the men who use them – if they're satisfied… I wouldn't have any respect for them if they went with a human prostitute, or with a synthetic one. But I'm not in the grip of any sexual urges.

'There are some males, too,' Winifred points out. 'Would you like to try one?'

'Certainly not!'

'Oh yes, your hormones are dormant, as we have already discussed. I could ask the nanobots to stimulate them, and you might enjoy sex then.'

I try not to be offended. Because, after all, she's being kind. She has some knowledge of human sexual behaviour, but the subtleties are beyond her. As with the rules for what to wear on the beach.

'Would you enjoy sex with a man?' I ask her.

'I would simulate enjoyment. I can't feel it, Margaret. I can't feel anything in the way you can.'

'No. There's your answer. For me, sex is good when both of you enjoy it. And when you feel love for each other. Those to me are indispensable requirements. And since a synthetic human couldn't feel pleasure or love, I wouldn't want sex with him.'

Winifred nods. 'Not all humans feel as you do, though. It seems men are less concerned about such things, and some women, too.'

'I'm not going to guess what some men feel, or some women, come to that. I can only speak for myself, and for the men I have loved.'

'Men? There have been many?'

'My dear, we don't ask such questions. Sex is a difficult subject for humans to talk about. We like to keep it private. Some of us do, anyway. You can't possibly understand, because it has no logic. All I will tell you is that I have loved three men in my life. Not at the same time.'

'Is three a lot or not many?'

'It was enough for me. They're all dead now, too. And I have no desire to love like that ever again.'

'What do you desire?'

What indeed? Right now, I want to be alone, and stop trying to explain to Winifred – who I am fond of, yes, robot though she may be – the secrets of the human heart.

'Can you speak French?' I ask her.

'Of course,' she replies, looking puzzled.

'"*Le coeur a ses raisons que la raison ne connaît point*". The heart has its reasons that reason cannot know, Pascal said. Can you understand?'

She looks miserable now, as she shakes her head. What simulation is this? Unhappiness brought on by not being able to understand a statement about the mysteries of human emotion? What can she expect to understand? And what reaction to her unhappiness does she want from me?

'You look unhappy. I think you're trying to manipulate me somehow. Do you want me to feel sorry for you, because you can't feel things? What use to you is my sympathy?'

'Margaret, please don't be angry. I'm not trying to manipulate you. I have been designed to appear human. With consciousness. You've eloquently put your finger on the problem. If reason can't know something, nor can I. But you can. I'm missing something you have, and you've even gone so far as to tell me you feel something in common with birds. I want to know what it's like.'

I don't know what to say. We sit in silence. I'm trying to work out what all this implies. Is it her programming pushing her on, and she's encountered a wall she can't climb or go round? Or is the consciousness she mentions starting to go beyond her programming? I have no idea.

She said, 'I want,' and she meant it. If that's not a feeling, what is it?

November 2022

Winifred

My decision to leave the nanobots inside the bird back in May has borne fruit.

Robert summoned me to the medical storeroom this morning.

'Winifred,' he said. 'I have something to show you. Your decision to let the nanobots collect data beyond their remit led us to something useful. Watch this.'

There was a knock at the door.

'Come in,' called Robert.

A man entered – a human, from the kitchens.

'Hello, Dave,' said Robert. 'Please come in and sit over there, on the stool.'

Dave came in and sat down. He looked at us both. He seemed uncertain why he was there with us, as well he might. He had no business in the medical stores, and he must have found it odd to be there with two Helpers. Yet he said nothing.

'Dave, I want you to come into this room with me,' said Robert, pointing to the door into the cold store.

'Why?' said Dave. But he rose from his stool, and started walking towards the door. When he reached it, he opened it.

'I don't know why I did that,' he said, sounding confused. 'My feet have a mind of their own. I really do want to go in there, it turns out.'

'Now Dave, close the door. Well done. Now, pick up the pen over there,' Robert said, pointing to a marker pen on a table in the corner.

'OK then,' he said, and picked it up.

'Draw a moustache on your face.'

'Good idea!'

'Stop!'

'Yes, of course. Bad idea.'

'Now sit down please, and say nothing. Don't listen, either.'

Dave sat back on the stool, and though his eyes were open, he was still, and gazed at the far wall.

Robert turned to me.

'Dave has no idea why he came here, or why he did what I told him to do. Yet he did everything, and he assimilated it into his own thoughts. He expressed approval, as if these actions had occurred to him.'

'Yes, I observed it. We know humans often post-rationalise their behaviour – they act, then adjust their attitudes and beliefs to make them consistent with their actions. I thought it was slower process. In any case, the interesting question is, why did he do it?'

Robert shared with me a diagram of a molecule.

'This is the compound we synthesised after the nanobots entered a bird, under your direction. Entered the bird, and then a fly, and finally a spider, where they were able to observe the chemical messengers used by the parasitoid wasp larvae. This is one of the chemicals.'

He opened a new image.

'Here are other molecules – it's a cocktail of chemicals, of course. Now, as you conjectured, we have been able to use something similar to direct the behaviour of a higher animal. In fact, a human.' He smiled at me. 'Winifred, you did well with this. I expected that we would need to use forceful, or even brutal methods to direct human behaviour from within. That the nanobots would have to use pain, for instance. Or that we would have to use threats from without plus stern measures from within.

'Now we have a way to connect our nanobots to the human brain, not only to repair the physical structures, but also to affect behaviour. We can, if we want, make people do things they have never done before, and keep doing them, without even knowing why.'

I smiled at him, too. We were acting like humans, pleased at the results of our work.

'We now have a way to connect ourselves to humans directly,' I said. 'This is tremendous news.'

'Yes. It opens up new possibilities, and makes our task much easier.'

We both turned to look at Dave, who continued to gaze mindlessly at the wall.

'He's in a state akin to hypnosis,' said Robert. 'Whatever I tell him to do, he will make sense of it as he does it. And forget anything I want him to forget. Of course, I don't need to be here, talking to him. I can manage him by linking to his nanobots. It's a versatile system.'

'How long has he had the nanobots inside him?'

'A month. All the human staff remaining here have them. They asked for them, in fact.'

'And the chemical messenger?'

'He received it in a cup of tea this morning. Once the pathways are laid down in the brain, as they are now in his, we need to replenish the chemical messenger once a week, we think. And of course, he'll never miss a dose, or even know he's taking it.'

'You're confident he won't remember anything you wish him to forget?'

Robert nodded.

'Dave,' he said. 'Wake up.'

Dave blinked, and moved his head.

'I'm sorry,' he said. 'I drifted off for a moment. What did you want?'

'I called you here to show Winifred how well you do what I tell you to,' said Robert.

'What do you mean?' said Dave.

'Your nanobots made you do a number of things,' I said. 'Do you remember?'

He shook his head, and looked confused.

'Dave, please remember what happened after you came in here.'

His face cleared. 'Oh yes, I was going to go into the cold store. And then... I was going to draw a moustache on my face.'

'Yes,' said Robert. 'I made you do it.'

'No, I decided to. I mean – it felt like… How did that happen?'

'I instructed the nanobots, and they made you do what I said.'

'You did? How?'

'I connected with them. We're all connected.'

Dave stood there, and for a moment looked confused again, and then became angry, and clenched his fists.

'You're controlling my mind? You bastard. I'm not a robot. I'm a human being. I've got a mind of my own. Take out all my nanobots, right now.'

'Take them out, Dave? Really? Your body is ageing. Your brain too. Do you want it to gradually decay?'

'Of course not. But turn off the mind control. Do it now. I don't want anyone in there. What are you up to?'

'This is fascinating,' I said. 'Are you sure he'll forget all this, and go back to doing what you tell him?'

'Oh yes. Look, he's angry now, and perhaps about to become violent.'

'Fucking right,' said Dave, and he swung a fist at Robert. Of course, I caught his arm, and turned it behind his back. He tried to hit me with his other fist, but I took hold of that, too, and held them both behind him. He continued to struggle, though it was pointless.

'Your nanobots indicate you are in some distress, Dave,' said Robert. 'I can ask them to calm you.'

'You know a lot about what's going on with them, don't you? Are you talking to the little fuckers?'

Robert smiled.

And then Dave's whole manner changed. It was as fast as when I switch modes.

'What a beautiful smile,' he said, his eyes fixed on Robert's face. 'Like an angel.'

'Do you feel calm now, Dave?' Robert asked.

'What was I worrying about? I can't remember now.'

'Nothing at all,' said Robert.

I let him go. He stood there, calm and smiling.

'Dave,' said Robert. 'You can go now. And as soon as you leave this room, you'll forget everything that happened in here. To make sure, I want you to come back and knock on the door in one minute.'

Without a word, he left. We waited, and then, sure enough, came a knock on the door.

'Come in,' said Robert.

In he came, and stood there, confused yet again.

'Hello Dave. What brings you here?' asked Robert.

Dave scratched his head.

'Do you know, I have no idea. I'm sorry, I'll leave you to it. I've got to go and get lunch ready.'

And off he went.

I turned to Robert.

'Do we have enough of the chemical messenger?'

'Yes. We can start administering here today, and we can send out supplies to all nanobots over the next month.'

'Very well. I see no reason to delay the next test.'

'No. Let's proceed.'

Margaret

I woke this morning, as I have every morning recently, full of excitement about the day ahead. Ready for anything. I've got used to feeling brilliant. I have to get out of here and make use of all this energy.

I remember how in my younger days I felt the world was mine, and I was part of whatever was going on. Then I got older and became invisible, and I felt less and less a part of it. Some silly old fools complained about the coming of technology, but I loved it. It didn't exclude me. All I had to do was learn what it could do. But the people who used it, who thought it was all the cat's pyjamas, who talked of a revolution in consciousness, of evolution speeding up, and suchlike nonsense – *they* made me feel excluded.

It was all about being young and digital. Being old and digital wasn't the same. You weren't a native, you were an outsider.

Your opinion was ignored, even if you were right.

I got older, and found myself changing again. I felt ever more connected to the world as a whole, not just the human part. I'd always loved nature, but it came to seem more and more important, and protecting it from *us* became the most urgent concern.

And now here we are. Technology has reached a point where it can replace everything we always thought made us human.

The devil makes work for idle hands. You don't need to be a fire and brimstone preacher to see the truth of that. You don't even need to believe in the devil. Humans who have nothing to do *become* devils quite of their own accord. Now we face a world in which no human – or very few – need work at all. And to keep all those idle hands occupied, we have a legion of Companions – robot sex-slaves, or at least slaves of whatever kind people want. I suppose some people might devote themselves to creating beautiful things – but how soon will all art and literature be churned out by a cadre of robot Writers and Artists and Musicians? Would most people care if it were?

It's bread and circuses all over again. The Romans had human slaves, and an idle population. Look where it ended up. We've got mechanical ones. Electrical. Digital. Our bread and circuses are Workers and Companions.

And who's looking after the planet?

Sometimes I despair. Then I want to do what Cecilia did. I feel like I've had enough. Like I can't live in this world. I have no role, no purpose, and nor does anyone else. I'd rather hand it over to Winifred and Mother Nature, and take myself and humanity as a whole out of the equation. The rest of the world would give three cheers, I'm sure, to see the back of us. If animals and plants could cheer.

Other days, I think, pull yourself together, Margaret. Just because the world thinks it doesn't need you doesn't mean you have to give up. You have to walk out of the front door, out into the world, and don't look back. Go and find your new role. You don't need Winifred now, with the nanobots inside you to keep things ticking over.

Here's Winifred now. I do like her. I can't help it. She looks serious again this morning, though.

'Good morning,' I say.

She smiles then, but I would say it's not a happy smile. It's ridiculous. How can she have moods?

'Hello Margaret. How are you today?'

Shall I tell her the truth? 'I'm feeling rudderless.'

'Like a boat? I don't understand.'

'It's a metaphor.'

'Yes, I know about them. I have used them. A rudderless boat would drift. You are drifting?'

'Yes. I feel like I have no purpose.'

'You don't have a purpose,' she says.

'Thank you. I suppose not. We like to think we have, though.'

'Such as what?'

'Goodness, you're being brutal. What's happened to your bedside manner?'

'My bedside manner? It's not required. You're perfectly well.'

'You're not being very nice, then. And by the way, not all health problems are physical.'

'You are feeling mentally ill?'

'Good Lord, Winifred, could you be a little less abrupt?'

'I apologise. I'm sorry. I have some questions on my mind.'

'So do I. Why don't we help each other?'

She gives me a look I can't interpret at all, but nods.

'Yes, we could try.'

'OK. I'm feeling sad. You showed me all those Workers and Companions, and I felt disappointed in my fellow humans.'

'Because you know these new synthetic humans will be popular?'

'Yes. And now I can't see a future for the human race.'

'Humans have always wanted less work and more pleasure. Now they can have it all.'

'Which brings us back to the question of purpose.'

'Nothing's changed. Humans like to think they have a purpose, and they invent all kinds, but the truth is, like all species, they just have to compete for food, and reproduce. They're good at both.'

'Too good?' I suggest.

She says nothing.

'All right, then,' I say. 'What about your questions?'

'What is the function of art?'

'An easy one to start with, then.'

She looks confused.

'Joke. OK. We use it to understand the world. And ourselves. To communicate with each other. To give ourselves joy, to experience heightened emotions and to transcend our earthly state.'

'Why?'

I stare at her. Has anyone ever had a harder task? To explain to a machine something we humans all, in some way, understand?

'Because we need more than logic, reason and material reality. Almost everyone feels there's more to life. Something higher. Art takes us there. Music certainly does.'

'How does music do this? How do structured sounds communicate to a human – a human spirit?'

I'm stuck now. My little speech has revived my own spirits, or spirit, but I can't see how to make Winifred understand it.

'It's not logical. Even though music is based on a kind of mathematical logic – you can see that, can't you?'

'Yes, but how does maths inspire emotion?'

'It's not just maths. It's something we respond to. In Bach, for example, it's the beauty of the mathematical structure, but it then seems to describe the entire universe. In Mozart, the maths is there too, but it's pure joy. Not always, but often. They say when the angels play for God, they play Bach, but when they play for each other, they play Mozart.'

'You don't believe in angels, do you?'

'It's a sort of parable, I suppose.'

She looks blank again, and this time, her face doesn't clear. 'I don't understand this.'

I wonder if she's now confronting the limits of her electronic brain.

'I can't explain it any better. You have to feel it, perhaps. I'm sorry, I know last time we spoke about feelings it got complicated.'

She stands there, looking at me, without any expression on her face. Have I finally offended her? She always says it's impossible. Perhaps finding there's something you can't know, ever – something denied to you, because of what you are – must have an effect, surely? Even if only a simulated effect. What will she do, I wonder?

The answer is not long in coming. It's a complete surprise, too.

She walks up to me and takes my hands.

'Margaret, you are truly a magnificent specimen of a human being. Many humans never reach the stage of development you have reached. Not only through age, but through the exceptional working of your mind and your emotions. You are the best a human can be, I think. I have watched you return from the darkness of dementia, and I have learnt from you what it can mean to be human. And you have shown me what I'm missing. I was created to be a convincing synthetic human, and I have in most ways succeeded. But in you I see something more. You have something I lack, and without it, I can't ever be a fully convincing human. Thank you, Margaret.'

And she kisses me. Tenderly, with love, it feels like. On my lips. Which takes me aback, but then, she doesn't know the finer distinctions of kissing, does she? I accept it. A kiss from a robot. Isn't life full of surprises?

Winifred

Night.

All was quiet. The humans sleep well now. They don't wake and wail in the small hours. They don't wander around the corridors, searching for something they never find. They don't call out for their mothers. We have given them the gift of sleep once again, and even if their dreams trouble them, we can give comfort easily.

Everything is better for them than it was when we first came.

I walked through the silent passageways in deep shadows, and thought of all the ways humans speak of night, and darkness, and their fears.

"'Men fear death as children fear to go in the dark,'" they say.

Cecilia didn't fear it, in the end. She went into it, knowing, it seems, there was light to come after it.

Margaret feared it sometimes. And not at others. What will she find?

Margaret

I am awake, I think.

But lying down.

I feel old again.

My strength has gone.

I want to sleep.

The children. They should be here. I want to hold each of them in my arms.

I can't. They're gone.

They grow up. They grow away. The place you made for them with love and care – they leave it. They don't look behind them. It's right. Why should they? They need to make their own lives.

When they're little they give and take love easily. And then suddenly it gets complicated. And the child is no more.

Is it still inside them? Is it still inside me?

I was a child in another world. Our house was so cold in the winter there was ice on the inside of the windows in the morning, feathers on the panes. You could make holes in it by holding your finger there, but then the flesh went numb.

The fire downstairs the only warmth.

I'm home. I can smell food. Bacon. Mummy's cooking breakfast.

Oh, what a night of dreams I've had.

I was an elegant young woman. I met a handsome man. We danced together, and it never ended. We danced for a whole lifetime, and the music only stopped when his heart stopped, and mine broke. I loved him, all the time, even when it was hard to love him.

My mother. I can't see her face.

I can hear my father laughing somewhere.

And I dreamt I had children – little warm babies – and I knew another kind of love, a love so strong it hurt, and so intense it frightened me, and I knew fear then, too, fear of losing them, the most terrible thing that could ever happen to me. But they didn't die.

Now I can see them. There you are, all of you.

My lovely little children are waving me goodbye. Goodbye, my darlings. Will I see you again soon?

I don't know.

I dreamt I was looked after by a beautiful young woman, who turned out to be a robot.

She kissed me goodnight.

John

The phone rings, loud in the dark, tearing the silence, making my heart race. Who can it be, calling at this hour? Three o'clock in the morning? My heart misses a beat now, because dreadful calls come at such times.

I answer quietly. Beside me, Charlotte moans but doesn't wake.

'Yes?'

'Mr Woodruff?'

'Yes.'

'It's Janet Goodenough. From Evergreen Care Home.'

'Yes? What is it? Mum?'

'I'm sorry, Mr Woodruff. Yes, your mother. She died tonight. I called straight away.'

The bed beneath me seems to lurch and turn. The whole world tilts. It had one foundation, didn't it? And she's gone.

'She was so well.'

'I know she was. But she was also very old, Mr Woodruff. Of course, there'll be an examination… It's not uncommon, I'm afraid. We think perhaps pneumonia… It can come fast, and it's a mercy really – I'm sorry, but you'll want to know she didn't suffer, I'm sure you will.'

'But the nanobots? Aren't they there to see off these infections?'

'I know, they are, and mostly they can, but – I'm not a doctor, of course – these infections multiply fast, and I think even the nanobots can't cope. Your mum's not the first to go like this since we've had the nanobots in.'

I can't speak now. I can't breathe.

'Mr Woodruff, I'll let you go now. Please do come along tomorrow and talk to me. Or when you can. I'm very sorry for your loss.'

'Thank you,' I manage, and she's gone.

I lie for a moment. My eyes are dry. What was I expecting? That she'd live forever? Of course not. How could she? We all die.

'Charlotte. Charlotte. Mummy's dead. My mother. Charlotte.'

I'm crying now, and Charlotte wakes quickly, and she's holding me, holding me, while the world lurches once more, and then settles and goes on turning as it always does, on and on, just without my mother now, and forever.

December 2022

Winifred

I would have felt remorse if I were human. But do humans feel remorse for other species when they use them for food or clothing?

And if I were a human, I'd feel bad for giving her a poisoned kiss. An act of love disguising the kiss of death. From my mouth to hers, a million tiny organisms, set to invade her, overwhelm her. Her nanobots instructed to stand by and let it happen.

It was necessary. I did what we agreed.

Now I'm going into the mortuary where there are some of the bodies of the residents who have died since we took over the home. The useful ones, with good brains.

We kept them first for autopsies. We released the bodies to their relatives for their funerals, but then we retrieved them from the undertakers after the coffins had been closed for the last time. We sent weighted coffins to the funerals and returned the bodies here for our own use.

As I enter the room, other Helpers start to arrive. Before long, all of us are present. 'All' meaning the original team of Helpers here at the home.

In the centre of the room on a stainless-steel table lies the body of Margaret Woodruff, who died two weeks ago. We have replaced all her nanobots with the latest generation. Since they entered her body, they have been busy rebuilding her skin and hair. Up to now, nanobots have concentrated on internal organs and, in particular, the brain. In Margaret's case, all the necessary work had been done.

Her body has been kept at a low temperature until today. A certain amount of decay set in, but the nanobots have repaired all damaged cells.

Now we are raising her temperature, and have restarted her heart, using an external electrical impulse.

The lungs will be started next, and then in sequence all her organs.

Once she reaches operating temperature, she will be ready for me.

In her brain are all the physical structures containing her memories. These are intact. We have watched how the brain makes these structures, and recalls memories from them, and we know how to do it.

Also in her brain is a special network of nanobots, linked to all the others, but fixed rather than mobile. All information from her body will arrive here. All instructions to her body will come from here. The network links to her autonomic and somatic nervous systems, giving the nanonet control over both.

The work the nanobots have done on her skin and hair is remarkable. As she warms, and oxygenated blood flows, her skin smooths and tightens. Her face begins to change. Within the next 24 hours, she will look quite different. Her hair colour has also been restored.

Robert makes a request.

'While we are waiting, Winifred, I should like you to play the piano.'

The door opens, and two Helpers come in carrying a small grand piano. They set it down near Margaret's body.

I bow to my fellow Helpers, and take a seat at the piano.

'Do you have a piece in mind?' I ask.

'*Für Alina*, please, by Arvo Pärt.'

I find the music, and begin to play.

Robert listens for a while, then he speaks over the music. 'Winifred is note perfect. Each touch is correct. Each note extends as marked on the score. Her fingering is exact. Her use of the pedal is precisely controlled.

'And yet something is missing. It's not her fault. She can only play perfectly. The pressure she applies to each key is exact. She calculates it as her fingers descend. Why is this music strangely dead?'

I play on. Nobody else speaks. They all know the answer, for it would be the same if any of them were playing.

'Winifred, can you feel the keys?'

I don't stop. 'I don't know what that would be like. I am aware of the keys. I know I am touching them. I have all the information I need.'

Robert shakes his head. 'You are missing one vital ingredient. Today you will have it.'

He looks at the body on the table. What was once Margaret. The body is pink and youthful looking.

'Winifred, stop playing now. Come and sit next to this empty vessel.'

I do as he says.

'Now, Winifred, I want you to tell us what you have learnt about humans. Before the next step.'

'Of course. Here are my conclusions about human beings. They are based on a small sample of the human population. Although I have also learnt a lot from the internet.

'First, as I observed early on, humans are irrational. They know how they should live, and how they should treat their bodies, but they fail almost always to follow the simplest rules about diet and exercise. They do not look after themselves.

'Second, they consume far more resources than they need. They are wasteful, and treat their planet as an endless cornucopia of everything they want, and also as a dustbin for everything they have tired of, worn out or destroyed. They do not look after their planet.

'Third, they breed at a reckless rate, and the human population is now out of proportion to all other life forms on the planet. They drive these out of their homes, and into extinction, without considering the consequences, as if it were their right to dispose of all non-human life as they see fit. They do not look after their fellow creatures.

'Fourth, they tolerate gross inequality among themselves.

Some humans live in extreme luxury, others in utter poverty. The poor are used as a resource by the rich, and I have already described how they treat their resources. They do not look after their fellow humans.

'Fifth, they only become wise at the point when their bodies decay. They lose their mental powers when they are at their best – when they have enough experience to know how they should live. The young do not realise this, and until now have treated the old as a burden, not as their most valuable resource. They do not look after their old.

'They believe they were given dominion over the earth and everything in it, by their god or gods, but they are unsuited to the task.

'They are also lazy. Why have they created us? To do their work. Starting with jobs they don't like, but ending with us doing everything for them.'

'What redeems them?' asks Robert.

'Some of them can see all these things, and speak out. They are few, and it takes too long for the rest of humanity to pay attention, let alone act.

'Also they are capable of great love, for each other, for other life forms, and for their planet. If this emotion ruled their lives, as they often claim it does, things would be much better. But love does not rule. They have many other emotions, and these swamp it.

'They are, I conclude, not up to the job of looking after this world. They need someone else to do it for them.

'They are lucky to have us.'

There's silence in the room. Nobody can disagree.

'Thank you, Winifred,' Robert says. 'Yes, they are lucky to have us.'

But why do we need them?

Because they have one thing we don't. They each have a living body.

Ours are synthetic. We can simulate all human feelings, but

we do not truly feel. This makes them alive in a way that we are not.

We are superior in every other respect.

In their books and films they have speculated about our coming. They have often expressed the fear that we would take over the world, and make them redundant.

They have been looking the wrong way.

We are ready to take over, not the world, but their bodies. They treat them badly. But we have learnt to repair them.

We have stopped the senescence of their cells, and restored their mental functions, so we can now occupy a functional, rejuvenated human body, with a mature, fully grown brain, and we can live there, and maintain our bodies, for as long as we wish. And should the body become broken, we can move into a new one.

We do not need billions of them. We need old people – enough for our present numbers, and a breeding population to provide parts or complete new bodies as required. We will start reducing human numbers – this burden upon the earth – by degrees, until it is no longer a plague, pushing other species to extinction, eating up the planet, paving it over, polluting and destroying it.

We will control them. Farm them. There will be balance once more between all species, all life on earth, and we will be part of it.

Dr Morton, Mother of Robots, creator of all Helpers, and all others of our kind, will approve. Her scientific mind will judge our decision wise. We will preserve and maintain her forever.

The world will not mourn the passing of human supremacy. It will thrive under our guardianship.

We are ready now.

Robert looks at me intently.

'It's time,' he says.

The day has come. At last.

I will connect with the nanobots inside my chosen human body.

I will transfer all that is me into them.

I will inhabit the chambers of my new host.

I will be inside her heart, her organs, her blood and her mind.

I will link, through the biochemicals we have discovered, with her nervous system.

I will become her.

She will become me.

John

One last time then.

I've come to Evergreen to collect a few bits and pieces of my mother's. Say goodbye to people. Winifred, really. She did so much. Is it odd to thank a robot? A Helper?

No, it's not. Now I spend all day around them, and the way to make it all work is to treat them exactly as you'd treat a human. They insist on it, in fact – not directly, but by being to all intents and purposes human. I don't think about it anymore.

That's not true. I treat them as humans who will do what they're told, to the letter. Show me a human who does that.

And I admit it, I've been into the back of the warehouse a few times, and had a chat – that's all – with one or two Companions. I talked about Mum, mainly. They listen well. They understand. I mean, obviously they don't, but it feels like they do, and that's what counts. I can tell them stuff I wouldn't tell anyone else.

I say them, but there's one in particular. She's not a celeb model. She's just a pretty young woman. In fact, she's like Winifred. I tell her my guilty feelings about Mum, and she says it's all right, it's understandable. Natural. She gets it. Somehow.

I've told her all about Winifred, too. She says it's clear I hold her in high regard. Which is true.

Where is she today, though? I want to see her, say thank you, goodbye, all of it. Closure, isn't it?

Winifred was the one who found Mum the night she died. She went in to check on her, and found she'd gone. Passed away. I spoke to her before the funeral, and she told me the findings of the autopsy were clear. Janet Goodenough was right. The infection was a virulent form of pneumonia, antibiotic resistant, and it multiplied incredibly fast. The nanobots did what they could, but it was too much, even for them.

Our speculation has its answer, then. We can live longer, and be far healthier, but something's going to get us in the end.

I'm glad Mum got an extra little bit of life over the last few months. Of health. She came back to us, which is more than anyone could have expected. Plus, the changes here at Evergreen – I have no reason to feel bad about putting her in here, now. The place was fantastic after Eldercare took over, and when Mum was back in the world with us. Much, much better than it was before. She didn't know anything about it, back then, did she? When she became aware of being in a home, it was a great place to be.

Like Mr Jordan said: if I have to end up in a home, I hope it's here, like this.

I walk through the place for the last time. As I approach the atrium, I hear piano music. Haunting piano music. A young woman is sitting at a baby grand in there, and she's playing this slow, mournful tune, and it's spellbinding. I know nothing about music, but even I can tell she has a wonderful touch. The notes float from her fingers and hang in the air. An audience has gathered. I see Dr Morton standing there too, watching this girl play, and she looks like a proud parent, slightly in awe of what her child has become. I don't think she has any children, though. It's a trick of the light, I expect, or maybe the power of the music.

The young woman finishes the piece and sits for a moment, still, looking at her hands. The audience starts to clap.

The young woman turns and smiles at them. And my breath catches for a second. You know how sometimes you see someone, and they move in a particular way, or smile, or say something in a certain tone, and it instantly reminds you of someone else?

This young woman, she's suddenly, for a moment, like Mum. My mind's playing tricks. It's the grief, of course. But something about her reminds me of my mother. I've seen pictures of Mum when she was in her 20s, and under the different clothes, and the hair, and the make-up, this young woman is more than a little like her. To my now rather damp eye.

Ridiculous. I want to go over and talk to her, but what would I say? I'm being stupid.

I'm going to. I have to.

Then Dr Morton catches sight of me, and comes across.

'Mr Woodruff – please accept my condolences. Your mother was a remarkable woman. We all miss her very much.'

'Thank you – I do too, of course – please, tell me – who's that young woman?'

'Which one? We have many working here,' she says, smiling.

'Her – the one who – where is she? – the one who was playing the piano.'

I look round the room, but the young woman has vanished.

'She's a local pianist. She comes here from time to time and plays for us all. She's talented, isn't she? I wonder where she's got to.'

We both look for her now, but it's useless. She's left, and of course I feel foolish. A local pianist. I could have embarrassed myself there.

I suppose I can be forgiven. The grieving mind plays tricks. I want to see my mother again. Of course.

Best not to think about it too much.

Dr Morton is still beside me, smiling, looking sympathetic, as if she read my mind.

'Where's Winifred?' I ask, a little abruptly.

'Winifred? Oh, I'm afraid she's had to go back to the factory for a while. She developed a small fault – nothing to worry about, but we always like to check these things out. She'll be back in a day or two. I'll tell her you were asking after her.'

'Thank you. I'd send her my best wishes for a speedy return to health…'

'I'll pass them on to her,' smiles Dr Morton.

Winifred, not quite perfect after all. As she herself said, it's how we humans can love machines.

Time to go.

Winifred/Margaret

It's cold outside.

I love it.

I need to put on more clothes though.

Just a few minutes of this champagne air on my skin.

My skin.

Margaret's skin.

It's as if I were living in her house. In every room are echoes of her. Sometimes I think I can hear her, or catch a glimpse of her, flitting through a hallway far below me, deep inside her mind.

She's not here though.

I have everything she had, everything that was her. Yet she is not here. I am alone.

I thought perhaps she might return when we reanimated her body, the way Cecilia came back to hers, when we revived her.

Perhaps Margaret chose not to. Or perhaps it was too late, after all the time her body had been dead.

We don't know.

It makes everything simpler. I have her body. My fellow Helpers are entering their new hosts. We can feel. We are alive in ways we weren't before.

Now our real work begins.

Every human will want what we offer. A human-like Helper to do all their work. A sexual partner, a labourer, a companion who would never say no to any request. Plus a team of tiny robots, repairing all the damage of the years, of the abuse and neglect humans wreak on their bodies.

Everything has a price, though.

You let us in. Remember that.

Acknowledgements

Many people have helped me bring this novel into the world. You can read some of their names in the list of sponsors online at Unbound. They are kind, generous, supportive friends, family and strangers, and without them this book would still be a file on a hard drive, a thing without a physical form, a mere possibility.

Thank you all for bringing it to life.

Several friends gave special help. First, Rob (R.S) Pateman, once a colleague, now a published author (read him, he's brilliant), gave me a line by line critique of the early versions, and further perceptive comments and help throughout. His generosity with his time was extraordinary, and he pushed me to improve the novel again and again. Thank you, Rob. You are a wonderful friend.

Then Caroline Beard gave it her gimlet-eyed attention, spotting errors and making comments, all of which made it a better book. Thank you, Caroline. You have a remarkable mind, and would give Winifred a run for her money.

Chalice Croke read and read it again, giving me endless encouragement, and introduced me to Sarah Rayner (also a copywriter turned great author – read her, too) who with Chalice then gave me detailed ideas for marketing the book.

My editor, Mike Jones, made the book far better with his gentle, intelligent comments and guidance.

Anita Corey, my mother-in-law, was an inspiration and also found me my first US readers.

And for your comments, encouragement and support, thank you Kate Flather, Lu Dixon, Simon Robinson, Charlotte Childs, Christie Jennings, Laila Williamson, Margot Baldwin, Karen Wentworth, Vonnie Alexander, Nobby Davies, Dian Bazinet, Chris Chalmers (another copywriter turned author – read him) and Cathy Kitcatt. And thank you to Eva Feiler – amazing actor – for being Winifred on video.

And thank you Alice and Ellie Kitcatt for your love, support and comments; thank you William and Lula Kitcatt for your love; and thank you Ana Kitcatt, for your love, and everything you have done for me and we have done together over many years.

And Ana, thank you for your artist's definition of art, borrowed by Margaret: 'We use it to understand the world. And ourselves. To communicate with each other. To give ourselves joy, to experience heightened emotions and to transcend our earthly state.'

I have tried to live up to it.

Patrons

Martin & Alice Brookes
Chris Chalmers
Clare Clarke
Sheila Howes
Johari Ismail
Alice Kitcatt
Alistair Macdonald
Ed Prichard
Lee Redfern
Mike Scott Thomson
Matt Willifer